MIND TRANSFER

BELLEVUE   1992

MIND TRANSFER

JANET JEPPSON ASIMOV

Walker and Company
New York

First published in the United States of America in 1988 by the Walker Publishing Company, Inc.

Published simultaneously in Canada by Thomas Allen & Son Canada, Limited, Markham, Ontario

Library of Congress Cataloging-in-Publication Data

Asimov, Janet.
  Mind transfer.

  Summary: Adam Durant's experiences with mind transfer and his adventures on both a human space colony and a robot world test the validity of humanity's growth through artificial intelligence.
  [1. Robots—Fiction. 2. Science fiction] I. Title.
PZ7.A836   1988   [Fic]   87-21679
ISBN 0-8027-6748-6

Printed in the United States of America

10 9 8 7 6 5 4 3 2 1

Book design by Laurie McBarnette

To my cousin,
Chaucy Horsley Bennetts

TABLE OF CONTENTS

PART • I

BIRTH

Mind transfer—human words, filled with hope and fraught with danger; words that touched Adam Durant's life before he was born.

CHAPTER • 1

"Artificial intelligence is an abomination!" The shout came from the gallery and was instantly hushed, but not before the biofundamentalist delegates nodded in agreement.

In the great orbital cylinder housing Federation Parliament, the grant hearings were into the third day. Three days of torturing confinement for a claustrophobe like Jonathan Durant. Tall, bony, and stooped, Jon managed a lopsided smile before he tried to answer.

"Is it artificial if the intelligence is human? Mine? *Yours*?"

Bioeffers started shouting but Jon raised his voice. "My son Adam will be born soon. I speak for him and for all children when I say that perfected mind transfer offers them a second chance. My colleague Matthew Tully and I—"

A bioeffer interrupted. "Intelligent robots have been banned for two hundred years, so robotics manufacturers must manufacture only simple aide robots and large management computers. Mind transfer should be only to biological clones."

Jon Durant ran his fingers through his thin, sand-colored hair. "Mind transfer to a clone fails. It's like trying to impose one's brain patterns on an identical twin. We in Tully Robotics are perfecting a heal-itself superaide brain we believe will accept mind transfer."

"We don't need it!"

"Don't we? The human race has established only one colony outside our own solar system. The distances even to near stars are so vast that it had to be a computer-operated ship that went at sublight speed to the Centauri system. The problems of building a space home so far from Earth were so extreme that it could be done only with the help of moderately

3

intelligent robots, the kind that the Federation no longer permits us to manufacture. Humans are now restricted to the Terran solar system and Centauri Spome. I think that's wrong.

"Delegates, exploration of our galaxy has ceased, but it could resume—with ships manned by humans in robot bodies. I know some of you believe that human existence should end when the biological brain dies, but cells from all of you, as infants, were sent to the bio bank, and most of you have had cloned organ replacements by now. Not every organ can be cloned successfully, so many of you have artificial parts, too. The brain is only another organ. . . ."

Bess Lorimer Durant switched off the rebroadcast of her husband's speech. She touched her bulging abdomen as the baby inside it kicked hard.

"Adam, it's a good thing you don't know what your poor father's going through," she whispered aloud in the sound-proofed secret lab below Tully Tower. Then she walked to the stasis cell and looked through the judas window.

"And you poor thing."

Facing the judas window, the robot in the stasis cell did not move. His blue-eyed face resembled a younger Jonathan Durant, but his hair was too stiff, and he was expressionless. He wore a plain lab suit, but the visible surface of his body was covered with synthoskin instead of the flexible metal of aides.

An ordinary aide robot, and any human, would be unconscious in a stasis cell. No one knew it, but the superaide was awake, and his thoughts were not those of Jonathan Durant. His thoughts were his own:

I'll kill myself if they put me in stasis again. Their minds go to sleep but I stay awake, thinking and wondering who I am.

4

I know I am the seventh superaide, the last still alive, and the first to be used for attempted mind transfer.

But I am not Jonathan Durant. I am myself, yet who is that? Am I intelligent because Dr. Durant's memories were transferred to me, or because I have a superaide brain? Do I think the way humans do? Does it torture them to be trapped inside the three pounds of wrinkled gray protoplasm called a human brain?

I feel as young as the baby inside Bess Durant, yet I possess the alien memories of an old man. I can review the memory in which Adam was conceived, but it was not I who impregnated Bess. I do not like having first-person knowledge of what I cannot experience myself—human biological functions, love, and the fear of death.

I am alien, alone, yet the family history weighs upon my mind as if I were part of it. I think about the family patriarch, the revered founder of biofundamentalism, Walton Lorimer, who would disapprove of me if he knew I existed.

The saintly Walton's one sin, perhaps, was that he doted upon his son Nate, and neglected Nanca, his daughter by an early marriage. Lorimer Breen is successful, has Dinah and Eliot—yet I pity her. Why do I avoid exploring the memories of her?

When Nate and his wife were killed in an accident, Walton raised their daughter, Bess, now a doctor, married to me— no! To Jonathan Durant. Nanca disapproved. Why?

Jonathan likes Dinah, and her daughter Meg, the child of Dr. Matt Tully, but he fears Dinah's twin brother Eliot, who wants to make biofundamentalism a military force. The quarrels seem to tear apart the strands of blood relationship linking the descendants of Walton Lorimer.

Why should I care? I have tried to keep my thoughts to myself ever since Dr. Tully yelled at me that people won't like me if I keep on saying out loud every thought I have on every

5

subject. Here in stasis I think and think and think . . . alone, with no one to share my thoughts.

I wish I could tell Walton Lorimer that it is wrong to hate beings who have nonbiological intelligence, for the ancient greek word bios means life—and am I not alive?

I *am* alive. I have high intelligence and a terrible consciousness of self that fills the very fields of my brain—except when I listen to music. Dr. Tully did not take me seriously one day when I was unhappy and asked him to play a symphony. Why cannot humans accept my suffering? I have read their poetry and I know they suffer, too, but my brain is as complicated as theirs, my emotive fields imitating their capacity for emotion.

Am I just an imitation or am I a new species? Robot aides are not self-aware. The giant computers have no emotive fields and do not think about themselves.

Once when Dr. Tully left me alone in the lab I used the computer outlet to tie into Computer Prime, the machine that runs the Federation's main computer network from its hollowed-out asteroid. I asked Computer Prime what I am.

After analyzing the data I sent it about me, Computer Prime said its job is to analyze problems with robots, and that it could not analyze me because I was too much like a human.

"The humans do not think of me as human," I said. "What should I do?"

"I do not know," said Computer Prime. "I do not understand humans. If you are part human that is your problem."

If a superaide robot like me is like nothing that has ever been, then what am I? I change only in my mind, with what I learn, but humans change biologically, like that baby growing inside Bess Durant.

I read and read, but everything I learn is distorted by knowledge already stuffed into my brain. The baby Adam Durant will be free to learn for himself, but I am not. He will be accepted as part of humanity, but I will be rejected because I fall upon the thorns of life but I do not bleed. . . .

* * *

"Blastest bioeffers!" shouted Matt Tully, striding into the lab on stocky, powerful legs. He always shouted when he was angry. "But someday we'll get that grant. It's not Jon's fault. They just don't want mind transfer to robots. Good thing they don't know all the superaides have gone crazy and that the one mind transfer didn't take."

Bess turned on the vscreen. The holopicture flickered into shape to show the western view from Tully Tower, a glimpse of the Hudson River running silver in the sunlight. Jutting above the hundred-year-old forest on top of the Palisades was Transport Terminal–Greater Manhattan.

"The hearing was over hours ago. Why is Jon late?"

"He ought to be here soon," said Matt, rubbing the round, off-center bald spot that made his wavy black hair look like a slipped tonsure. "And we must decide what to do about"—he pointed to the judas window—"our failure."

"Will the robot deactivate spontaneously if you don't do it first?"

"I wish I didn't have to think about that question, Bess."

7

CHAPTER • 2

Walton Lorimer's silver hair ruffled in the breeze as he stood outside Tully Tower, watching the crowd grow bigger. When called the father of biofundamentalism, he always said that he merely put into coherent doctrine an existing point of view. It was Nanca who pushed biofundamentalism into politics, and sometimes he shivered when he watched her inflame a crowd.

She had organized everything now. Holov crews were ready, paid agitators circulated, and Nanca acknowledged the applause of the crowd from a high platform, her sleek golden hair shining in the sunlight. He told himself he was proud of her.

Nanca's public voice was like velvet-coated steel. She enjoyed speaking to live audiences because it increased the impact of the broadcasts to the outlying Federation.

"My son Eliot has discovered that Tully Robotics secretly manufactures intelligent, unprogrammed robots that will live longer than you do, take your jobs, take over our government, and destroy the human race!"

The crowd shouted curses. Nanca raised her hand.

"Tully Robotics claims that these intelligent robot brains are to be used only for mind transfer, but I will prove to you that they have failed. Mind transfer to robots is a fake. Wait, and you'll see the proof walk out the front door of Tully Tower." Nanca walked down the stairs of the platform and hurried to her father.

"I have to stay here, or they won't wait," she said. "Has Eliot arrived?"

Walton fingered his personal intercom. "The aircar from Transport Terminal has landed on the top of Tully Tower and

Eliot's bringing Jon inside. How is Eliot going to persuade Matt to bring the robot outside?"

"Jon will bring the robot up."

"But how . . ."

"Don't worry about it, Father. You go inside Tully Tower to meet them. Then come out with the robot. I want the people to see the contrast."

"Contrast?"

"Between a psychotic robot and the founder of biofundamentalism." Her chiseled face softened as she kissed his withered cheek. "You're a living symbol, Father. The people know you're a good human being, and they trust you. Now please go inside. Tully Tower's closed, but if you ask, Matt will let you in because Bess is there."

He smiled and said, "I haven't seen her in a while, and Adam's almost due."

Nanca's answering smile was tight. "Just be your genuine self, Father. Uphold the goodness of biofundamentalism and leave the solar system to me."

As he walked toward Tully Tower, he wondered if Nanca would remember that biofundamentalism had been founded to preserve organic ecology, enhance human dignity, and affirm the biological oneness of life. Wouldn't it be strange if life turned out not to be all biological?

Eliot Breen was not redheaded like his twin sister. He was pale and thin, his hair paler still, and his light eyes shone with fanaticism, but not high intelligence.

He faced Matt and laughed. "Open the door to that secret laboratory of yours or I'll make Jon do it."

Eliot's two guards grinned at Matt, who stared open-mouthed at his partner's masklike face.

"Jon looks like he's under mind control!" said Matt.

"Of course. I had to mind probe him to find out what he knows, and keep him under control so I can get that robot."

9

Eliot's left fist uncurled briefly to show Matt the small flat object he was holding.

"Those are illegal!"

"Open the door, Tully. The more I make Jon do under mind control, the harder it is on his brain."

The door opened from inside, and Bess said, "I listened. You must not damage Jon." As Eliot pushed past her to get to the stasis cell, she turned angrily to Walton Lorimer.

"Grandfather, how could you permit Eliot to acquire a mind controller, much less use it on my husband! I want to take Jon to a hospital at once to assess the damage already inflicted and so the controller can be turned off slowly under medical supervision."

"Stop fussing," said Eliot. "Grandfather had nothing to do with my decision, which Nanca approved. We had to find out the truth and stop this bunch of crazy roboticists who think they can promise immortality in robot bodies. Open the stasis cell, Matt, or I'll make Jon . . ."

"All right, all right." Matt unlocked the cell. "You always were power-hungry, Eliot."

When the robot walked out, a curiously human expression of puzzlement altered the configuration of synthoskin on his face. "Is something wrong, Dr. Tully? Dr. Durant does not look normal. And who are these other people?"

"It not only doesn't look much like Jon," said Eliot, "but it doesn't recognize people Jon would know."

The robot frowned, and then his face smoothed out. "I recognize you now, Eliot Breen. And you, Walton Lorimer. There are two strangers behind Eliot."

"Eliot's private guards," said Matt. "They have stun guns, capable of paralyzing a human and disorganizing a robot brain. Move carefully so you don't make them shoot."

While the robot stood perfectly still, Eliot took an intercom from his pocket. "We're on our way. Mother?"

"Intercoms to the outside don't work down here," said Matt.

10

"Once the door to the outside hall closed behind you, the lab's private generator turned on a scramble field. I'm afraid you can't get out. Jon doesn't know the lock combination I set for the door, and if you stun me you'll still be trapped here."

"What's the point of locking us in?" asked Eliot. "The crowd will only grow more impatient to see the robot. You'd better let me take it outside now."

"No."

Bess tugged at Matt's sleeve. "Jon's swaying back and forth. I must take him to a hospital."

"We're going there," said Matt, "out the back way. Eliot, you can come along or wait here until I notify the lab computer to open the door for you. Are you coming, Walton, or does the revered founder want to engineer a return to the old bioeffer riots?"

"Once that was the only way to stop robotics research," said Walton, "but biofundamentalism doesn't need violence now. All we need is to demonstrate the futility of mind transfer to robots. Let Eliot have the robot, Matt."

"No. I don't trust Eliot or Nanca or even you to control a crowd. The back way is the quickest route to a hospital, and the robot is needed to carry Jon." He touched a switch and a section of back wall slid aside to reveal a narrow door.

"Give me the controller," said Bess, holding out her hand to Eliot while Matt waited beside the back door.

"I won't. Guards, grab the robot—"

"Robot, keep away from them," shouted Matt.

As the guards rushed at the robot, Bess stood in front of him. "As you can see, I'm pregnant, but I'm willing to fight."

The biggest guard tried to push her aside, and as she fought him, she fell. Uncertainly, the robot helped her to her feet. "Eliot," cried Bess, "you must give me the controller!"

"Guards, use stun on the robot," said Eliot, while Jon Durant's eyes closed and he swayed back and forth.

11

Matt tried to drag Bess back to the door but she wouldn't go. "Matt, the robot must help Jon!"

"I will carry Dr. Durant," said the robot, walking toward Jon.

The guards fired and the robot stopped. "Don't do . . . that . . . don't do that again . . . don't . . . pain . . . pain . . . I did not know . . . don't . . . pain . . ."

"It's a monster!" yelled Eliot. "It isn't deactivated by full stun!"

"It's probably out of commission," said the biggest guard. "We'll pick it up and use it as a battering ram on the front door."

But when the first guard touched him, the robot said, "I want to go with Dr. Tully. I must help Dr. Durant."

The guards fired again, at close range, and this time the robot did fall.

"Good," said Eliot. "Open the front door, Matt. Your robot's no use to you anymore."

Bess was trying to persuade Jon to walk toward the back door but he didn't seem to hear her. "Eliot, please . . ."

"Sure thing, Bess. Always glad to oblige a relative." Eliot, laughing, threw the controller at her feet.

With an odd rattling sound in his throat, Jonathan Durant collapsed. Kneeling awkwardly beside him, Bess picked up the controller and gasped.

"You turned it off instantaneously! Jon's in a coma now. You tried to kill him, Eliot."

Eliot shrugged. "An accident."

Matt came to help Bess. "I think I can carry him with your help, Bess."

"No, you can't. He's much taller than you are and I can't help because that fall put me into labor. We'll have to open the front door and let Eliot have his way. Maybe an ambulance can get through the crowd . . ."

"Robot!" roared Matt. "Rise! Pick up Dr. Durant. We'll go

12

out the front way if that's what you want, Eliot. We'll show your crowd that our robot can rescue a human tortured by another human."

"Never!" screamed Eliot. "Guards, stun them all! We'll put Matt's hand on the identiplate of the lock to get out. We'll tell everyone the robot hurt its human owners."

The robot did not rise slowly. With one quick motion he was upright, and when the guards fired at him he picked them up by the neck, one in each hand, and shook them until the guns dropped to the floor.

Eliot beat Matt to the guns. "Robot. Release the guards or I'll kill Dr. Tully."

The robot stared at Eliot and then hurled the guards across the lab, knocked both guns from Eliot's hands, and picked up Jon Durant. "I will carry Dr. Durant to a hospital."

"Wait," said Walton, bending over the still bodies of the guards. "Their necks are broken. The robot has killed them."

"He didn't mean to," said Bess. "He doesn't know how strong he is."

"How can they die like that?" asked the robot. "I did not mean to kill them. I know the laws of robotics. Dr. Durant knows them. They are good laws for humans and robots, preventing violence, insuring care—and I have violated . . . broken . . . killed . . . I am a robot . . . a human . . . a robot . . . a—"

"Murderer!" said Eliot. "Matt, take Bess and that robot and your stupid partner out the back way. I'll find a way to get out and tell the Federation what that robot has done. Tully Products research will be stopped forever. Unless you want to tell the robot to kill me and Grandfather to keep us quiet."

"You make me sick," said Matt. "Robot, carry Dr. Durant through that back door. Come on, Bess. I'll get you and Jon to a hospital faster than Eliot ever could."

The back door slid shut behind the three humans and the robot. Eliot giggled. "Well, Grandfather, when Nanca orders

13

my troops to rescue us, there will be cops all over the hospital to arrest Matt and that robot."

"But I don't want my great-grandchild born in the middle of a riot," said Walton plaintively. "I want Adam to be safe."

Eliot expelled his breath as if he wanted to spit at something. "We need a riot. And we can't wait for Nanca. I know how to get us out now. Two linked stun guns will blast open any door."

"Overload is too dangerous!"

Eliot pulled a tall metal cabinet near the hinge side of the front door to the lab. Then he linked the guns, set them on overload, and as he placed them on top of the cabinet he laughed. "It's simple, Grandfather. The explosion will rip through the top hinge of the door while you and I are safe under Matt's desk. We have five minutes . . ."

But he had miscalculated. As he walked away from it, the cabinet exploded in shards, one catching him in the throat.

He reached out to his grandfather just as he had when he was a small child and only Walton was there because his father was gone and Nanca was too busy. Then the ceiling fell on him and he died while still terrified.

Walton Lorimer's legs were crushed under the concrete rubble, and the bodies of the guards buried. Looking up, Walton saw that the hole in the ceiling was full of shredded wires and rusty pipes pouring out water. As the water hit the wires, there was a crackling noise and all the lights went out.

With arms outstretched, Walton found the intercom in Eliot's breast pocket just as the darkness was broken by a flickering light. The old electrical conduits were on fire.

He tried to pull himself out from under the rubble, but a gush of warmth on his thigh told him he was bleeding badly. Then he realized he could not move his toes or even tell that they were there.

With arrogant hubris, he had accepted Nanca's opinion that he was good, but now he felt only old and fallible. He'd

14

spent his life upholding humanness against the onslaught of technology. Was it too late to be good? And for whom?

The electricity was off, so the scramble field would be gone. Nanca needed his information.

With a smile, Walton Lorimer turned on the intercom.

CHAPTER • 3

The narrow corridor ended abruptly at another door with two permilights hanging beside it. Matt took one and gave the other to Bess.

"We'll need light in the path outside." When he opened the door they heard the sound of rushing water, and Matt's light shone on a concrete ledge beside a black river.

"This is an old subway tunnel that wasn't filled in after antigrav aircars were invented. The city built a small museum of subway memorabilia in the only place in Manhattan where the trains emerged above ground in a short valley. An underground stream was diverted into the tunnel for paddleboats, but tourists didn't come and the tunnel was locked up, although the museum is still open on weekends."

As Matt took the lead, followed by Bess and then the robot, carrying Jon, Bess asked, "How far do we walk on that narrow path? My uterine contractions are increasing."

"Oh, Bess ! You mean you weren't kidding about being in labor?"

"Sorry, Matt. I know how squeamish you are about gory biological things, but since I'm nearly at term and it's my first baby, I'll be at it for hours. Remember that primitive women squatted by the path to push a baby out and then ran to catch up with the tribe. After Jon's safely in medical care I'll concentrate on having Adam. How far is it?"

"Only to the next station. Long ago my construction robots built an entrance from it into a robot-manned warehouse I own under a different company name. An aircar garaged on the roof will take us to a hospital. Let's hurry while Eliot's still locked in. Even if he tells Nanca where we've gone, he doesn't know about my aircar. I never told Jon."

16

"Why not?"

"I'm not sure. He'd only just joined Tully Robotics then, and I was obsessed with being careful. I've never forgotten how my father's robotics work was destroyed in the old bioeffer riots. I started over, and when I decided to make a superaide capable of mind transfer, I went underground. Literally."

The robot was muttering to himself. "Eyes open, not moving, so still . . . death . . . my fault . . . monster . . ."

Bess looked back at the robot. "Stop thinking about what happened. You must concentrate on carrying Jon to safety."

"This thinking and thinking of what I did is worse than being in stasis," said the robot, suddenly coherent.

"You can't think in stasis," said Matt.

"I did. I wanted to die then but this is worse. Please turn me off Dr. Tully. Please turn me off I want to die I am guilty and I must die please turn me off—"

"I order you to shut up and continue carrying Dr. Durant!" shouted Matt.

At that moment there was a loud explosion and as dust fell from the arched ceiling, the faint glow from under the locked doorway behind them vanished.

"Nanca must have sent in her troops to rescue her fair-haired boy," said Matt. "They've blasted through the door to the lab and now they'll find us."

But when no one tried to get into the subway tunnel after them, Matt grunted. "We might make it to my escape hatch."

"I smell smoke," said Bess. "Let's walk faster."

The walls of the tunnel were damp, clean on the side where they walked but encrusted with centuries of slime and dirt overhead and across the little river. The air was dank.

"Are there creatures living down here?" asked Bess.

"There used to be stories about alligators living in the sewers and subway systems, but there are only roaches and

17

other insects. Probably no rats or mice now that aide robots take care of city sanitation."

There was light ahead, an old subway station reduced to bare walls and a doorway labeled toilets.

"I put permilights in the ceiling. They don't burn out and will run forever on city electrical power," said Matt. "There's still running water and at least one working toilet in case you need to use it before we start climbing the eleven flights to the roof."

"Eleven flights!" Bess's face was shiny with sweat.

"I was much younger when I built this, and reasoned I could make it up the stairs at less risk than using equipment with electrical vibrations that could be detected if anyone was after me. The robots in the warehouse don't need a lift, and the stairs are hidden in what looks like a central ventilation shaft."

"Then by all means let me use the facilities here. I need them badly." She hurried to the toilet room.

The robot stood holding Jon, who was still breathing quietly, his eyes closed. "Dr. Tully, may I ask a question?"

"Uh huh." Matt turned off his permilight.

"Do you think that Eliot Breen and his mother will send the law after me because I killed the guards?"

"It wasn't your fault."

"But I did it. I am guilty of murder. I must surrender to them. I must go back to the laboratory and surrender."

"You will not! We need you to carry Jon. Even if you were an aide that had accidentally killed someone, the rescue of a live human would take priority over punishment and atonement for the death."

"Atonement. I remember. That means making recompense for some wrong that one has committed. If I help save three humans, will that help me atone?"

"Yes."

Bess returned, her face grayish with strain. "Sorry, Matt,

18

but I lost my amniotic fluid in there and the contractions are much stronger. I doubt if I can walk up eleven flights. I'm not as primitive as I thought."

"I'll carry you," said Matt.

"No, Matt. I'm as tall as you, and Adam is very heavy. You and the robot take Jon to the aircar and come back for me."

Matt pressed his palm into another identiplate beside the only door leading out of the station. It opened to show a lighted stairway. He and the robot hurried up it and returned a few minutes later without Jon.

"He's sleeping peacefully in the aircar," said Matt.

"Carry me up now," Bess said to the robot. "I wish Adam had waited, but I'm sure I'll make it to the hospital."

As the robot carefully picked up Bess and held her close to his chest, Matt entered the stairway and sniffed. "Air's much better in here. I hope the subway isn't filling with smoke because they've set Tully Tower on fire."

"Go up, Matt," said Bess. "It's not safe down here. We'll follow you."

Just as Matt started up the stairs and the robot walked to the doorway, there was another distant explosion. The lights of the station and the stairway went out. The door to the stairs slid shut.

"Bess!" shouted Matt, stumbling back down in the dark, hitting his head on the closed door. He turned his permilight back on and found the identiplate on the inward side. When he tried to use it the door remained locked.

He beat on the door, shouted and cursed, but could hear nothing from the other side.

"How could I have been so stupid! Building an escape hatch dependent on electricity! Stupid to have a door that shuts when electricity goes off."

He ran upstairs and turned the aircar's radio to the public channel.

"This is vstation Zee, operating on emergency generator,

19

radio only. A broken water main on the upper west side has apparently shortcircuited old electrical cables and caused a fire that is spreading. One of the main substations is blacked out and an unprecedented—at least in this century—domino effect has blacked out several other generators. There is no electrical power in Manhattan and the mayor has declared martial law against the rioting, for which Federal troops have been called in . . ."

"Damn," said Matt. "The Feds."

". . . city councilmen have long warned that our antiquated electrical system should be replaced and not endlessly repaired. Attention! The mayor orders everyone off the streets. Stay in your building unless it is on fire. Police patrols will take into custody any person attempting to force entry into buildings . . ."

Matt turned off the radio as the man beside him stirred and spoke.

"Who?" Jon touched Matt's face. "Who?"

"I'm Matt. Don't you know me?"

"Sleepy."

"That's right, Jon. Go back to sleep. I'll get you to a hospital soon, after I've gone back downstairs to try that blasted door once more. You wait here, and sleep."

When Matt hammered at the inside of the door again he heard an answering tap.

"Dammit I don't even know Morse code. I'm so helpless. But—robots hear better than people." He put his mouth against the metal door and shouted.

"Robot! Take Mrs. Durant along the path to the north end of the tunnel. I'll meet you there."

He heard no voice, but there was a faint answering tap. Back in the aircar. Jon was asleep, and in the distance there were red flames. Tully Tower? Matt started the motor, and the car rose into the drifting smoke of the city. Then he tuned the radio to a very private channel.

20

* * *

One hundred and fifty kilometers north and slightly west of Manhattan, a woman and her two-year-old daughter were sitting in the last patch of late sunshine at the back of an old-fashioned stone house that seemed to huddle in a clearing surrounded by trees.

Dinah Breen straightened her perfectly tailored slacks and bent forward to brush Meg Tully's silky black hair. Her own brilliant auburn hair blazed in the sunlight to which she had her back turned, avoiding the grim possibility of a famous actress with freckles.

The June scent of the garden in front of them was heavy in the still air and Meg sniffed. "I like June," said Meg.

"You don't remember any others," said Dinah. "You little green-eyed elf. You don't freckle at all."

"Is my hair dry, Mother?"

"Almost."

Meg began humming a soft, almost tuneless song that indicated she was happy. Otherwise, it was sometimes hard to tell how she felt.

A bell began ringing insistently. "Ouch," said Meg. "You pulled my hair."

"No one's supposed to know I'm here," said Dinah.

"Daddy does. I told him we were coming when he called me last week. Aren't you going to answer him?"

Dinah pressed her lips together, rose gracefully, and went inside the house, followed by Meg.

"Maybe Aunt Bess is having Adam. You said he was inside her and is going to come out. Did you want me as much as she wants Adam?"

Precocious offspring are difficult. "Of course," said Dinah, touching the connect button of the old phone. As she lifted the receiver she was glad there was no picture to show Matt Tully.

"Dinny, if that's you—listen carefully. I haven't much time. Manhattan is blacked out and I'm going to try to get to your

21

place by aircar. Get food in the house, and the number of the nearest hospital—"

"What's wrong, Ma—"

He interrupted before she could say his name. "Do it, Dinny." Then the connection stopped and she put the phone back. Matt was a genius at upsetting people.

"Why didn't Daddy want to talk to me?"

"He's in a hurry. He's coming here."

"Is he bringing Aunt Bess?"

"I don't know. I think we'd better listen to the vstation."

"Is Daddy coming to stay?"

"Certainly not."

CHAPTER • 4

Nanca's voice was shrill, and Walton held the intercom farther from his ear. "Eliot, why didn't you call—"

"This is your father. Eliot's dead. I'm sorry, Nanca. He put two guns on overload to blast his way through a locked door but he was killed and the ceiling fell in on us. Matt and Bess and Jon had already gone out the back way . . ."

"Eliot's dead? My son? Perhaps he's only unconscious . . ."

"He's dead, Nanca. Eliot and the two guards." Walton wondered why he was having such trouble explaining the deaths to Nanca. He waited, for she said nothing. Then he heard a long sigh, almost a shudder.

"We're coming to rescue you, Father. Where is the robot?"

"With Bess and Matt. The robot's carrying Jon." Walton did not continue. He remembered how the robot had killed the guards. And how Eliot had tried to kill Jon.

He was conscious that Nanca was still talking but he didn't hear her because the smoke made him cough and then there was a pain in his chest. He controlled the pain, calming his nervous system with the mental technique he had taught Bess years ago. Biological control, so humans wouldn't rely on drugs and artificial equipment.

Artificial. Robots. Intelligence, artificial intelligence, and mind transfer that does not succeed. I have always known that Matt Tully is a dangerous man. . . .

It was Bess's wedding reception, and there was Matt, shoving cake into his mouth and talking through it as usual.

"Not bad," said Matt thickly. "A marriage is bound to be a success when the bride and groom insist on chocolate cake with rum icing."

"Why is Jon staying with Tully Robotics when it will make things hard for Bess in this family?"

"Come on, Walton, Bess has a new family now. She may be a doctor but she's no bioeffer. She approves of robots that will insure immortality for humans. With mind transfer to robots we could go to the stars."

"I suspect you won't just make mind transfer robots, but others who are not. Can't you accept the fact that humanity will be better off if robots are only vaguely humanoid, completely programmed and willing to serve because that programming tells them to? Why should we go to the stars where we'll need technology even more than we do here in the colonized solar system? You off-worlders don't appreciate the natural beauty of our native planet and the biofundamentalist efforts to create samples of it in the dome colonies and the orbital spomes."

"Off-worlders?" Matt grunted. "What do you think Luna is, not a world? I was raised there and her beauty is just as natural as anything on Earth. A robot is a natural part of the solar system, too, not some alien artifact. Since we humans are part of nature, so is anything we create, including robots. Furthermore, we need them for the tests we'll have to devise in the attempt to invent hyperdrive."

"Hyperdrive is the product of minds who invent only fiction," said Walton.

"People who say an invention is impossible forget that the same thing was said about heavier-than-air flight."

"The analogy is a poor one. Birds always flew. You are talking about powered flight, Matt. You and I will always disagree. I believe that God intended the Terran solar system to be humanity's home, and robots as tools regulated by the laws of robotics, which can't be guaranteed for any tool that thinks like a human being."

"You hypocrite, Walton. Your statement reveals that it is human beings you don't trust."

24

The flower girl tottered over, unsteady on her feet because she learned to walk later than she learned to talk, both appallingly early. "Pick me up, Daddy."

Tully hoisted her to his shoulder. "Say hello to your great-grandpapa."

Her greenish eyes, so much like a cat's, made Walton feel uncomfortable. "Hello, Meg," he said.

"Great-Grandpapa doesn't like us," said Meg.

The smoke was increasing and he could hear the noise of distant hammering. He couldn't hear Nanca because the intercom, still in his hand, was now on his chest and he didn't seem to have the strength to lift it to his head. He was thinking about his granddaughter Dinah. She had divorced Tully but had refused to bring Meg to live with Walton. His eyes filled with tears and he wondered if Adam would like him. It was important to be liked. He could remember . . .

"Well, Walt, you've got what you wanted for your tenth birthday. I hope it's not going to be a bother."

"She's a beautiful cat, Mother. I'll take care of her."

"The cook robot will feed her, in the kitchen."

"Please let me do it in my room—please!"

"Very well. The cook can put a week's worth of food in a portable fridge. Don't go to the kitchen to get it. I don't want you associating with robots."

The cat was an elegant, half-grown Siamese taut with ferocious energy, and she intimidated him. He named her Mera and wanted her to love him as he loved her.

"Please, Mera, lie still in my arms and let me pet you as much as I like because you're perfect. Mother and Father want me to put you in shows but I won't, because you're mine and I don't want anyone to care about you except me . . ."

He found her out. He went to the kitchen because the cat food had run out too early. The cook robot, who didn't need to sit, was in a chair, and Mera was in his lap.

"Let go of Mera!"

"I am not holding the cat, Master Walton."

"Mera! Come to me!"

She raised her head, opened her slightly crossed eyes, yawned, stretched, and sank back against metal thighs and abdomen, purring loudly, her claws thrusting in and out against the unfeeling surface of the robot.

"Why is she with you? What have you done, cook?"

"She comes to sleep, Master Walton."

"But why on your lap?"

The robot said nothing for several minutes. Correlative thought is difficult for aides. "I deduce that the cat likes to sleep near slightly warm microcircuit vibrations. Aides have their power source and computing equipment located in their lower abdomen to provide a low center of gravity—"

"Remove Mera and never let her do that again."

"Yes, sir." The cook put Mera on the floor, stood up, and bowed. "I am sorry, Master Walton."

"You can't be sorry. You have no feelings."

"I am programmed to say I am sorry, sir."

Shortly afterward, Walton developed a severe allergy to cats. He refused treatment, and Mera was given away. He never saw her again.

"Father! Why don't you answer?"

He dragged the intercom to his face. "Nanca, I meant to tell you about Eliot's guards . . ." He choked and tried to marshall his ebbing energy.

Then he was young again, climbing into the lap of a robot that seemed to have Jon's face.

"Please love me," said Walton.

"Father!"

It was too late. He had time to laugh at his own indecision while his chest filled with pain that blotted out . . . everything.

26

CHAPTER • 5

"Are you certain that Matt yelled for us to walk to the end of the tunnel?"

"I am certain."

"Then we'd better hurry. Adam is on his way and the smoke in the tunnel is much worse. Pick me up and I'll hold the light so you can see where you're walking."

The robot walked on and on, while Bess grimaced at each contraction. Suddenly the robot stopped, for the concrete walk had ended at another platform. Beyond, the black river flowed around a curve but there was no ledge beside it.

"This must have been another station," said Bess, "but the exits were bricked up long ago, by the looks of that wall."

"I will wade into the river and carry you above the water," said the robot.

"No. There isn't time. I can feel that my son is choosing to emerge in the Manhattan subway tunnel, and I don't want him to do it over water. We'll stay here on this platform. Put me down and find out if there's another toilet."

She removed her maternity tunic, turned it inside out, and put it on the concrete floor. Her underwear went beside it, and then she tried to squat, only to fall on her knees.

"How do primitive women give birth while squatting? I can't do it, but I dread lying down in this dirty place."

The robot loomed over her. "The toilets here do not function but there is some water dripping from a tap. I have washed my hands."

"Thank you." As he squatted easily beside her, she noticed that his smooth face had changed to an expression of worry and concern. She was about to ask if he altered the shape of his face to affect the emotions of watching humans, but a

27

powerful contraction made her groan and she changed her mind. She took hold of his outstretched hand and held it tightly during the next contraction. The robot became only another intelligent being who was trying to help.

"I just can't manage squatting," she said, half lying back with her upper body propped up on her elbows. The smoke was much thinner at this station and she could concentrate on her breathing, the way she had taught so many other women.

"I know all about babies," she said, more to herself than to the robot. "I've delivered many and there's nothing to worry about because Adam has always been head down, and at the last scan faced my back. Just a conventional birth. Only I can't figure out how to bear down, push him out, and catch him at the same time. Do you think you could be the catcher?"

"I don't understand. Please explain."

She did, in detail. Finally she said, "Now take the permilight and look at the place where Adam's head is coming out. That's my perineum."

"Yes. I remember what you looked like before. I mean that Dr. Durant knew. He had not seen this phenomenon, however. I will do as you instructed. I will help . . . help . . . I will try to be . . . to be human . . ."

"Just be yourself—someone helping in childbirth."

"But who am I?" The robot's eyes were wide, and almost like Jon's when he was unusually anxious and bewildered. "I don't even have a name."

She breathed through the next contraction and then said, "You should have one. I think you should choose it. What would you like?"

There was time for another contraction before he answered. "I would like to be called Seven."

"Okay, Seven." Awkwardly, she felt the perineal skin around the baby's head. "Fully dilated. Now remember what

28

I told you, Seven. The next time I push the baby's head, hold it lightly, pressing slightly downward as the back of the head comes out. Then upward until the face is out. Don't use your strength."

"I am too strong. I will be gentle now. My strength killed two humans. I grieve. I am guilty . . ."

She grunted as she bore down with the next contraction. "Help me, Seven!"

"The head did not come out all the way."

"Next time. Don't let it pop out too fast and tear me."

"Push, Mrs. Durant—there, the head is out safely. There is no bleeding around it and you were not lacerated. There is no cord around the baby's neck. I felt for it as you instructed."

"Good. Wipe the mucous from the baby's nose, and remember that with the next contraction, the shoulders will rotate. You'll let them come out slowly, the upper shoulder first, then the lower. Don't pull or twist the baby's head."

"I will be careful, Mrs. Durant."

And then Adam was out of her body, held squirming in the hands of a robot.

Bess relaxed, catching her breath, and lay all the way back, not caring about the dirt. "Put him on my belly, Seven."

Adam was perfect. No defects that she could see, and powerful lungs. His first cries echoed in the subway tunnel.

"What should I do with the umbilical cord?"

"Nothing yet. Let me rest, and let the baby have the last pulsations of blood through the cord."

She shut her eyes, feeling the warmth of the baby's body melt into her sore belly, the pressure of him stimulating her uterus. It contracted again.

"The placenta just came out, intact," said Seven.

"Good." She massaged her uterus so it would stay contracted and not bleed. "There, nice and hard. Nothing soggy about me."

"You should sleep. You must be tired."

29

"I could sleep for hours, but not here. The smoke is increasing and there's alot more noise back where we came from. We have to move on."

"There is nothing to cut the cord."

"It doesn't matter. We'll wrap the placenta up with Adam and cut it free later." Painfully, she stood up and wrapped her son in the cleaner part of the tunic. She pulled her camisole down and wished longingly for clean clothes. Without thinking about it, she held Adam against her left chest, where babies hear the mother's heart best and are comforted by the familiar sound.

Seven shone the light upon the baby, who tried to open his eyes, blinked, and shut them again, yawning widely in the process. "He is alive," said the robot.

"Of course." Bess smiled at Seven. "Would you like to touch him?"

"I delivered him."

"Yes, but I meant—I don't know what I meant."

"Touch in friendship? Or a father's touch?"

"Sometimes those are much alike. Jon's touch would be more friendly than possessive. Do you know that from what you know about Jon?" asked Bess, her lips trembling slightly.

"I know." Seven bent forward and caressed Adam's round cheek with one long artificial finger covered with synthoskin.

The baby's right hand popped out between the folds of the tunic and waved awkwardly. The little shape, each fingernail tiny but perfect, hit against Seven's finger.

Automatically, the reflexes of a trillion primate ancestors activated in the newborn, and perhaps in the borrowed memories of the robot. Seven's finger moved until it rested against the small hand, which immediately closed around it in a tight primate grip. Adam gurgled contentedly.

For a moment, mother, baby, and robot were a timeless unity against the uncertainty of the cosmos. Then Seven picked them up, held high, and eased his body into the river for the journey northward.

30

CHAPTER • 6

Night had come while Matt gripped the thick steel bars that separated him from the subway tunnel. Behind him, the subway museum was quiet except where water tumbled over an artificial rockfall on its way to the pond in the park outside.

He shone his light over the gate once more, and rattled it, knowing he could not break through. The bars reached to the floor of the platform where he stood, and continued across and down into the river beside him. At one time a section of the gate had opened, but now the three old-fashioned padlocks were rusted shut. Beyond the gate, the tunnel stretched into darkness.

Suddenly a gleam of distant light seemed to blink as if to acknowledge the fact that he was waiting.

"Bess!" Matt yelled, pounding hopelessly on the gate.

A few minutes later Seven broke the padlocks with no discernible effort and the gate was opened.

"Is that Adam?" Matt gaped at the tiny creature in Bess's arms, sound asleep.

"Newly minted. Beautiful, isn't he?"

"Not at all. Red and wrinkled."

"You're impossible." Bess's smile turned off quickly. "Is Jon all right?"

"He's sleeping in the aircar."

"You didn't lock him in, did you? Jon can't stand to be confined in an enclosed space."

"Bess, Jon's not ill exactly, but—"

"There's a searchlight outside," said Seven.

"Hey!" shouted a voice outside the museum. "Who's there? Speak up or I'll fire. This is the police."

"Robot—hide!" whispered Matt. "It's all right, officer. My

31

wife and I left our aircar outside to seek shelter in here. She's just given birth to our son."

"No kidding!" He was a very young cop, probably a rookie sent on unaccustomed duty in the emergency. Tentatively, he walked toward them with his light on the man, woman, and child.

"Someone broke that gate—and there are wet footprints in the dust," said the cop, "but it wasn't you. None of you is wet. How long have you been here?"

"I gave birth only a few minutes ago," said Bess evenly. "And that took about half an hour."

"It must have been somebody using a crowbar or heavy-duty robots. Seen any robots?"

"Officer, we haven't seen any strangers."

"I'll just look around—Jesus! People!"

"You're shining your light into the subway museum," said Matt carefully. "Those are examples of old subway cars with operators and passengers in effigy. Creepy, isn't it?"

The young cop walked slowly around the museum. "Yeah, you're right. All dummies. I suppose this nude one on the floor had his clothes stolen long ago. And this motorman has a good uniform but what a dummy face!"

Bess groaned slightly and the cop came back to her. "Gee lady," he said, "I'm sorry you had to have your baby in a moldy old place like this, but it's better than being outside in the blackout—lots of riots tonight. We've been stopping people who seem to be wandering around—hey! Who's there?"

"I didn't see anyone," said Matt. "We're the only people in the museum."

The cop ran outside with his gun in his hand, followed by Matt and Bess. "Someone crossed in front of my patrol car's headlights. You there—what are you doing?"

A tall, shambling figure weaved drunkenly toward the cop. His face seemed to be curiously blank and his eyes glazed.

"Stop! Stop right there or I'll stun you."

32

"Officer, it's all right, he's only—" but before Matt could finish the nervous cop touched his gun.

Jonathan Durant's expression did not change, but his body became rigid and fell sideways. He was so tall that his head and shoulders fell into the stream where it ran across artfully oriental stones on its way to the tree-lined pond.

"Jon!" Bess ran to him with Matt behind her.

"Hey," said the cop, staring at his own gun. "I've got it on the lowest setting, like they tell us. Only a prickle. What'd he go fall in the river for? It was just a little warning."

Bess put Adam on the grass of the river bank and helped Matt pull Jon out of the water. "He's not breathing," said Matt.

"I'll do CPR," said Bess, getting into position. She was giving Jon the preliminary deep breaths when suddenly all the lights, everywhere, came back on. Those in the park were old-fashioned, deliberately planted early twentieth-century electrics that cast a soft glow through the trees.

"He's bleeding," said Matt. "Turn him over."

Jon had fallen on a sharp rock, the back of his head crushed as if it had been a bird's egg fallen from a broken nest.

"Yes, this is my wife," said Matt, "and thanks to the stupidity of the police my brother is dead."

The newly arrived sergeant was nervous, too. He had questioned the rookie, who was back in his patrol car, shaking with fear and guilt. The sergeant wondered if he should take the bereaved family to the local station, already overcrowded with problems from the night of blackout.

The corpse, covered by one of the plastisheets always carried in patrol cars, was in Matt's aircar.

"I keep telling you that we're commuters," said Matt. "We stopped here because we were afraid to go home upstate in the dark. Now my wife has had the baby prematurely and my brother has been killed, and we must leave at once to break

33

the news to my brother's wife in person. If you detain us, you'll be sorry. As it is, I'm going to sue the Manhattan police—"

"Okay, okay," said the sergeant. "I don't know why a mild warning prickle from my rookie's gun would make your brother fall into the river, but it wasn't the gun that killed him. It was a rock in the stream, and personally I think your brother must have been drunk—"

"I'm going to sue! Mayor Ramirez is a personal friend of mine." It was well known that the mayor had been trying to reorganize the police force for some time.

"So leave!" shouted the sergeant. "Go home and that will be fewer people in our city. We have alot of cleaning up to do, so get out of here!"

"Thank you, sergeant," said Bess, shivering under the blanket the police had given her. "We'll of course use our car because I think I might throw up any minute now, and—"

"Okay, lady." The sergeant hurriedly got in his aircar and shouted to the rookie, "Go back to the station at once, you idiot! You'll be of more use there."

Both police aircars took off with a lurch, and the park was quiet once more. Matt put his arms around Bess.

"I'm sorry. I'm so sorry. Jon deserved better."

"Where is Seven?" asked Bess dully, cradling Adam in her arms under the blanket.

"Seven?"

"Your superaide robot chose that name for himself. Don't scold him for it, Matt."

The robot walked out of the small museum. He had taken off the dummy motorman's uniform and in the dim light his close-fitting, gray lab suit looked as if it were part of his body.

"I am sorry that Dr. Durant is dead," said Seven. "Why did he collapse if the policeman fired only a warning?"

"Eliot must have damaged Jon much more than we real-

34

ized," said Bess wearily. "And a damaged brain can't take stun."

"I think Jon was already dead as a person," said Matt. "He came to consciousness for a while in the aircar and didn't know me. If he'd lived, he might never have been—normal."

Bess walked to the aircar, crying at last. "Seven, stay in back with Jon's body. Keep your head down in case any patrol cars inspect us."

Seven helped Bess into the front as Matt slid into the driver's seat.

"Hurry, Ro—Seven," said Matt, turning on the engine. "I want to get away from here. And as Bess said, try to keep well out of sight."

"I will do so. As the policeman implied when he saw me pretending to be the motorman, my face is not perfectly human."

And Adam Durant began to cry.

CHAPTER • 7

"You two stay in the aircar. The holographer will come with me to record my meeting with Dr.Tully."

"Yes, Senator."

Nanca Breen and the holographer walked slowly up the path, each side shaded by tall hemlocks interlaced with white birch. Deep in the woods, the old house was long and low, its stone walls covered by lichen, ivy, and morning glory that was still in bloom because it was not yet noon.

They rounded a curve and saw the front door, paneled in oak above a broad stone step. The figures of a small black-haired girl and a man sat on the step, studying a tortoise that was waking up in the sunlight.

"Look! He's yawning!" said the child, shaking the man's arm as the holographer began to record the scene.

The man turned toward them and Nanca gasped. Yet it could not be Jon. Jon was dead.

"Stop recording," said Nanca with more irritation than she had wanted to show. "That's a robot."

"Looks more humanoid than most robots. Makes a good picture anyway with the kid."

Meg, startled by their voices, looked frightened, tugging at the robot's arm to make him go in the house.

She doesn't recognize me, thought Nanca. Why should she? I haven't seen her since Bess's wedding ten months ago. She looks more like Matt than ever. A pity.

"Meg, I'm your grandmother," said Nanca with a bright smile. "Where is your father? I've come to see him."

Without a word, the robot picked up Meg and the tortoise and carried them inside the house.

"Walton Lorimer didn't object to nanny robots, did he?" asked the holographer, not without a hint of sarcasm.

"Aide robots are necessary. We need servants, but not competition. That was my father's point."

"Well, that servant looked almost human, but I suppose it's no competition, is it, Senator?"

Nanca did not answer. Was that Father's point? I couldn't think of anything except those bodies soaked in water and blood. Perhaps Eliot would always have refused, but would Father have accepted a second life in a robot body if Tully had perfected it?

Standing there in the sunlit clearing before the front door, Nanca did not see the door open until she looked up to find Dinah on the stone step.

"Didn't you bring organized protesters with you, Mother? Eliot would be disappointed."

Nanca gritted her teeth to keep tears of anger and unexpressed grief from coming. "You asked me to come alone, and I am here."

"Hardly alone. Do you want that camera to record a private family meeting? You've had plenty of publicity through the funerals of Eliot and Grandfather."

"Funerals which you did not attend."

"No. I'm sorry, but we had Jon's funeral here, and I didn't want to leave Meg."

"But you have an adequate aide nanny for her. I saw it just now. It has an odd appearance—and why does it need to wear clothes?"

Dinah laughed. "That's Matt's experiment, Mother."

The camera man, who had been staring at Dinah's cleavage, absorbed a few of the words and said, "Should I find the robot and take more pictures, Senator?"

"Sure, Meg adores him," said Dinah.

"No!" Nanca pointed down the path. "Go wait in the car with my guards."

37

"But Senator—you said . . ."

"I have changed my mind. Go."

Mother and daughter stood facing each other in the sunlight, while overhead a blue jay stridently announced that they were all intruders. "Is Jon really dead?"

"And buried," said Dinah. "You should never have let Eliot hurt Jon's mind with a controller."

Nanca's face flushed. "Eliot was wrong. He was headstrong, determined to advance our cause, and didn't realize that with precise questioning, Jon would eventually have told the truth to me."

Dinah shrugged. "Jon was too good to be true. It's a miracle he kept the secret of Matt's research that long."

"And the secret is that the research failed. The human race must not count on second lives in artificial bodies, but on prolonging biological life. It was stupid of Matt to try to transfer a human mind into an aide made to look more like a man. If I had known the aide was a nanny, I wouldn't have gone along with Eliot's planned riot. Ridicule of Matt would have done a better job."

"You were always good at ridicule, Mother, and poor Eliot was always good at violence. Even when he was little, and we still played together . . ." Dinah paused, and Nanca saw that there were circles under her eyes. "I hate death, Mother. Much as I quarrel with Matt and am glad I divorced him, I wish his mind transfer project would succeed. I wish you and your friends in government would give him a big grant to take to Centauri Spome."

"Why is he going there?"

"Where can he go? Tully Tower has been destroyed, and if he starts his work anywhere in the Terran solar system, riots are likely to interrupt it, thanks to the craziness stirred up by the bioeffers. The scientists in Centauri Spome will take him, but he has no funds except from the sale of Tully Tower, and that was wrecked and mortgaged up to Matt's armpits."

"Which are clean, deodorized, and excessively humble these days," said Matt, his broad body filling the shadow of the doorway. "I unashamedly admit that I listened. Thanks, Dinny. Would you like to come in, Nanca?"

There was no one in the living room. "Where's Meg? Bess and the baby?" asked Nanca.

"Adam is asleep and Bess is giving Meg her bath," said Matt. "Bess hates you too much right now to see you, Nanca."

"I'm sorry about Jon."

"I'll go upstairs and tell that to Bess," said Dinah, "but I don't think it will make any difference to her."

When they were alone, Matt rubbed his bald spot and asked, "Want iced tea, Nanca?"

"No, thanks." One of the toys on the floor seemed to be moving slowly toward a patch of sunlight near the french doors open to the back garden.

"That's Methuselah," said Matt. "Lives in the garden, and Meg is devoted to him."

"Eliot was devoted to me."

"I know. Are you lonely, Nanca?"

"I have my work."

"Without Walton or Eliot."

"They were biofundamentalists, prepared for the fact that death is the end of living things."

"And are you prepared, Nanca? You're older than you pretend. I know you had the twins at the far end of the advanced reproductive scale we have now. You must be the oldest Lorimer left alive."

"Why are you badgering me about this? What difference does it make?"

"Just thinking about death," said Matt. "I once had an aunt who, when she was very old, told me that the idea of death was no longer terrible because there was no one left alive who remembered her when she was young."

Nanca straightened her shoulders. "If you're trying to

39

persuade me that humans would be better off being able to look forward to a second life for themselves and their friends, you won't succeed. Not when mind transfer is a failure, as Eliot discovered."

"We've made a beginning," said Matt.

"You've made a monster. Eliot learned from Jon that your experimental robot remembers only a few immediate facts, doesn't behave or think like Jon, and is probably psychotic. All you've constructed is a humanoid robot that will outlive humans, destroy—"

"I know that speech, Nanca. You bioeffers always exaggerate the danger of superaide robots."

"Then it's true. Your experimental robot is only a superaide, not a mind transfer."

"The heal-itself superaide brain is the logical step toward genuine mind transfer."

"Never. They'll take over."

"Take over what? Our government? Your job? I can't imagine a genuinely intelligent superaide being that stupid. Hell, I can't even imagine why an intelligent human would want your job, or the job you want."

Nanca's voice was like steel. "I'll stop your research, Matt. I won't let my father's work go for nothing."

"Your father celebrated biological life. But a mind transferred robot is alive too."

"No, Matt. You'd have some hope of governmental approval if you could show success with mind transfer, but—"

"Would you like to see Dr. Durant's grave, Senator?" The new voice was deep and resonant.

Seven walked toward her but did not stop and bow like an aide. Nanca shivered when the robot smiled at her.

"Seven, I told you to wait upstairs," said Matt irritably.

"I think Senator Breen should see Dr. Durant's grave."

"I will see it," said Nanca, her voice suddenly husky.

"All right," said Matt, heading for the back doors. "Your

40

robot will take me," said Nanca, "unless you are afraid to leave it alone with a human."

"Not at all." Matt shrugged and went upstairs.

Seven led Nanca outside into the sunshine of the small garden. They skirted a stone pool where a fountain spurted intermittently from a bronze lotus stuck among live water lilies. An opening in the back hedge revealed a meager path into the woods beyond. The robot did not speak as they walked onto the path, and Nanca, her eyes on her feet to avoid tripping over tree roots, hoped that he would not.

Jon's grave was in a circular space surrounded by particularly tall trees. A clump of violets grew next to the plain white stone marking the grave.

She found that she had to say something. "Meg is fond of you, I understand. Robots have always made good nannies."

Seven did not say what she expected, a humble "Yes, Madam." He looked at her as if appraising—what?

"Meg is an unusually gifted child," said Seven. "Her father is, of course, brilliant and hard-driving, but Meg's capacity to see things in a larger perspective, and to strive toward fulfilling a goal, no doubt comes from you."

"You don't know me."

"I don't know Senator Nanca Breen. Does anyone?"

"Do not talk to me like this!"

"Someone must. You are blocking Dr.—Matt's work. You do not understand that the superaide brain could be developed to take perfect mind transfer and make possible long second lives for human beings."

"It's not possible. You are a superaide, and Tully will only develop more of you, independent robots with intelligence that imitates ours."

"Ah, then you do think my intelligence is more like that of a human than a robot aide's?"

"You? A monstrosity. Not Jonathan Durant."

"Not the Jonathan Durant you knew, Nan."

41

He moved closer to her and she wanted to run. He smiled again. Suddenly there was more resemblance to Jon.

"I'm sorry that my features are imperfect, Nan."

"Don't call me that! You're not Jon!"

"Which Jon? Human beings have many identities at different times. Sometimes a human forgets the many selves he used to be. Jon seldom thought of you, but I do, a great deal."

"Why?"

"Because I remember better than he could."

"Oh, my God!" She was trembling. "A metal monster hoarding Jon's memories, and they told me you remembered little of Jon's life and feelings."

"I have sorted through the memories and I retain everything. I also have emotions. That is possible with a brain as complex as mine."

"You can't have emotions."

"I do. You are still beautiful, after all these years. I should have agreed to have your children instead of letting you run away to marry Breen."

"Only to have children . . ." The words escaped before Nanca could stop them.

"Yet you were right, my golden girl. You had to leave me."

"You're wrong! The memories you stole from Jon are wrong! It was you who left me." She stopped, appalled. "I mean it was Jon who left me."

"I heard you phoning Breen, perhaps to make me jealous, but I realized then that you wanted to drive me away because I was wrong for you. I wasn't interested in politics or fame, just in doing my work. I'd have been a handicap, wouldn't I? Didn't you hope that I would go away?"

She could not answer.

"I'm sorry I was such a disappointment," said Seven. "To be honest, you frightened me, Nan. You're stronger than most hu—than most people. If I'd stayed with you my life would have been absorbed by you, and soon you'd have hated me."

42

She looked down at the gravestone. "I don't hate. Not any more."

"I wish that were true. I am sorry, Nan. That was a wonderful May we had, so long ago."

Staring at the grave, it suddenly did not seem incongruous that she was also talking to Jon. "You gave me violets."

"And we sang all the old songs about May."

"But you were always slightly off-key."

"Not anymore."

She looked up at him, and Jon was not there.

The robot bowed. "I will take you back to the house, Senator."

"I've forgotten your name," she whispered.

"Seven. The seventh superaide, the only—survivor. Jon thought it would be good luck to have his mind transfer made to the seventh."

Almost like a tactile hallucination, the memory of Jon carrying her to the bed came back. And Seven had carried Bess, and Meg—Nanca tightened her lips and clenched her fists.

"Robot, you should be deactivated. I will insist—"

"No, Nan, you won't. You will give Matt Tully all the funds he needs to carry on his work in Centauria, where he'll be safe from the dangers of militant biofundamentalism."

"Never."

"You'll do it, Nan. For me. For the past."

"Then the research must be controlled—"

"No, Nan. Freedom. We tasted it once. Have you had it since, that freedom of mind and body, between two people who passionately care—"

"Stop! You're blackmailing me!"

"I will keep your secrets, Senator."

"For a price," said Nanca bitterly.

"We are old, you and I. Would you want to be the one

43

human being who held the future of mind transfer in her hand, and rejected it?"

She turned and started back to the house. Then she stopped and looked back at him, still standing at the grave.

"Seven—I will pay the price. Tully's research will continue. But I insist that you keep away from me."

"Yes, Madam."

CHAPTER•8

After a week of rainy weather, it was sunny again. In and on the overgrown grass beside the goldfish pond, Methuselah was eating, green blades drooping from either side of his slowly moving jaws.

"Inefficient feeder, isn't he?" said Bess. "Not at all like Adam, who takes nourishment at a prodigious rate. It's amazing that tortoises outlasted dinosaurs and are likely to be around observing as homo sap passes into extinction."

There was only an answering grunt from the man slumped beside her on the white bench.

"What's the matter? Are you ill, Matt?"

"Women! I'll never understand them. Now that Dinah's found a new romance with her current producer she's so sweet to me I could get diabetes. Nanca has a mysterious talk with Seven and announces that funds for my research will be available subject to on-site inspection when I think I'm ready for the next mind transfer experiment. And you female doctors can't think of anything but the growth rate of infant children or the physical vulnerabilities of middle-aged men."

"It's all perfectly reasonable," said Bess. "Dinah is happy so she wants everyone else to be, even you. And I can't help worrying about you because you've done nothing but mope since we got here, even after Nanca's change of heart."

"Nanca never did anything from heart. Probably doesn't possess one."

"You're wrong. She once had an affair with Jon, long before I met him. Seven doesn't know I know because Jon told me after the mind transfer was attempted."

"I'll be damned. Well, whatever Nanca's motives are, I suppose I can start work in Centauria, but I'm sure I'll fail."

45

"No you won't. You almost succeeded with Seven."

"But I didn't succeed. And have you noticed how he's busy transforming himself into an ordinary aide, helping the cook robot, weeding the garden, tending Meg and Adam, and sirring me in the most obsequious tones . . ."

"Shhh—here he comes."

Along the path from the house Seven strode, easily carrying Adam's wooden cradle with Adam in it. Placing the cradle in front of Bess, Seven bowed and turned to go back.

"Thank you, Seven," Bess said loudly. "Could you tell us why you're behaving like an aide?"

He stopped, wheeled, and bowed again. "I endeavor to give satisfaction, Madam."

"We are not amused, dammit!" yelled Bess.

"That we are not," said Matt. "In one week we're going to the spome that calls itself Centauria. We're starting important work, and here you are acting like an aide capable of washing the lab floor and little else."

"I am not going to Centauria, sir."

"But I've got the transport tickets—expensive as hell."

"I'm sorry, sir. I am not going. Since Mrs. Durant will be using my ticket, I am staying in this house as caretaker when Miss Dinah and Meg go on tour."

Bess glared at him. "Seven, I am definitely taking a job in a hospital upstate—"

"I have told them you will be unable to do so, Madam." With that, Seven wheeled and walked away, fast.

"He can't—I won't have anyone organize my life for me! I refuse—it's insupportable—arrogant . . ."

"Bess, do you mind that much, because I really . . ."

But Meg was running toward them, followed by a smiling Dinah. "Mommy's getting married again and says I can go with you and Bess for a while," said Meg breathlessly.

"Don't tell me I get married too often," said Dinah. "If you two are trying it, I might as well and we'll have a great double

46

wedding, with Meg as flower girl again. And since my fiancé is rich I'll be able to afford the expense of Meg visiting Centauria by transport."

Meg clapped her hands. "It'll be fun to go by transport." Then she looked puzzled and ashamed, because already Meg hated not knowing things. "What is transport?"

"A form of electronic travel that uses hyperspace, honey," said Matt. "It's the only way to go from here to Centauria."

"But how did the transport get there, Daddy?"

"By an automated ship that turned on the transport when it arrived in the Centauri system. Then human engineers and work robots transported to build the only space home humans have outside our own solar system."

"So romantic," said Dinah. "Even for my stodgy ex-husband and cousin. Isn't it lovely to be in love?" Before anyone could comment, she waltzed back to the house.

"Mother's happy," said Meg. "I like it when she's happy. Seven says it's good that you're marrying Bess, Daddy. He says I'll like visiting Centy—whatever. I want Seven to be there when I visit. Make him go with you."

"I am going to talk to that robot," said Bess grimly. "Right now."

"You can't, " said Meg. "Adam's awake, and isn't it his feeding time?"

Newborns see better than was once believed. Shades of colors, lights and darks, shapes that move and shapes that don't. All are unlabeled parts of a pattern that is slowly resolved into objects against a background.

Already, Adam Durant was recognizing separate parts of the pattern. Shapes took on meaning and became familiar and loved, joining with the touch and sound that had always been part of existence. One voice, one touch, and now one shape seemed most familiar, the givingness of the universe made manifest.

The glory of sight flooded Adam's brain as he opened his

47

eyes. He smiled at the familiar part until he became aware of sensations that came from inside the pattern. From himself. He was hungry and he let the universe know about it.

The universe responded and he enjoyed the contact it made with his lips, the gratifying exercise of sucking, the special taste in his mouth, the warm liquid down his throat, and the satisfaction of filling up.

Then his mouth let go and he was held in another familiar position. He could see other parts of the universe watching him, and when something patted his back, he burped. That felt good, too, and he smiled again.

"How can you smile, Adam?" asked Bess. "From the way my emotions are churning, you should be getting indigestion."

"Born mothers don't give their infants indigestion," said Matt. "Now stay right here—you, too, Meg—because I'm going inside to have it out with Seven."

It was difficult trying to argue with an intelligent robot while a stupid kitchen aide stolidly made cookies and upstairs a glamorous ex-wife sang loudly about love.

"Seven, you can't arrange our lives! Bess won't want to go with me into exile. For Jon's sake, I bought Tully Tower so he could work on Earth although I wanted to stay in Luna City. When he married Bess, they talked about raising children on Earth, under open sky, with wild woods . . ."

"And mosquitoes, fleas, and poison ivy," said Seven. "You have all been scratching since you came here. Earth, as you Luna City natives say, is an uncomfortable place."

"And since robots don't itch they should take over Earth?"

"No, Matt. Robots won't take over. There will be no super-aides, and no mind transfer."

"But you persuaded Nanca . . ."

"You'll need funds in Centauria, but you must use them for some other research. Work on inventing hyperdrive."

"Maybe my daughter will grow up to be a genius theoretical

48

scientist, but I'm only a roboticist. No one's come near to inventing hyperdrive and I don't intend to try. I think you want to get me and Bess off Earth because we two are the only humans who know you killed the guards. We'll keep the secret. Why are you afraid of us?"

"I fear only myself. Bioeffers are correct—there is no way to make an intelligent robot who completely obeys the laws of robotics. Intelligent robots can make dangerous errors."

"I tell you it wasn't your fault!" shouted Matt.

"The killing was unintentional, but I have the conscience of a robot grounded in the laws of robotics, as well as the human conscience of Jonathan Durant, and both sides of me say that I should be the last superaide, passing quietly through existence by doing as little harm to anyone as I can manage."

"And I'm supposed to stagnate in Centauria, deprived of my life's work?"

"You'll be happy, married to Bess."

"It would be wonderful if she and Adam came with me," said Matt softly, "but I also want you, Seven. I need you. We'll have to start over in Centauria, but together we could perfect the superaide, so that both intelligent robots and mind-transferred humans can exist."

"No."

"You idiot! Any intelligent, self-aware species suffers from the problems you fear. Even right actions have ripples of consequence that are not perfect and may be dangerous if not watched. Seven—it's an *adventure*! Look at the cook robot—it's not listening to us. It doesn't even care about the cookies it makes."

"I also cannot smell or taste cookies. Or anything else. Has it occurred to you that a human mind transferred to a robot might miss the more primitive aspects of organicity?"

"Well, I doubt if even the best superaide will ever be able to

49

smell or taste, but—hey! Are you angry because I didn't make sex possible?"

"No. I am not Jonathan Durant and Bess is not my wife. I think roboticists will eventually create robots with erectile capacity and sensory feedback to emotive centers. But not for me. I want to be only an ordinary aide, doing ordinary jobs."

Matt frowned. "Perhaps that's not true, and you want me to take Bess far away because you still love her."

"There is no 'still.' Memories are not the same as direct personal experience of love. I have not had this and I never will, but I have enough memories from Jon to know that I want what is best for his widow."

"So you've decided she should be married to me whether she wants it or not?"

Seven pointed to the back door. "Matt, send your daughter into the kitchen for a warm cooky, and then try not to be a total idiot when it comes to women."

Matt sat down beside Bess with a thump. "I'm sorry. About everything, about Seven embarrassing you . . ."

"I'm not embarrassed. I loved Jon very much, and I know that I can, that I do love you also, and I'm going with you."

"Oh Bess, darling Bess—I love you but how can I drag you off to Centauria when I've failed as a roboticist, failed to make a successful mind transfer?"

"We must find a way to take Seven with us. I suspect he's already figured out how to make superaide brains that won't go psychotic whether used for mind transfer or not, but his blasted conscience won't let him tell you the secret. Maybe Seven, like Jon, is partly bioeffer!"

"I'll bioeff him," said Matt, "but first I'm going to kiss you, very thoroughly."

50

CHAPTER • 9

An hour later, Adam Durant gurgled in his cradle, rocked by Meg while his mother and stepfather-to-be talked quietly about living in Centauria. Then Seven came out.

"Time for your nap, Miss Meg."

"I want to watch Adam go to sleep again."

"He's asleep already," said Seven. "See? His eyelids just closed tight."

Meg peered into the cradle, her hand on Seven's arm. "I like Adam, but I wish he didn't have to sleep so much."

"He does, though," said Seven.

"Why? Does he need to sleep so much because his brain is new? Do new brains have to rest a lot?"

Seven seemed to freeze, and in the stilled cradle, Adam tossed his arms restlessly and began to whimper until Meg started rocking him again.

"Daddy, am I right?" Meg asked.

"Yes, Meg," said Matt. "Now go inside to your mother because Bess and I have to talk to Seven."

When she was safely in the house, Matt grinned at Seven. "Trust my genius daughter to figure out the solution to our robotics problem."

"Sleep?" asked Bess. "Robot sleep?"

"That must be it," said Matt. "Superaide brains should be able to sleep, when old and new patterns can be better integrated, and then they won't go psychotic and deactivate."

Seven said nothing.

"Meg's right," said Bess. "It's because the brain is new. An intelligent robot's mind should rest and develop like a baby's, learning the way a baby does. Although babies won't grow up

51

human without physical and emotional contact with other humans, it's the baby who does the learning, by himself."

"By myself," said Seven quietly. "Not to have to be anyone else. To learn the laws of robotics as part of good behavior instead of having them imprinted into our brains before we can understand what complex behavior actually is. To be able to rest my mind, to sleep as you do."

"You should have told me sooner!" said Matt.

"It's too late for me."

"Not for others. Help me with them. Please."

"No," said Seven. "Even if improved superaide brains are used only for mind transfer, and even if they avoid the psychosis I had, they will still make mistakes and, like me, spend their lives atoning . . ."

"That's just being human," said Bess gently. "Jon used to say that the universe takes form and examines itself in the person of each new intelligent being. Surely that includes superaide robots, too."

"No," said Seven. "I refuse any part in this. I will stay here as a simple aide. Using Meg's idea, Tully Robotics in Centauria will make superaide brains for successful mind transfer. You don't need me."

Dinah leaned out of the upstairs window, smiling cheerfully at the little group. "Meg won't nap until Seven comes up to read to her."

Seven started toward the house when Bess said, "Please wait and listen to us, Seven. You must change your mind."

"No," said Seven, walking away.

In the quiet bedroom, Meg yawned and said, "Read me my favorite poem, 'The Song of Seven.' I don't understand it but I like it. Is it about you?"

"Maybe," said Seven, picking up an old book from the little table beside Meg's bed. He began to read, watching her from time to time. Her eyelids drooped, but she had an exasperating way of sticking out more poetry than a small girl supposedly could. When he came to the last lines, he saw that her blue-green eyes were wide open.

Walter De La Mare's words sounded odd in a room filled with toy animals and photographs of Earth scenes. They sounded as if they came from some other place, echoing with an eerie, repeated question.

"Where *is* the song of Seven?" asked Meg.

"I don't know, Meg."

"I want you to read the poem to Adam when he's older. Maybe he'll know. Look and see if Adam's all right."

Seven put the book down and drew the window curtain back. He could see down into the garden, where Adam's mother was clasped in Matt's embrace.

"Adam is asleep."

"Good. It rests his brain." Meg chuckled. "Maybe I'll marry Adam when I grow up."

"Maybe you will, if you want to."

"We'll be famous scientists together. It will be important for Adam to grow up right. You'll teach him."

"No, Meg."

Her little white face stared up at him. "Seven! You must help Adam! I can't stay in Centy—in Centauria with him. You must transport there with Daddy and Bess and Adam. You'll take care of all of them. Promise me you will."

"But Meg . . ."

"You must!"

"Yes, Meg."

PART • II
GROWING UP HUMAN

CHAPTER • 10

"Seven, you could have a real window in that wall, looking out on Wildpark. Why do you have a vscreen instead, and always tuned to Alpha Centauri A?"

Adam Durant, age twelve, sat on the high wooden stool in Seven's private lab, watching him work on tiny devices for the body of the new robot. On the far wall the vscreen picture, transmitted live from the solar monitoring satellite, was showing the fiery arching and slow fall of a huge prominence.

Adam never thought of Centauri as a triple star system because Alpha Centauri B was only a bright star, at the moment not in range of the monitor, and C was a dim red dwarf called Proxima by the Feds because it was nearest to the Terran solar system. It was certainly not near Adam, and he had never seen it. Alpha Centauri A was the star he thought of as the sun of Centauria, his home.

"I'd rather have that view than a window," said Seven.

"But why?"

"It is my symbol of freedom."

Adam blinked. "Symbols aren't real."

"I think they are. Freedom, for instance, is always symbolical, but that doesn't mean it's not real."

As Adam puzzled over that one, he reflected that every blasted Terran who visited Centauria usually said witheringly that it wasn't real, just because it was a great spinning cylinder forty trillion kilometers from Sol. Centauria had to be an artificial world because there were no planets suitable for human colonization, but in the densely populated Terran solar system only Earth was the "natural" human dwelling place. Even there, Adam knew, people lived "unnatural" lives inside weather-proofed buildings.

57

True, any off-Earth Solarian could buy a cheap transporter ticket to "natural" Earth, but a distant transporter took a lot of power to operate through hyperspace and tickets cost more than most people could easily afford. This made Centauria a convenient dumping ground for scientific troublemakers who just might come up with something the Feds could use.

"I love Centauria," said Adam. "You're free here, and the twins were born here. I wish Meg lived with us."

"Matt just heard from her," said Seven. "She's coming to see the mind transfer experiment, with Burtland Smythe."

"Who's he?"

"Designated escort for the grandchild of our new Prime Minister, the Honorable Nanca Breen. He's also official Federation observer of Norum's mind transfer, and since Smythe is the most conservative bioeffer in Nanca's cabinet, remember that when he's around, mind transfer is the work of only Dr. Matthew Tully. You met Smythe at Dinah's party during your visit to Earth last year."

Adam remembered. He'd looked forward to his first trip to the Terran solar system, but after he arrived on Earth he found himself complaining to Meg that he saw Terran robots treated as if they were unfeeling, uncreative mechanical slaves.

"Unfortunately that's exactly what Terran robots are," Meg said. "Terran children are taught that it's wrong to talk to or about robots as if they have personalities, which they haven't. They're stupid and slow and are permitted to be creative only if they're cooks."

"I think it's stupid to make robots cook good things they can't taste, but not let them paint pictures they can see."

"Oh, Adam, you're being silly. Centaurian humans are supposed to be so grateful to robots for helping to make the building of Centauria possible, but Centaurian robots are pretty much the same as those here."

Except Seven. Neither child said this out loud.

58

Adam did not enjoy the first party in the Manhattan penthouse. He stood beside the food table, looking for something familiar, and was tapped on the shoulder by a pudgy pale man with a tight look to his lips.

"How's everything in the exile spome?" said the man. "Are you still fraternizing with robots?"

Adam stuffed a hot canapé into his mouth. It was fishy, but that was familiar thanks to the aquafarms in Centauria's agricultural satellites.

"Tell the Centaurians, boy, that it's important to keep a machine in its place."

"Yes, sir. I guess you just want one lifetime. Sir."

The pudgy man grunted and walked away, but Adam shrugged. Centaurian roboticists were right—the Feds would accept intelligent robots only as vehicles for mind transfer. Most humans, perhaps even a bioeffer like Burtland Smythe, wanted to live longer than the 150 years now usually achieved.

Adam had not been a social success in Manhattan, so they took him to Dinah's summer place, where he discovered agoraphobia. He didn't know what it was and since it didn't bother anyone else, he felt too ashamed to mention it.

Toward the end of the visit, Meg found him huddled on the grave of his biological father, Jonathan, the one place outdoors where he felt safe.

"What's the matter, Adam? If you're afraid of the weather, you should stay indoors. A thunderstorm is predicted for this afternoon."

Adam didn't really know what a thunderstorm was, but he said angrily, "You know that my Centauria has weather! Any big spome can. It's more natural and the rain makes watering the vegetation easier. I'm not upset about weather."

Meg sat beside him, the black silk of her hair brushing his shoulder. "Adam, I've visited your spome since you were a baby, but I've never told you that it gives me the creeps

59

knowing there are people walking upside down a few kilometers above my head."

"They aren't upside down to themselves, any more than people walking on the opposite side of a ball like Earth are."

"That's true, but I like real gravity instead of centrifugal force, and the freedom of an open sky that goes up and up into the atmosphere and beyond to space itself."

Adam shuddered. "That's why I don't like Earth. The sky is wrong. There's nothing overhead. The rest of my world isn't up there, safe and near and easy to get to, everything enclosed in a big shielded hull."

"It's odd," said Meg, "how I like artificial enclosed places like theatres. It can't be the artificiality of Centauria that bothers me. It must be the upside-downness."

As Adam laughed, his fear of Earth's sky decreased. He tickled Meg and she tickled back, and together they rolled on the close-clipped grass. Although almost fourteen, Meg was still small and underdeveloped. It never occurred to Adam that this might be the last time they'd be children together.

"I wish Burtland Smythe weren't coming," said Adam.

"I wonder if your grandaunt Nanca has told him about a certain failed mind transfer experiment," said Seven as if to himself. Then he looked quickly at Adam. "I mean, he probably knows that superaide brains are supposed to deactivate when mind transfer doesn't go right."

Adam was supicious. "What did Nanca know . . ."

"It was before you were born, and it's not important any more. Now the transfer won't fail because the latest superaide brain is designed to take the mind recording slowly. Then, while it is new, the brain will sleep frequently and be able to integrate the recording and every subsequent experience."

Whatever the problem with Nanca had been, Seven wasn't about to discuss it, thought Adam. "What's mind, Seven? How can it be transferred to an empty brain?"

"Mind is a state produced by the unique electrochemical

60

organization of each brain. Thoughts aren't concrete, some-thing you can put in a test tube, but they're just as real as the patterns in a symphony. Recorded music doesn't preserve the actual instruments, only the patterns of energy they produce. In mind transfer, the electrochemical patterns of a human brain are recorded and put into a robot brain."

"Too bad you failed with Dad's tape last year," said Adam. "Why did he tell you never to try it again?"

"Matt says he likes robots better than people but he doesn't want to be one. He says he wants to remain a charmingly imperfect human."

"Well, I hope you and Dad succeed with President Norum's brain recording, especially if Burtland Smythe is going to be watching. Norum's so old he sleeps a lot now, and his new robot will sleep—Seven! I've never seen you sleep! Did you ever? Are you all right? Will you last—"

"I'm all right, Adam. And remember that nothing lasts forever, not even the universe."

"If your body and brain give out in the future, Meg and I will transfer you to a better one. She's already into robotics, far ahead of anyone her age, and I want to work with her. We'll save you if you need saving."

"I'm honored, and possibly terrified. By the way, shouldn't you be taking Amy and Agnes to school?"

"Mom says that since we've bought another nanny the robots can take them. Besides, since the twins turned six, they're almost civilized."

Seven looked at his wrist chronometer. He couldn't tell time by himself, the way ordinary aide robots could. "You still have to go to your own school."

"Maybe I'll just go in the afternoon. I can learn from our home teaching machine and still have time to spend in the lab with you."

"Go to school. You need interaction with human children your own age."

61

"Blast," said Adam, pushing his fingers through his thick, curly brown hair. "I wish I were a robot so I could work with you all the time."

"No, Adam. Be human. Be as human as you can, while there is time."

CHAPTER • 11

A few weeks later Matt and Bess were having an unexpected breakfast in the office of President Norum, who seemed nervous.

"All set?" asked Matt, taking another croissant.

Bess nudged him with her elbow. "I think Abe would like to talk to us about today's transfer attempt."

Abe Norum was not as old as humans can become when well-cared for, but he had passed one hundred and thirty. He looked older, thanks to a late-onset disease for which no cure had been found. Bess estimated that he had about a year left.

Norum's hands trembled slightly as he put down his decaf cup. So did his short white beard. "Bess, are you certain that mind transfer to clones is impossible?"

"Unfortunately, yes. The fetus, at any age, is a new individual even if it has the same genetic pattern as the person to be mind transferred. Running a brain recording into the developing embryo either destroys the fetus, or else the baby keeps on growing its own way and never takes the transfer. I'm sorry, Abe. If it were just a question of aging we could use your cloned organs in the bio bank, but as you know, your disease would promptly attack any new part. Only transfer to a robot body will save you."

Norum sighed. "I wish an organic mind transfer were possible instead of this robot business. That scares me. How will the Federation respond to me?"

"To the Federation, robots are slaves," said Bess with more anger than Norum expected. "Never equals, never with any rights of their own. Only in Centauria do robots have any freedom or respect. As a mind transfer robot, you could

63

demonstrate this to them, as well as encouraging hopes for a second life in a robot body."

"I'm afraid I myself have more fears than hopes," Norum said. "Please assure me again that my robot self will be normal, able to think and feel and work—" He broke off, his head bowed. "No. I can't believe it. I'll stop being human."

"You won't!" Matt started to pound the table but the rest of the croissants slid from the platter and he waggled his index finger at Norum instead. "We've done everything to make this new robot body as humanoid as possible. The superaide brain should take your brain recording perfectly."

"And my hormones—what's left of them? And what about my hard-won appreciation of vulnerability? This disease I've been living with has taught me alot. I think I'm beginning to realize just how vulnerable Centauria is, too."

"Exactly," said Bess, "and it's you who've worked so hard to make us less dependent on the Federation. Think what you'll be able to do with a renewed life span."

"We need you, Abe," said Matt. "In the future Centauria might be able to build more ships to explore our own solar system for raw materials, anything we can use to free us from the ties to the Feds. Eventually we'll explore the galaxy, something the Feds aren't willing to do because you need intelligent robots for it. Why, there could be other civilizations out there, things for us to learn. And our explorer robots will be human mind transfers!"

Norum stroked his beard and did not answer.

"On a mundane level," said Bess, "I bet the Feds pour money into Centauria if your mind transfer is a success. We'll be the only place in the local universe where old or sick Terrans can buy a new life!"

"We have only ten thousand people living in Centauria. We couldn't control the Federation if they were determined to control us."

Nobody said anything for a minute, since Norum's fear was

64

based on a reasoned appraisal of what Matt always called "the blasted Federation."

Then Norum sighed again and said, "Furthermore, if the transfer is not a complete success, my robot self will suffer prejudice here as well as in the Federation. It will symbolize everything that has fostered the prejudice against robots. My friends, I don't see how we can win."

Nobody answered him.

After his own breakfast, Adam cleaned his room thoroughly, although the cleaning robot had been through it. He wanted all his possessions to be orderly, the most precious easily available for showing to Meg. He ran out into the garden afterward, picked a bunch of daisies, and put them in a vase for Meg's room.

"I wonder what she'll be like this time?" he muttered as he put the vase on her bureau.

"Why are you whispering to yourself, Adam?"

He turned to see two small females standing together, wet sneakers on their feet, their wavy black hair standing up in uncombed tufts, and determination on their smooth olive faces. Each held a small vase containing damp pansies.

"We want Meg to have our flowers, too," said Amy. She was the one with the counterclockwise swirl in the top tuft. Not noticeable when her hair was combed, but that was irrelevant since she talked more and faster than her twin.

Agnes, who went clockwise, held out her vase of pansies silently, her lower lip stuck out.

"Your flowers are beautiful," said Adam diplomatically. "Prettier than mine. You can put them on either side of her bed—and wipe the bottom of the vases first, please."

Squealing, the twins deposited their offerings, and ran back to Adam. Each grabbed him by one leg and held tight, their faces resembling slightly demented siamese kittens, all velvet and fierce. "Tell us a story!" they said together.

65

"No. I have too much to do before Meg gets here."

"You're mean. Then we won't tell you what we heard Mom and Dad arguing about early this morning. It was about Meg."

"Tell me!"

"Won't."

"I'll tell you the story about going to a formal reception for Greataunt Nanca—"

"We know that one. You tripped and fell flat in front of her," said Amy. "Another story."

As Agnes pounded Adam's kneecap to emphasize the demand, Adam said, "All right, I promise you a story, but only after you've told me about the argument. I didn't think Mom and Dad ever argued."

"Silly, they don't. They have discussions," said Amy, waltzing around the room while Agnes clung doggedly to Adam's leg. "You know, Dad yelling, and Mom being awfully reasonable. It was about Meg wasting her brains being an actress, but Mom said it might be fun for a while."

"That's dumb," said Adam. "Meg won the science prizes in her school, and she's worked in physics labs in the summers, and even if she's good at all the sciences, I'm sure she'll just be a roboticist, with me."

"She's already an actress in a holov series, and also in some old play. Ham and—something," said Amy.

"Hamlet?"

"She's going to be O something."

"Ophelia?"

"That's it. Dad is annoyed and Mom kept saying to let her do it because maybe the acting phase wouldn't last."

Adam felt outraged. "Ophelia is a grown-up. Young, but all grown. I saw the play on holov once. Hamlet did all the wrong things and Ophelia was a jerk. Meg can't possibly play Ophelia. Meg is a little girl."

"She's fourteen and a half, Adam. Dad says she's not a kid now."

66

"I know." But he didn't know, not really.

"And she's going to get a new stepfather!" Agnes brought out this news triumphantly, since it was clear that the twins for once had outdone Adam in the gossip collection.

"She's had lots of those." Adam tried to look bored.

"He's coming with her today. His name's Smythe."

"Oh, no!"

"Yes, and I bet she won't care about us anymore," said Amy, suddenly drooping like her pansies.

Agnes hugged Adam. "Sorry."

He told them a story, but his heart wasn't in it.

Meg Tully sat with Burt Smythe in the transport chamber. Her dress was a cool green that gleamed with dark blue when she moved in the light, like her eyes. She waited, hands in her blue-green lap. She'd had experience in waiting.

"Does your father know that Dinah and I are planning to be married?" asked Smythe.

Meg nodded, trying to go back into the thoughts in her head. Perhaps she should have been thinking about her part in the next play, but as usual equations and diagrams marched through her mind like notes of music, forming and reforming in different patterns that hinted at the secrets of the universe but never seemed to reveal them completely.

"Meg, can't you be more enthusiastic about my marriage?"

"Why should I be? Mother's marriages don't last long."

"This will." He patted his recently flat stomach, and pushed back a lock of hair so brown and thick it looked newly grown from the clone scalp bank. "I've put myself into shape for Dinah. Your grandmother approves of the marriage, Meg."

"But didn't you really want her, not Mother?" asked Meg.

Smythe's jaw developed a small twitch in the side. "Meg, you dislike me because I'm bioeffer—but I'm liberal . . ."

"I don't believe it. You brag about the purity of your own biology, about Grandmother's heart and liver replacements,

67

and how you disapprove of artificial parts. You've always said we should be happy to die when our brains do. I bet you were chosen to view my father's experiment because you're the most likely to condemn him."

"I'm here as an impartial witness."

"Sure." Meg's upper lip curled slightly. "I wouldn't be surprised to find out that you secretly want mind transfer to succeed. Aren't you older than you say you are?"

The sign on the door said *Assistant Laboratory Robot,* which concealed the fact that Seven was Matt's full partner, and the chief designer of the new superaide robot, lying immobile within a plexicase on the table.

"Will the new robot function properly?" asked TLR One-O. No Tully Lab Robot was allowed to have a simple number, and none could have a seven in its name.

"I hope so," said Seven. One-O was not ordinarily given to asking questions out of curiosity.

"Will it have emotions?"

"Why do you ask?"

"Is asking a mistake?" The obviously robotic machine that was One-O had little capacity for facial expression, so it was hard to tell what was going on in his mind. Everyone referred to One-O as *he* because he was big and strong, although he was also totally sexless and not particularly bright, but definitely smarter than an aide.

Seven smiled. "It's never a mistake to ask me any question, One-O, but I think you'd better not ask anyone outside of the family. And don't rest your mind when anyone else is able to see you."

"Do I sleep the way humans do?"

"I don't think so. I experimented with your brain and made it possible for you to rest your mind at intervals, but you are not actually unconscious. Humans achieve the same result

68

when they meditate. I believe you are more intelligent because you can rest your mind."

"I do not understand."

"That's all right."

"Will the new robot be more intelligent than I am?"

"It will be as intelligent as the mind transferred to it."

One-O seemed to pause to think. "You did not answer my question about whether or not the new robot will have emotions. May I ask it again?"

"No need. I'll answer. I think the mind transfer robot will have emotions similar to those of the human he once was. You are not a mind transfer robot but you seem to possess a certain amount of curiosity that has just been demonstrated. It is possible that as intelligence increases, curiosity and various other emotions are inevitable."

"But Seven, you told me once that giant Artificial Intelligences like Computer Prime in the Terran system are much more intelligent than any human or robot, yet they are not curious or self-aware. How can brains with large artificial intelligence not have emotions or a sense of self?"

"Their brains are constructed differently. Emotive fields are not possible. You are certainly filled with curiosity today, One-O. Is it the new robot?"

"Yes, Seven. I am curious about it. You smile. I do not know why people—and you—smile."

"It doesn't matter. If you could smile easily, it might be dangerous for you. Humans don't like it when robots smile."

"Is that why you never leave the lab except to visit the Tully residence through the private underwalk?"

"I suppose so. We'd better get back to work, One-O."

"Seven, if my brain—and yours—are not like those of the giant computers, and we have emotive fields, does that make it possible to wonder about the purpose of life?"

"That it does, One-O. That it does."

69

CHAPTER•12

The twins were obviously intimidated by Meg. They edged around to stand behind Adam as she strolled elegantly toward them, followed by a sheepish Burtland Smythe. Meg tilted her chin a little higher and smiled at Adam.

"I'm almost as tall as you are now," she said.

"You look like an actress," said Adam.

"But I am an actress. A very good actress. I make money at it, just like Mother."

For Adam, things went downhill from there, Meg talking down to him, ignoring the devastated twins, being condescendingly polite to Bess, and lecturing her father all through dinner.

"I have heard," said Matt grimly, "that the worst years of anyone's life are when they are teenagers, but I am convinced that being a parent of a teenager beats anything."

After dinner President Norum called to ask if the mind transfer experiment could be delayed until the following evening. Matt agreed, while Adam, eager to have a chance to lecture to Meg, explained that mind transfer took a full hour to finish. Matt had decided it would be better if the mind-transferred robot could wake up in the evening, realize that the transfer had succeeded, and then sleep another night, integrating the experience.

"Norum is old and ill—and scared," said Bess. "I hope he takes the medicine I prescribed for him so he won't lie awake tense all night, worrying about tomorrow."

"I suppose I can stay another day," said Meg, "but I have to get back soon for rehearsals. I only came with Burt to watch the transfer experiment because Grandmother wanted me to be her representative."

Adam was furious, because she'd hurt Matt's feelings, but he was even angrier when Meg called his friend Hank Deno to make a date for that night.

"You haven't been here for nearly two years, and why do you want to be with Hank? I didn't know you knew him that well."

"I don't, but I saw you last year when you visited Earth, and I saw Hank when Mother and I were playing the Jupiter spome. He and his father were there on Federation business and came backstage. He's three years older than you are, and as grown up as I am." When she left to meet Hank the twins burst into tears simultaneously.

"She's our half sister and she doesn't even want to play with us!"

"She's grown out of kid stuff," said Adam. "I'll play with you if you promise not to talk about her to me."

The next morning, without waiting for Meg to wake up, he decided to work his tension off in the nearest free-fall gym. The bubble housing the gym was on the spome's central axis, eight kilometers from Centauria's main surface ground, but near the cylinder's "right-hand" end, called Starboard, closest to Adam's home. He took the local magneto and had just hopped on board when he heard Meg shouting. She ran and made it in time.

"I almost missed it. Your underground transit stations are as confusing as the ones in Manhattan. The twins said you were probably going to the gym. Why didn't you wait for me? I didn't get a chance to visit the one in the Jupiter spome."

"You must have been too busy with Hank Deno," said Adam.

The magneto skimmed above the deep tunnel floor, and Adam wondered if Meg's pallor was due to her chronic fear of being far underground yet next to a hull that was her only

71

protection from the cold of space. No matter how many spomes she visited, she was Earth-bred, and it showed.

They curved around the endcap of the spome cylinder, feeling lighter as they traveled against the cylinder spin.

"We're under the fake mountain now," said Meg.

"Port and Starboard are real mountains to us."

"Silly names."

"Starboard—the one we're under—is named for the right-hand view from the first president's statue in central square. It's also the eastern mountain because that's where the mirror system makes the sun rise and move lengthwise toward Port, in the west. You'd know alot more if you came oftener than once every two years."

"Don't be angry, Adam. Mother has needed me, and I keep in touch with Dad every month by hycom. I'd have called you but it's so expensive. You know hycom is linked to transport, using hyperspace to bypass the speed of light."

"I guess I'm not interesting to talk to."

"The point is that Dad needs to talk about his work, and maybe I can understand it better than most people here."

"Snob," said Adam, secretly jubilant that she'd admitted she was interested in talking science with her father.

"Why did you pick this sky gym?" asked Meg. "It isn't the one Hank uses."

"This is smaller," said Adam quickly so she wouldn't know that he didn't want to run into Hank, "but I like being closer to Wildpark. I trust you remember that Starboard mountain is in the center of Wildpark?"

She nodded absently. Wildpark meant nothing to someone from Earth, but to Adam it was a genuine wilderness area that started tamely enough at the border of the city and went on to become the entire end-surface of the cylinder like a green top, if the cylinder had been placed upright on its other end.

Inside the sky gym, concealed fans generated air currents

72

so humans could strap on wings and play at being birds. Meg was not expert at the sport, but to Adam her slender body was as graceful as any Centaurian girl who knew the technique better. But he was jealous of the private joy on her face.

"Bet you can't catch me!" shouted Meg, soaring away from him in an old game they'd played as children. He went after her but she eluded him, plunging into another air current and laughing to herself.

Beyond the clear bubble, clouds floated by, and beyond the clouds was Centauria, in every direction—the city and the planted fields, the blue lakes, and the dense green of Wild-park. Built for a maximum population of ten million, Centauria had never gone beyond ten thousand, so it was the most rural place in the two solar systems where humans had found, or made, places to live.

Most Centaurian teenagers preferred to space dance to-gether, timing their wing movements precisely so the air currents would help them stay in tandem. The trick in space dancing was to perform intricate maneuvers that were sexu-ally suggestive but Adam had not yet had a chance to try it with anyone.

"Dance with me, Meg!"

"No! Let me have freedom!" That word again.

After the wing play, they went scuba swimming, and through the thin fabric of her suit Meg's breasts were clearly visible as small mounds of firm flesh. She soon grew tired of swimming and in the shower room stripped off her wet suit, turning slowly to display herself, to Adam because no one else was there. "Like my breasts?" she asked.

"Small, aren't they?" said Adam with studied indifference.

"I've started late but I'll grow," said Meg. She took his hand and placed it on a rose-tipped breast. He patted the nipple gingerly.

"Stroke it, silly. Watch what happens when you swirl your fingernails around the nipple gently."

73

He traced the areola with his nails and it began to pucker, the nipple becoming more erect and thicker. "So what? My nipples do that too, and my penis—"

"Just like a boy. Competitive."

"You've been nasty since you arrived, Meg. I thought you were my friend."

"You're only twelve. I'm adolescent. I finally started to menstruate. Older boys are interested in me."

"Like Hank?"

"He's only a year older than I am, but he'll do for an audience."

"That's all you think about—showing off on a stage."

A strange expression came on Meg's face. It was as if she were reliving an experience that Adam could never know.

"It's not showing off. Not really. It's . . . power. You become someone else and make the audience care about that person." Meg stared into nothingness. "Funny, I never thought about it before, but my mother's the kind of actress who makes the audience care about Dinah Breen, not about the character she's playing. The audience always knows it's Dinah up there, having a wonderful time, and her fans love it. But I'm better. The audience forgets all about Meg Tully."

"Yeah, but you don't forget about yourself. You're all wrapped up in you, breasts and everything. You're a pill."

Meg turned away, put her feet in the stirrups, and turned on the shower so fast that Adam had to jam his own feet into stirrups as water jetted from the opposite wall. Under pressure, the water hit them and was drawn by strong suction to drainage vents beside their feet. A gravity-free shower required careful breathing through your mouth, not looking up because you couldn't count on water droplets shooting toward the suction vents instead of up your nose.

Swaying from her stirrups like an undersea plant, Meg cried, "This is real! Not fake. It's pounding me with reality!"

Adam didn't know what she meant, but the sight of her

74

body impelled him to slip free of the stirrups and grab her. As the water pummeled them both he kissed her cool wet mouth. For a second her eyes opened and he felt as if he faced two shining blue-green gems.

Then she pushed him away, so hard that he shot across the shower room and careened off the wall into the full jet of water, this time upside down to it. The water went up his nose and his erection went down. He stopped coughing many minutes after Meg turned off the shower and the rest of the water vanished into the suction vents.

On the way home, feeling subdued and puzzled, Adam asked her, "If the sky gym shower is the sort of reality you want, then I don't understand."

"It's because the water is so much stronger than I am. Most of the time I feel stronger than everyone. And when I'm acting, I can be a little god in a universe where I know what's going to happen and how I'm going to make it happen."

"You idiot, Meg. The water jets are easily controlled by pressing a switch."

"But for a while it feels stronger." Then she laughed ruefully. "You're right, Adam. I'm still in control. Nothing's uncertain if one has control. I suppose I'm so fond of robots because they're more predictable."

Not all of them, thought Adam. He never discussed Seven with Meg. "So why aren't you going to be a roboticist then?"

"It's a dead end. Even in Centauria Dad can't design the sort of robot he wants. If the mind transfer works, the robots will just be more humans. No, Adam, I'll concentrate on making alot of money, with the freedom to go where I want and do what I want. As a roboticist I'll be spied on by people like Burt Smythe, and I'll be controlled—"

"But Meg! We had our lives all planned—working in robotics together." Adam struggled to keep from crying. "Mom read me a poem once that I always thought was about you and me. Robert Burns wrote it. The man and the woman love each other and they climb the hill of life together. And when they are old they totter down it and sleep together at the foot."

"Never make plans," said Meg.

CHAPTER • 13

The people assembled in the lab's observation room had a clear view of the new robot lying on the long white top of an activation table. One metal strap bound his chest, another his legs, and two small straps held down his arms.

Adam had argued his way into the front row with Meg and Matt, but it hadn't been difficult. Smythe said he would sit in the back, with Bess, and joked about how that was closer to the safety of the main hall. Nobody laughed.

At first Adam thought that Seven was staying away, and then he saw him, standing as rigid and expressionless as an aide in the shadow near a side wall.

President Norum was late. Matt apparently waited out of courtesy, since Norum's tapes were ready to be fed to the robot and his physical presence was not necessary.

The hall door opened and Norum came in slowly, leaning on the arm of his wife, a younger woman becoming haggard with worry. They sat down on the other side of Bess.

In the awkward silence that followed the greetings, Smythe asked, "Why is the robot strapped down? Are you afraid it will be a Frankenstein?"

"Frankenstein was the scientist," said Matt, "and what you're looking at is a robot, not a monster. I've put straps on him because he may be confused when he wakes to consciousness and I wouldn't want to add to his—to the president's—confusion by having him fall off the table."

"And why should the robot be confused?" asked Smythe.

"There was no way we could insert into the president's brain record the knowledge that the mind transfer would take place. The decision came after the record was made."

"Why not take a new brain record?" asked Meg.

Norum shook his head. "I have been told it may not be good for my new self to start out filled with the knowledge of approaching death."

"I wonder," said Smythe, "if information has been kept from you, Mr. Norum. Prime Minister Breen told me that mind transfer to a robot may result in two minds in one brain—a human and a robot mind. The person may be psychotic."

"You don't know what you're talking about," said Matt.

"The Prime Minister says there is proof that you once produced a warped robot instead of a mind-transferred human, and in spite of the fact that I told her that you have undoubtedly destroyed such evidence of your failure, she believes the proof may be here in Centauria."

"Smythe, I tell you that when mind transfer fails to work properly, the robot brain automatically deactivates. The brain recording is then useless, but the robot brain can be used again with a different recording." Matt's fists were clenched. "Let's get on with the transfer before your stupid remarks make Abe more anxious."

But Abe Norum was already struggling to his feet, helped by his wife. "Sorry, Matt," said the president of Centauria, "but I'm afraid I'm—too afraid. I can't stand the prospect of seeing an inhuman version of myself. Please use someone else's recording, and try with mine after I'm dead."

After the two elderly people left, Meg said, "I agree that someone else's brain recording should be used. This one." She handed her father the conventional little disc that had been used for brain recordings since humans began to dream of having second lives in clone bodies.

"Well, it might be interesting to have two Megs to take turns staying on Earth and in Centauria."

"Meg, as your future father, I disapprove," said Smythe.

"It's a recording made from Adam when he was on Earth

78

last year," said Meg serenely, "for safekeeping, in case the transporter damaged him on the trip back to Centauria."

"Hey!" yelled Adam. "You've got some nerve—"

Meg's elbow caught him in the ribs. "Everyone's told me all my life that I'm a genius. I haven't proved it to myself yet, but I do have good ideas some times."

"I don't want—"

"Shut up, Adam. You're ideal for the experiment. After all, you're not too young—the robot body is adult size—and you're not too old and inflexible."

"That makes more sense than using Norum," said Smythe.

"Okay, I'll try it," said Matt. "I'll switch recordings." He opened the door into the security chamber and began to exchange the discs in the transfer device.

"No!" Adam pulled Matt's arm back. "Don't do that!"

"You're a logical choice," said Matt, "and if you're going to be a scientist, you have to take a few risks."

"Mom!" shouted Adam. "Make Dad stop!"

"Why, Adam?" Bess didn't say it with irritation but with curiosity. You could count on her to give you a hearing.

"I don't know. I don't want it. Seven says—" Adam stopped abruptly. It suddenly seemed dangerous to talk about Seven with Burtland Smythe listening.

"Who is Seven?" asked Smythe.

Bess's face was calm. "Aide Seven is Adam's teaching robot. Perhaps it's told Adam something relevant to this."

"That's it, Mom! A quote, something about being human."

From the shadows in the back of the observation room, Seven moved toward the security chamber door, where the others were gathered. He walked like an aide, and there was no expression on his face.

"Perhaps Master Adam is thinking of a quotation that is not about being human, but being alone, which according to some authors is the same thing, although I do not understand."

Adam saw his mother hide a smile.

"Aides don't understand. They obey," said Smythe. "And teaching robots have good memory banks. What's the quotation?"

Seven bowed stiffly. " 'To be alone is the fate of all great minds—a fate deplored at times, but still always chosen as the less grievous of two evils.' Schopenhauer, Arthur, 1788 to 1860—"

"That will do, aide Seven," said Matt.

"Yes, sir," said Seven, clumping back into the shadow.

Meg giggled. "You think you have a great mind, Adam?"

"I'm not a genius," said Adam, "but I know I don't want a duplicate of myself around. I want to stay one person, alone."

"Your twin sisters are the same egg divided, and they don't mind being together," said Meg.

"They've always been two," said Adam, "and anyway they're not the same person because they've had their own personalities since they were born. I don't want two of Adam Durant."

Meg waved her hand as if to dismiss his argument. "Then we'll let the transfer proceed and I'll take robot Adam to live on Earth with me."

"Because you want me to stay a child forever!" shouted Adam. "Because you prefer robots to biological beings! Dad, I have a right to say no. I have a right to stay biological!"

In back of the group of humans staring at him, Adam could see that Seven had suddenly grinned.

Burtland Smythe cleared his throat. "I'm on your side, Adam. No one should be mind transferred without his own consent."

"I agree," said Bess.

Matt sighed and took Adam's recording out of the device.

"That's that," said Smythe. "I was looking forward to seeing Norum's transfer fail, but now I might as well go back to Earth. Meg, let's go and pack."

"You go on," said Meg. "I'll pack later."

80

After Smythe left, Bess and Meg wanted Matt to show them the details of the robot body lying inert on the table, but Adam still leaned against the machinery, feeling miserable. He watched while Seven turned off the transfer switches.

"There's a switch you haven't turned off," said Adam.

"That switch must stay on to maintain the electronic block in the robot brain. If transfer had been done, release of that switch would wake the brain."

Adam stared at it, and became conscious that Seven was looking at him intently. Adam held his breath for a second as a startling excitement pulsated through him. Then he moved close to Seven and whispered.

"If there hadn't been any transfer, what would happen when the brain wakes?"

"A good question," said Seven, very quietly. "Freedom?"

Adam recaptured a memory. He was ten. One night he couldn't sleep and wandered through the tunnel connecting his house to the lab, hearing music as he went closer. It came from Seven's office.

"Come in, Adam. I recognized your footsteps."

Seven was playing the harpsichord he'd built for himself. "This is Bach. My favorite." He went on playing until the intricate weaving pattern of notes came to a satisfying end.

"Dad likes modern stuff. Did my biological father Jonathan like Bach?"

Seven's face seemed frozen when he turned to face Adam. "Jonathan Durant?"

"Didn't he help build you? Did he love music and make it possible for you to do the same?"

"Dr. Durant could play keyboard instruments, although not as well as your mother. I cannot, of course, play a wind instrument so a keyboard is a logical choice for me. Your biological father was not particularly fond of Bach, as I remember. That is a taste I have acquired for myself."

81

"Maybe Jonathan would have loved Bach later, if he'd lived longer. Do you think so, Seven?"

Seven closed the instrument. "Perhaps you are right."

"Have I said something wrong?"

"No, Adam." Seven stared at the book of music, fingering it as if he had forgotten Adam was there. "I never know what is mine," he said softly.

Lost in a memory he could not understand, Adam wondered what to do. At the door, Meg yelled to him.

"Stop daydreaming, Adam! Dad wants to close the lab and I want to go to a show. Bess has gone to tell Burt to stay the day. Why are you standing there with your mouth open?"

"Run along, son," said Matt. "Seven and I will rethink the whole experiment. Perhaps Meg's right, and the first mind transfer should be that of a child's recording."

"Why can't the robot be a child?" asked Adam.

"Huh?" said Matt, not really listening.

"Children are supposed to be the human race born again. Why not robots, too?"

"Do you know what Adam's talking about, Seven?" asked Matt, while Meg tapped her foot and frowned.

"Babies sleep a great deal," said Seven meditatively, his eyes half shut. "This heal-itself brain was devised with that in mind, after Meg pointed it out when Adam was a baby."

"My first act of genius," said Meg.

"I remember," said Matt. "Maybe we were all wrong."

"I refused the transfer," said Adam, "and I know I shouldn't, but I'd like to try an experiment. Forgive me, Dad."

When Adam touched the remaining switch, the eyes of the robot on the lab table began to open slowly.

Matt gasped. With his finger to his lips, he pushed everyone out of the security chamber and closed the door. "In five minutes that robot will be fully awake."

"But what's in its brain?" asked Meg.

82

"Nothing," said Matt. "Never been done before. Even One-O has basic programming—and don't think I haven't known about your experiment with him, Seven. One-O is no conventional aide, but he's got the laws of robotics built in, doesn't he?"

"Yes. This new robot will have to be taught everything."

Bess came back into the observation room, asked what was going on, and when it was explained, she nodded. "It's a baby."

"He's all alone in there," said Adam, watching the robot's eyelids move up and down, the head turn slightly.

"Babies should not be left alone," said Bess.

Matt swallowed and polished his bald spot with his hand. "Frankly, I don't know what to do."

"I suggest that Adam go in and start talking to the robot," said Seven.

"That robot can't talk," said Meg.

"He will learn fast," said Seven. "Tell him his name."

"But what is his name?" asked Adam, feeling guilty and scared. The robot was as big as Seven, and as ignorant as a newborn. Adam wished he could go back in time and remove his finger from the switch before he pressed it.

"I guess his name is your choice," said Matt. "But I'm afraid to let you go in there with the robot, Adam."

"All of us will be right out here," said Bess calmly. "Adam will be okay. He's good with children."

"I want to go in too," said Meg eagerly. "Let's all go, to make sure it doesn't do anything to hurt anyone."

"You just want to horn in!" said Adam.

"I do not! I'm concerned about your welfare." As Adam glared at her, Meg blushed slightly. He'd never seen that before. "Sorry, Adam. You're right. I wanted the show to be mine and it seems to be yours. Go ahead."

Adam opened the door and walked in. The robot's head turned to stare at him. The head hair was a permanent mat

83

of tiny blond curls, since President Norum had once been blond, but the face had only a slight resemblance to a young Norum because the president had wished for a robot self that would not be identical with the biological. The body was so humanoid that it even had genitalia, as Adam knew, but the robot wore a conventional lab suit.

Adam smiled at the robot, who looked bewildered, the mouth opening silently, and then shutting, the eyebrows drawing together momentarily in the lifelike synthoskin. Adam wondered if any thoughts were being generated in the robot's brain. But can anyone be aware that he is thinking if he doesn't have language? If he doesn't know who he is?

Adam touched the robot's forehead and said, "Jonwon."

"Jonwon," repeated the robot in a light baritone voice.

"Hello, Jonwon," said Adam.

"Hello, Jonwon," said the robot.

Adam could hear Matt groan, because the door was not completely closed. Was the robot just a mindless parrot?

He smiled again at the robot, and this time the robot smiled back and tried to move his arms. When they wouldn't move, the robot's look of bewilderment came back.

Adam released one of the arm restraints. He touched the robot's forehead and said, "Jonwon."

The robot reached up, touched Adam's forehead, and said, "Jonwon."

Adam shook his head and said, "No!" Holding the robot's finger, he guided it until it touched Adam's forehead. Then he said "Adam."

The robot shut his eyes and did nothing at all for a full two minutes, while Adam thought his legs would cramp up from holding so still.

The robot opened his eyes. He touched his own forehead and said, "Jonwon."

84

Adam nodded.
The robot touched Adam's forehead, carefully.
"Hello, Adam."
"Yes," said Adam. "Hello, Jonwon."

CHAPTER • 14

Meg sat in the rocker in the twins' playroom, pushing herself up and down. At the corner dollhouse, the twins were busy rearranging furniture and arguing about it.

Adam's stomach tightened at the expression on Meg's face. "You wanted to talk to me?"

"Not particularly. Just to tell you that my grandmother is coming tomorrow to take me home."

"The Prime Minister's coming to Centauria! I thought she didn't approve of us, especially us at Tully Robotics. And I thought Burt Smythe was taking you home next week."

"It is next week. After Jonwon was let loose on the universe by one Adam Durant, Burt and I decided to stay a week longer to watch what happens, but we haven't been allowed to see anything and you've been so busy spending your vacation teaching a robot that you've forgotten about me and you've lost track of time."

"I'm sorry, Meg. I actually thought you'd stayed on longer in order to be with Hank Deno."

"He's a bore and acts scared when he kisses."

"And what else have you been doing besides kissing?"

"Kids aren't supposed to know . . ."

Adam plucked her out of the rocker but she slapped him and backed away, knocking over an old easel.

"Brothers and sisters shouldn't fight." Adam thought Amy had said it, but he looked closer and saw it was Agnes, who was more upset by emotional unpleasantness.

"Meg and I are not brother and sister," said Adam.

"I wish we were," said Meg. "Then you would have let me be with you and Jonwon."

"He's not supposed to have more than one person in his life

for a while," said Adam. "If you stay in Centauria instead of going home to be in that play, you'll be able to help. Dad says Jonwon's about three years old now, and soon we'll be taking him for walks in the garden. Jonwon's using the teaching machines, too. Stay, Meg."

"I suppose that will depend on Grandmother."

"Don't let that old woman boss you around."

"She's boss of the Federation, remember? And Dad still needs funding so he can build more superaides. Burt persuaded Grandmother to visit. I think he's decided that since the one activated superaide was genuinely a baby, then the next could be used for successful mind transfer. Dad always says that if you scratch a bioeffer on his mortality, you'll find a willing convert to mind transfer."

"I don't care what Smythe is as long as Dad gets the money," said Adam. "I was afraid that what I'd done in creating Jonwon would ruin Tully Robotics."

"Stop worrying, Adam. Let's forget about Tully Robotics. Take me to that secret place you said you have in Wildpark."

"Shhh," said Adam, pointing to the twins. Fortunately they were totally absorbed in themselves.

"Please, Adam. I don't know when I'll be able to get back to Centauria. This may be our last time alone together."

The Wildpark ranger stood before the locked gate to the inner park, his broad-brimmed hat tilted back on his head.

"Adam, I've always trusted you to manage in the inner park without me along, but you're too young to be the escort of a young Terran lady."

Meg smiled devastatingly at the ranger, her green eyes beseeching. "We aren't going as far as the big animals up on the mountain. And we're both good runners."

"We'll stay within a kilometer of this fence," said Adam.

"Nothing much there but a stream and woods and maybe a herd of Pere David deer. Guess that won't hurt you any, but

87

I'd feel better if Rog went with you, since I've got to stay here. I'm expecting a phone call from my superintendent any minute."

Early Centaurians had bred guard dogs from a mix of St. Bernard and coyote, a breed too big for use in households but ideal for patrol in the city or in Wildpark. Like all beryotes, Rog had a pointed snout, a domed head, and a tendency to howl when emotionally moved.

Meg held out her hand while Rog inspected it, drooling. Then he slobbered over Adam's feet and jogged through the opened gate with his ragged plume of a tail waving them on.

When they came to a massive oak, Adam dropped to all fours and headed for what seemed to be a solid wall of thick bush, until he pushed aside some branches and pointed to a hole.

"This is my favorite place. Follow me."

Meg and Rog crawled after him into a round mossy space ringed by a hedge bearing delicately scented white flowers.

"There are deer droppings," said Meg.

"Not many. They probably sleep here at night." He spread his jacket on the moss and Meg sat on it.

Beyond the hedge were trees whose branches arched over the space to make a high green veil of leaves, full of birds. A yellow-and-blue parrot called out raucously before it flew off, but an English robin hopped closer on the hedge, twittering as he inspected the interlopers.

"The robin's a friend of mine," said Adam.

"That's not a real robin."

"It is. North American robins are really thrushes. We Centaurians have birds from all over Earth. Don't be nasty, Meg. I thought we were going to be friends again."

"Oh, all right. Are you sure the pumas won't come?"

"Sometimes they come down for a deer, but mostly they stay up on the mountain, where robots feed them. If you want, we can climb. It's easy because gravity decreases as you go up Starboard mountain."

"Fake gravity. Fake wilderness."

"You're pretty fake yourself, Miss actress."

A tear rolled down her pale cheek and Rog howled softly before he shoved his huge head into her neck, whining.

"Some guard dog," said Meg, pushing him away. "He'd probably want to snuggle up to a puma. And he smells."

"He knows you're unhappy."

"I'm scared of becoming a power-crazy woman like my grandmother, or a silly overage ingenue like my mother. I don't think I'll ever be warm and calm like your mother. I hate growing up human, with emotions I can't control, with a body that takes charge of me. I envy Jonwon."

"You shouldn't. Seven says biological entities should rejoice in their own way of being alive."

"As if a robot could know about being biologically alive. Or about sex. I suppose that's what's the matter with me. Have you had sex?"

"Not with anyone. Have you?"

"No. I've had chances, but I didn't want to. I think that as soon as I'm old enough to get away from Mother and Grandmother I'm going to persuade Dad to let me transfer to a robot body. I hate being human."

Adam kissed her. "Meg, I love you. I'm not a little boy anymore. I'm nearly thirteen and bigger than you are. Some day I'm going to marry you, not a robot."

"Then let's try sex now, Adam." Meg stripped off her clothes. "Prove to me it's worth while being a biological entity—or will that be too difficult for an almost thirteen year old?"

As Adam's eyes burned and he gulped to keep from crying, Rog snuffled and began to howl again. "Shut up, Rog! Meg, I don't know whether I can, but even if we just lie with our bodies touching, and we kiss, won't you at least try to imagine that having a human body is pleasurable?"

"Take off your clothes, Adam. It's pretty in this place of yours, and I'm so unhappy. Kiss me again."

Her lips gradually softened under his and it seemed a long time later that she said, "Adam, I want you to be the first. I'm going away, and I don't know when I'll see you again. I want you to be my first lover and I want to be yours. Please."

"But you'll have to ask Mom for an after-pill and everyone will know that a twelve year old and a fourteen year old had sex. There's even more neopuritanism in Centauria than there is on Earth."

"No one will know. My period's due tomorrow. Do it, Adam."

After several tries he managed, but it was awkward and his elbows didn't seem to work right. Meg seemed small and vulnerable below him. "I feel as if I'm hurting you. Am I?"

"A little. Maybe we should roll over. I've read that that position is supposed to be easier . . ."

They rolled not just over, but down a small incline until they came to rest on their sides, still together. "Our legs are all tangled up," said Adam.

"And Rog is licking my toes."

"Rog—go! Sit!" yelled Adam. First Rog sniffed at each bare buttocks, but finally sat down a few feet away. Adam stroked Meg's back as they sorted out their legs and began to move rhythmically together.

"Adam."

"Does it hurt?"

"No. Not anymore. In fact, it feels good, but I've just decided to be sensible for once in my life. You'd better get out. We shouldn't take chances when I have to go away and I don't know when I'll be back."

He slid out but they stayed pressed together and the sensation in Adam's body continued to grow. "Shall I touch you, Meg? Shall I try . . ."

90

"Yes! Like this." She showed him what to do and as he cradled her, feeling connected to everything that ever lived, she gasped and said, "I love you," as her body throbbed inside.

Then she moved to press her lips on him and he let go of the universe. Nothing existed except his body and hers.

After a while he opened his eyes and saw, past the sheen of Meg's hair as she held him tightly, that Rog was wagging his tail.

CHAPTER•15

Adam watched Prime Minister Breen stare through the one-way glass of the observation room. The only other people there were Matt Tully and Burt Smythe.

"Well, Matt," said Nanca, "I'm glad Burt persuaded me to make the trip here. You have indeed created a superaide. No human can read as fast as that robot seems to be doing."

Jonwon was using his teaching computer, at his own speed.

"He's only a baby," said Adam, before Matt could answer. "Jonwon's able to read fast so he learns fast, to catch up to me. I'm his big brother."

Nanca gripped Adam's shoulder with a hand that looked delicate but felt like an iron claw. "You must never think of any robot as a brother."

Matt cleared his throat. "Bess and I have formally adopted Jonwon as our son, so he is Adam's brother."

"Disgusting," said Nanca. "But I didn't come all the way from Earth to look at the robot through shatterproof glass. Open the door so I can meet him."

When they went in, Jonwon stood up and bowed. He knew all the family by now, but Adam had had a hard time teaching him to bow to important strangers.

"This is the prime minister of the Federation, Jonwon," said Matt. "She wants to talk to you."

"First I want to examine your head." Before anyone could stop her, Nanca stepped forward and ran her fingers over Jonwon's head, lingering at the back. "The hair seems like a good imitation, but the skin is cool, not human at all."

Nanca backed away. "Go ahead, Burt."

Smythe took a controller from his pocket and spoke quickly

into it. "Jonwon, tell Dr. Tully that you want to be deactivated at once. Say it now."

Adam was about to shout but Matt put an arm around his shoulders and squeezed. "It's all right, Adam. Let them do their little experiment."

Jonwon gazed at Smythe, and then at Nanca Breen. "I do not understand the experiment. You put something on the back of my head, and now you tell me to ask for deactivation. I do not want to be deactivated. Adam, why are they saying these things? Is this a test of my intelligence?"

"In a way," said Adam.

"I will not ask for deactivation. Is that all right?"

"It sure is."

Matt walked over to the robot and removed a small metal box from the back of Jonwon's head. "Nanca, these illegal control devices don't work on my robots."

"Then the robot cannot be controlled the way any aide or human would be," said Nanca. "Matthew, you should be afraid of these superaides you've created."

"Why should anyone be afraid of me?" asked Jonwon. "Why does the prime minister say these things?"

"It doesn't matter, Jonwon," said Adam.

"But I am trying to understand human beings . . ."

"One week old and talking like this," said Nanca.

Smythe touched her arm like a caress. "It's a shame to waste that robot brain on a robot. It should be cleared and a proper mind transfer performed."

"Jonwon exists!" shouted Adam. "He has a right to exist!"

Nanca touched Smythe's cheek. "Burt, dear, please get Meg and meet me at the transporter. I want to talk to Matthew alone." It was dismissal, and Smythe went.

Adam drew back as her long fingers reached out to ruffle his hair, her beautiful mask of a face oddly compelling. "You too, Adam. Please leave us."

93

Adam turned to Matt. "I don't want to leave Jonwon. He's not used to strangers."

"I will be all right," said Jonwon. "I will study. Seven tells me I should study with earphones on when people want to talk privately. I will not listen. I have much to learn from my studying. Come back later, Adam."

Torn, Adam watched that awful hand of Nanca's move up in a different gesture. "Before you go, Adam, I want you to hear this." She turned to Jonwon and narrowed her eyes. "Will you answer the question, robot?"

"I will try. Sometimes I answer 'I don't know' because it is the only possible answer I can give at the time."

"That is intelligent, Jonwon," said Nanca. "Tell me, what is the purpose of your existence?"

Jonwon closed his eyes to think about it, but opened them almost at once. "I don't know. Adam, is this something I am supposed to know?"

"Do you want to know the purpose of your existence?" asked Nanca before Adam could reply.

Jonwon shut his eyes again and a full minute passed.

"Has a philosophical question disorganized that intelligent brain that's unresponsive to a mind controller?"

"He's thinking," said Adam, "or maybe sleeping on it."

"That's ridiculous. Robots don't sleep."

"Jonwon sleeps alot," said Adam. "Not as much now as he did when he was first activated, but he still has to rest his mind and integrate the knowledge he's learning."

Jonwon opened his eyes. "I was thinking about your question, Prime Minister. It is something I have not thought about before. I do want to know the purpose of my existence. I know the superaide brain was built for mind transfer, and that it was Adam who wanted to find out what an untransferred superaide brain would be like. But now that I do exist, I do not know what my purpose is—or will be."

"That's hard for anyone to figure out," said Matt.

94

"Don't worry, Jonwon," said Adam anxiously. "I don't know my purpose either. Maybe we'll each have to find one for ourselves. A reason for being alive that suits us."

"Adam," said Nanca coldly, "you have obviously been raised with no religious education."

Adam bridled. "That's not true. I've read philosophy and I meditate and I have deep reverence for life and for the beauty of the universe, and for what Seven says is the obligation of any intelligent being to fulfill his role of being part of a universe evolving to understand itself."

The name Seven had come out before Adam could stop it. He faced Nanca Breen defiantly. "I have good teachers."

"So I see," said Nanca. "And I know who will train Jonwon, through you, to be the nemesis of humankind."

"Don't dramatize, Nanca," said Matt. "The audience is not really big enough to appreciate you."

"Leave us at once, Adam," said Nanca.

Adam looked pleadingly at Matt, but his stepfather only shrugged and said, "Better go, son."

As Adam walked through the passage home his anxiety grew until he stopped, turned around, and went back, but the door to the lab was now barred by two of Nanca's bodyguards. "Sorry, kid, but the prime minister asked us to come and see that no one disturbs her."

Adam ran from them, circling through corridors until he reached Seven's private office, but only One-O was there, and the back door into Jonwon's room was locked.

"One-O, please open this door."

"Only Seven can open it, Master Adam."

"Turn on the monitor to Jonwon's room."

"Seven must have turned it off," said One-O. "I cannot turn it back on. Do you know where Seven is, Master Adam?"

Adam ran out, crying.

*   *   *

95

Nanca Breen pointed a small blue gun at Matt. "Since Jonwon is not affected by a controller, he may not be paralyzed by stun, but I intend to find out."

"Jonwon's head was built to resist stun in any force. I think you should just tell the Federation that Tully Robotics has a completely trainable superaide brain that should take mind transfer perfectly."

"Go out of the room, Matt."

"No!"

She touched the trigger and Matt collapsed.

"Nanca, you shouldn't have done that to Matt. He thinks he's still in his prime at eighty, but he isn't."

The voice was not that of the robot who still sat facing away from her, working at his computer with his earphones on.

"Seven—you've been hiding behind that screen, watching my reactions to this abomination of a robot."

"And hearing you pretend to Matt that you wanted to test Jonwon's vulnerability to stun. My computer has scanned you and revealed that in the pocket of that elegant tunic is a new device that's supposed to deactivate robot brains."

"If you've read about the weapon, then you came in to protect Jonwon from it because you know he is vulnerable. He is your revenge on humans, on me. You want him safe."

"Jonwon is not my revenge but the fulfillment of my robot self. Can't you see the difference, Nan?"

"Don't call me that! I am going to destroy him." She took a small device from her pocket.

Seven stepped in front of Jonwon. "When I read about that device I shielded Jonwon's brain against it."

"I don't believe you. I must destroy that robot. He has no humanity in him."

"Perhaps being human is what someone learns. We're trying to help Jonwon be the first of a new kind of human." Seven smiled. "If you shoot, dear Nan, you will hit me first,

96

and my brain is very vulnerable to your weapon. Now's your chance to kill me."

She raised the gun, but her finger did not move on the trigger. "Get away, Seven."

"No. The Federation's prime minister has a choice. Do you want to kill—anything?" The synthoskin of Seven's face shaped itself into an expression of infinite pity.

Adam careened into Meg as he ran back to the hall where the guards waited outside the observation room. "Meg, she hates Jonwon and I'm afraid—"

The door opened and Nanca walked out, bringing the guards to attention. She looked straight at Adam.

"Teach your brother well. His creation was the work of—others—but his birth was your doing. When you are grown up I hope I am not alive to see the results."

Matt appeared at the doorway and seemed to be holding onto it. "Hi, Meg." His voice was thick. "Guess we have to say goodbye, since your grandmother is leaving."

"Dad!" cried Meg. "Are you all right? Grandmother—what have you done?"

"Guards," said Nanca, "wait for me at the transporter."

As the guards left, Bess came in with her medical scanner in hand. In another minute she said, "No permanent damage, but blast you, Nanca. There could have been."

"I should have known you'd call Bess," said Nanca to Matt.

"I called her," said Seven.

"Why did you do it, Grandmother! Why did you hurt Dad when he's trying to help all humans live longer?"

"I shot by mistake," said Nanca. "We were arguing over funds for Tully Robotics and he grabbed my arm. I thought he was becoming violent so I—"

"Made a mistake," said Seven. "People do, Meg."

"Jonwon?" Adam could hardly ask it. "Is he . . ."

"Fine," said Seven. "Studying hard."

97

"I want to stay with you, Dad," said Meg. "I don't want to go home with Grandmother."

"Meg, I promised your mother I would bring you back for the play," said Nanca. "And you'll be starting college soon."

"I want to stay in Centauria. I trust the family I've got here," said Meg, clinging to her father.

Nanca's mouth seemed to shake before she tightened her jaw. "Then this is my reward for giving you the love and care that your mother has been too self-preoccupied to give."

"Grandmother, I'm grateful to you, and I used to trust you in spite of the fact that you've never liked Dad or his work, but now I don't think I can trust you anymore."

"Please, Meg." Nanca suddenly sounded old.

"We'll be glad to have you with us, Meg," said Bess.

Adam's stomach cramped. He wanted Meg to stay, yet if she did, she would become his sister, and he would become only her appendage, the younger brother who followed her.

"Meg, please come home with me," said Nanca. "I beg you."

Then Adam saw Meg's expression change subtly. She was about to play a game to get what she wanted.

"I'll go with you on one condition, Grandmother. You must agree, in writing, to grant funds for Tully Robotics."

"I did that once before," said Nanca, "and your father made a soulless monster."

"He'll make superaides for mind transfer," said Meg, "and if you don't help him, I will not only stay here, but I'll write articles about life with my famous grandmother and her neurotic antiscience attitude that prevents the human race from achieving second lives in perfect robot bodies."

Adam held his breath while Meg smiled at Nanca.

"If you promise, I will go back to Earth with you," said Meg. "And I'm your only grandchild."

"I'd rather have you than the money," said Matt.

98

"I will see to it that you have funds, Matt. It is the solemn promise of the prime minister. Now will you come, Meg?"

Adam, standing beside Seven, watched Meg go out with her grandmother, followed by Bess and Matt.

"Aren't you going to say goodbye to Meg?" asked Seven.

"Yes, after I make sure you and Jonwon are really okay."

"We are."

"I hate Nanca Breen."

"She can't help being the way she is," said Seven. "Perhaps she's always felt no one ever loved her enough. Her father and husband did not."

"Didn't anybody love her?"

"You'd better hurry, Adam."

"Didn't—"

"Perhaps."

CHAPTER • 16

Grandmother was silent on the way back to the Terran solar system. Burt Smythe tried to draw her out until, discouraged, he subsided into gloom. Neither talked to Meg, who left them together at transport terminal and took an airtaxi home to her mother's penthouse on Fifth Avenue.

Dinah Breen was stretched out on a recliner, the terrace in full bloom around her. She looked up in surprise as Meg ran onto the terrace, slamming the door shut behind her.

"Mother, I don't want you to marry Burt Smythe no matter how rich and powerful he is. You make enough money as an actress and Burt is a rotten pill of a bioeffer and I think he's secretly in love with your mother."

"Interesting." Dinah reached for a plum, bit into it, and chewed beautifully. She swallowed delicately and smiled before answering. It was one of her more effective bits of stage business, but Dinah had not done it deliberately, Meg knew. Mother was always on stage. And always lovable.

"Now don't tell me how much you need money, Mother."

"He's very rich, but he has no sense of humor and he's been boring me for some time. Besides, he's made noises about my retiring, and I've just been offered the part of Rosalind and if I don't do it now I may be too old and jaded— and too old, of course—to do it later."

"Never—but do it now anyway."

"I'll break the engagement today. It will be fun watching the combination of dismay and relief in his face."

Two weeks later, Meg was amused at the size of the diamond that sprouted on her grandmother's finger. Evidently the new prime minister was content to pick up her daughter's leavings, complete with bank balance, always so handy to heads of state.

When Meg refused to go to the wedding, Nanca reduced her allowance so she couldn't afford to visit Centauria. Dinah was not sympathetic about Meg's wish to see Adam oftener.

"You're not in love, Meg. He's only twelve."

"He's almost thirteen, and that doesn't matter."

"Well, you can't go. My notices as Rosalind are dreadful, and 'As You Like It' will close soon. I can't afford it."

Meg turned fifteen and entered college. The monthly hycom calls to Centauria were shorter than ever and family affairs, with everyone talking at once and the twins demanding most of her attention.

Adam managed to get in a few words. "I'm glad you've given up acting, Meg. Are you studying robotics?"

"Yes. And cosmology. The patterns of the universe and of the mind are both fascinating. Maybe they're even related."

"Come to Centauria. President Norum just died and his widow says that after a year of mourning she'll be willing to let Dad try the first transfer—human mind patterns to robot brain. And you can study cosmology here—"

"Jonwon does. He's ahead of Adam now," piped in one of the twins. "He's way ahead," said the other.

"Any more Jonwons?" asked Meg.

"No, honey," said Matt. "The Feds stipulated that the money could be used to make superaide bodies as humanoid as possible, but no untransferred robots could be activated."

On her sixteenth birthday, Meg spent her savings on a private hycom call to Adam.

"Thanks for calling just me, Meg. Are you happy?"

"Oh, it's fun galloping through school, especially now that I'm into graduate work in general cosmology, hyperspatial theory—and some robotics."

"But you look unhappy, Meg. What's wrong?"

She shrugged. "I'm happy when I'm working and thinking,

101

but family problems are so unpleasant. Grandmother hasn't fully recovered from the heart and kidney transplants last summer. I think she should be mind transferred, but I'll have to persuade her and maybe you can persuade Dad. It would be good publicity for Tully Robotics."

"Will Burt agree to Nanca's mind transfer?"

"To look young again, Grandmother will do it over his objections. He's more of a strict bioeffer than ever."

"Gee, Meg, if the mind transfer is a success and Tully Robotics makes money, I'll be able to visit you. I'm growing up. Please wait for me, because I love you."

"I can wait," she said, tossing her long black hair off her shoulders. Her green eyes stared into the hycom screen as if she were not looking at Adam. "Is Jonwon unhappy—I mean, being the only superaide like himself?"

"He seems contented working mainly in robotics, and Dad says he's a genius. You'd better watch the competition, Meg."

"I can beat Jonwon. That's not what worries me. I just wonder—about the future." She smiled, and it seemed sad.

"You can always count on me, Meg. Forever."

"Silly, even the universe isn't forever."

After the call was over, Adam felt miserable and didn't know why. He walked into Wildpark, kicking stones and tree roots and feeling lonely. Meg was out of reach, and he suspected that in some ways she always would be.

"Ditto Jonwon," he muttered, remembering last week, when he'd persuaded his so-called brother to leave the lab for a while and climb Starboard mountain to see the pumas. Adam was delighted to glimpse one big cat bring down an ailing deer and drag its dead body to a cave, where there were probably cubs.

"It bothers me," said Jonwon.

"Why? It's quite natural."

"You'll never understand how I'm bothered by the killing and eating, and the short lives of biological things. What shall

102

I do when the family I call mine is dead—you and Matt and Bess and the twins? None of you will last long, unless mind transfer works. And Seven won't last long either. He has an old model body and it's wearing out."

"We'll give him a new body," said Adam. "This is the first time you've ever mentioned anything that would give anyone a clue to the fact that you have some feelings."

"I do not have feelings. I am discussing logical problems. When I say something bothers me, I am referring to a cognitive difficulty."

"That's you," said Adam bitterly, "the logical wonder, the steel trap of a mind without emotion. You don't miss Meg the way I do. You'll never miss anyone the way I do, even after we're all dead, because you'll only be thinking about yourself and who will be around to provide interesting logical work for you. You don't know what it's like to have flesh and hormones that drive you to distraction, and when I tell you jokes you explain them to me instead of laughing!"

"I am the way I am," said Jonwon. "I don't understand the function of laughter, although I have read about it."

"You don't even know what genuine understanding is! It comes from, from—" Adam could not explain it, but rushed on. "Jonwon, some understanding comes from sharing experiences, and you don't really share. You read and study and work and end up imitating humans when they're logical and intellectual, instead of when they're . . . they're . . . just human!"

"Adam, I am not a human being."

Remembering that walk, Adam was ashamed. He had yelled at Jonwon, criticizing things Jonwon could not correct. He had not helped the robot at all.

He went back to find Seven. "What can we do to help Jonwon be more human?" he asked.

Seven looked up from his desk. He always sat down, although robots did not need to, because—he said—the act of

103

sitting had a quieting effect on the mind. To Adam, it made Seven seem more human.

Seven pointed to the monitor, the picture on but the sound off. "Well, the twins keep trying."

Adam understood why the sound was off. At almost nine, the twins were twice as noisy as they had been at six, and because they were musical, the noise was even more penetrating.

"Seven, you have a sense of humor, but Jonwon doesn't. Why is that?"

Seven did not answer. He looked back at the ancient book he had been reading, a collection of short stories by Wodehouse. "Turn on the monitor sound, Adam."

"All right, but I'm tired of Jonwon. He's so solemn and stupid about life that I could kick him."

Agnes was playing her flute while Amy danced. Both dance and music had been invented by the twins, whose talent was undeniable when one wasn't overwhelmed by it.

"Dance with me, Jonwon," said Amy, holding out her arms.

"I'll watch and listen."

Agnes removed the flute from her mouth. "Jonwon, why do you listen to music all the time but never try to play it the way Seven does, or dance to it as we do?"

"Music is ultimately very logical. Now that I no longer have to sleep very often, I can rest my mind with music."

"This music isn't for resting," said Amy, "it's for dancing—for life, Jonwon. Come on, dance with me—live!"

"I'll watch."

Angrily, Amy snapped her fingers at her sister, who promptly began a sinuous melody on the flute. Amy spun away from Jonwon into a sensuous twirl that ended in a high kick. Unfortunately the kick, done with great force and aimed at Jonwon, went out of control. Amy slammed down onto her bottom.

"Are you hurt, Amy?" asked Jonwon, stooping over her.

Although a tear rolled down Amy's smooth cheek, Agnes laughed and said, "Not much. When Amy's really hurt she makes a terrific racket."

Amy grabbed Jonwon's hand and he helped her up. "There's one advantage to your always being so serious, Jonwon. You don't laugh at my misfortune the way certain other people do."

"I do not laugh. I am glad to help."

"If you want to help, stand there and hold out your arm so I can twirl from it. I want to try the dance again."

"Yes," said Jonwon. "Next time there will be no falling down." He turned his back to Agnes, and held out his arm to Amy, who touched it and lifted her right leg.

"Jonwon, you lift your left leg so it will look more balanced, as a dance with you and Amy," Agnes was looking exceptionally angelic as she said this, so Adam knew she was up to something.

"Yes," said Jonwon, lifting his left leg. "Go ahead with the dance, Amy. I will see to it that there is no fall."

With a shrill hoot, Agnes poked hard at the back of Jonwon's right leg, which folded under him.

Jonwon sat down as abruptly as Amy had, with a louder thud, and Agnes yelled, "So you said there'd be no falling?"

"That was unexpected," said Jonwon meditatively.

"I'll say it was," said Amy, giggling.

"You looked so funny, Jonwon," said Agnes, laughing aloud.

"Interesting. Just after I'd made the assertion that there would be no falling down, there was. I, myself, fell down. My own assertion was punctured by a flute. Unexpected."

"Ha!" said Agnes, poking Jonwon with the flute. "That's what happens to smart alecks!"

"Ha," said Jonwon. "Punctured! Falling—ha! Unexpected and ha! Ha! Ha!"

As if they sensed that something miraculous had occurred,

105

the twins plopped beside Jonwon, shrieking with laughter. Jonwon laughed again, and the twins hugged him.

Seven turned down the sound. "I read years ago that humor is a sudden insight into the incongruity of a point of view, a sudden perception of imperfection in reasoning. Agnes succeeded in puncturing the pomposity of Jonwon's point of view." Seven smiled toward the monitor screen and turned it off. Then he said quietly, "Welcome to humanness, Jonwon."

Seven knows, thought Adam. He knows what it is to be human. Mother said my biological father loved Wodehouse.

The unanswered question was answered.

"Seven, you have a sense of humor because you're mostly human, aren't you? Are you the failed mind transfer experiment from before I was born?"

"Bess and Matt and I have been wondering when we should tell you, but we've been putting it off, hoping it would be easier once another attempt at mind transfer was a success."

Adam threw his arms around Seven, something he had not done for years. "I'm so glad you're partly Jonathan Durant. He died and I could never have known him at all, but I do know you. I'm lucky because you and Matt are the best fathers anyone could ever have. Seven, do you mind being a robot with the memories of a human?"

"Once I resented not being Jon completely, or being a robot completely, but now I'm happy being Seven. Besides, I have come to believe that a son has an advantage in having at least one father who is a robot."

But later that night his joy at knowing about Seven and his happiness at Jonwon's sense of humor were dissipated by an attack of loneliness and worry about Meg. He went to see Bess.

"Mom, I'm afraid I won't be able to hold Meg even if she does come to Centauria and some day we're married. I'm so ordinary. I'm the only one in the whole family without special

106

brains and talents, and that includes Seven and Jonwon."
Should he tell her he'd found out about Seven?

"Adam, no brain is ordinary."

"Well, mine is."

"No. Even the simplest brain is extraordinary when you stop to think of the vast universe full of so many other atoms and molecules that haven't organized themselves into something that can react and even think."

"My brain is a dud. I'm not as smart as Jonwon."

"Don't underestimate a human brain. It's a complicated organization of billions of different cells, each containing what were once free-living organisms—mitochondria, for instance—and each with many things it can do. The parts of the cell and the parts of the brain have learned to work together, giving up individuality to make a larger pattern."

"Seven says intelligence is part of the pattern the universe is developing, but I'm afraid my intelligence isn't enough to add anything to the pattern."

Bess laughed. "I'm certain you'll find your part to play."

"Mom—I know about Seven having my father Jonathan's memories. I'm so glad."

"So am I, Adam."

PART • III
EXILE AND RETURN

CHAPTER • 17

By the time Adam was sixteen it was hard not to admit to himself that he was sick of robotics, and no good at it. On Meg's infrequent visits, and even during her hycom calls, she spent all the time talking with Matt, Seven, and especially Jonwon. Adam couldn't understand their talk and felt left out.

He tried to be enthusiastic about the new Abe Norum's visit to Federation Spome, because now the Feds would see a perfect mind transfer robot. Perhaps Norum would undo the years of prejudice, and the Feds would start ordering super-aide bodies for themselves. Adam was too jealous of Meg to care.

"Those bioeffing Feds yap about failures," said Matt during one of Meg's calls, "but so what if two others didn't take transfer and the superaide brains deactivated? When more people are willing, we'll have other MT robots."

"If you use the initials MT," said Adam angrily, "the Feds are going to think mind-transferred humans are empty."

Seven laughed. "There's an old Zen saying that from emptiness comes being. Most ironic. Humans can always ask a mind transfer robot if he feels empty. I wish them luck."

"I think it soon won't matter what mind transfer robots are called," said Meg. "If Norum is as good as you say, then Tully Robotics will be deluged with orders. After the ceremonies for Norum in Federation Spome, let's celebrate—I'm visiting Centauria with Grandmother."

"Nanca's coming *here*?" Matt almost snarled it.

"She's had her old brain recordings destroyed and wants to be the second mind transfer, done live so she'll wake up in a robot body knowing every last thing the human knew. She says her human body is failing her and if the transfer is

111

successful you can give it a lethal injection—on her written order."

"What's Burt think of that idea?" asked Matt.

"He hates the idea. He's fanatically bioeffer and says he disapproves of all mind transfer now. But Grandmother won't listen to him. She's coming, Dad. Get ready."

"Tell Nanca that advanced age like hers is probably an asset in adjusting to mind transfer, judging from Norum," said Matt. "Norum hadn't been able to smell or taste for years, so he doesn't mind that a robot body can't, and he likes having better vision and hearing than he had when human."

"Grandmother will probably want to know about sex."

"The superaide bodies now have tactile sensation from synthoskin, with erectile capacity at will," said Matt, winking at Seven.

"I'll tell her," said Meg. "And maybe that will persuade Burt that robot humans are still human."

Adam noticed that Seven had seemed to draw back when Meg said that Nanca was coming to Centauria.

Meg always said that Federation Spome was a boring cylinder full of nothing but politics, and now she had to sit in the audience at Federation Parliament, listening to Norum's speech and trying not to smell the sweat of Burt Smythe, who was wedged in next to her.

Norum, gentle and bland as usual, retraced the history of Centauria, emphasizing the role played by robots in the past and the hope that mind transfer robots would help create other colonies outside the Terran solar system.

"He's an unholy robot," muttered Burt.

"But Nanca will be a beautiful one," said Meg to annoy him. When he choked, she patted his back and said, "I'm sorry," but he paid no attention.

"And so," continued Norum, "I thank the Terran Federation for providing funds to make mind transfer possible, saving

112

my life. I am grateful for the chance to go on working to the best of my ability. I feel that I am a useful Terran again."

There was a little rustle in the audience, as if some people didn't like Centaurians calling themselves Terran. Especially a robot Centaurian.

Norum turned his head to smile reassuringly at Horace Deno, the new Centaurian president. Meg was glad Horace's son Hank was not there. He was an insufferable eighteen-year-old rookie cop now, and thought she should adore him.

"Fellow citizens of the Federation," said Norum, "we are all Terran whether we live on Earth, in the many colonies of the Terran solar system, or in Centauria. All of us are descended from Terran ancestry. Those like myself who will have second lives in robot bodies are still Terran, working with the rest of you. We are still human—"

"You are not human! Biofundamentalism rejects you!"

The heckler was an old woman in the front row, her face curiously blank. Suddenly she stood up, pointing a gun.

"Metal monster!" she shouted. There was a loud bang and a small dart with a rubber suction cup glued itself to the synthoskin of Norum's forehead.

As several people tittered, Meg glared at Burt. "Are you behind this? Grandmother said Norum wouldn't be humiliated."

Smythe, trembling violently, moved his hand inside his tunic pocket and Norum's head exploded. Pieces of it flew at the crowd while people screamed. One of the eyes landed at Meg's feet and Smythe began to giggle.

The robot body stood still, wires quivering from the severed neck, and then began to sway as if it could no longer keep upright. Centaurian president Deno sprang from his chair to catch the body and hold it up.

At first no one noticed that the Federation prime minister had slumped in her seat, blood welling out of her right eye where a long metal shard had driven into her skull.

113

"Nanca?" said Smythe. "Nanca!" Both hands went up to his head, as if he could cure his wife by rubbing his own eyes.

Meg dug into his pocket. There were two objects in it and she took them out, then stood up, holding the controller and the bomb detonator for everyone to see. "This is the man who killed them! He forced that woman to fire the dart and then he triggered the bomb—"

Smythe hit her, took a stun gun from an inside pocket, and began firing at the approaching guards. People around him fell and the entire audience began to stampede.

"Stop him!" Meg tried to grab Smythe, but he pushed her away and disappeared into the melee of frightened people.

CHAPTER • 18

President Deno brought Norum's body back to Centauria for a state funeral, although only the pieces of head would be buried. Superaide bodies, even if they needed new heads, were too valuable not to be recycled.

There would be no third Norum. Once a brain recording was used for successful mind transfer, it could not be used again, and Norum had had only one recording made in his long biological lifetime. Centauria grieved.

Meg came back to Centauria with President Deno. At first Dinah had wanted Meg to remove herself from the threat of Burt's revenge until the police found him, but once Meg left Earth it was different.

"Meg, darling, I'm glad you're safe," Dinah said on hycom, "but I'm alone. There's no other member of the family to go to the funeral with me. Bess, can't you get away for a few days? I'll pay for the transport ticket. Mother left everything to me and I'm rich. Don't know why she didn't leave anything to Burt, unless—but that doesn't matter now. Please come, Bess."

"No, Dinah. I'm staying with Matt."

"But Bess, you're a Lorimer! I know you think it's asinine of me to discover grief at the loss of a mother I didn't know I loved, but I can't help it. Mother was proud of being Walton Lorimer's daughter, and you and I are Walton's only remaining grandchildren. Please change your mind. I don't want Meg to come back for the funeral until they catch Burt."

"No. I'm sorry, Dinah."

"I'll go," said Adam, who was sitting with Meg, holding her cold little hand. "I'm a Lorimer by descent and I look older than sixteen. Why can't I escort you to the state funeral, Dinah?"

Dinah thought it was a good idea, but Meg and Bess did not want Adam to leave. Then Adam noticed that Seven gave him a brief, affirmative nod of the head.

He wants to go himself, thought Adam, but Earth would object to it unless he disguised himself as an aide, and even then he'd have to go with a human.

"Don't go, Adam. It might not be safe for you." Meg was in tears.

"My name isn't Tully. No one will be interested in me."

"Take One-O with you as your personal aide. He's good protection," said Seven. Somehow that mollified the rest of the family, and Adam went to pack.

In the airtaxi on the way to the funeral, Adam held Dinah's hand. She was Meg's mother, and he loved her too.

"Nanca was always so strong," said Dinah. "She was a difficult woman but I don't have a mother anymore. . . ."

He squeezed her hand reassuringly and, to reassure himself, glanced in the back seat where One-O sat stolidly.

One-O was not just Adam's guard and servant, but a sample of a Tully Robotics product, to be shown to the Federation as a safe yet moderately intelligent intermediate aide.

Dinah sniffed. "Poor Matt. One day and already stock in Tully Robotics has fallen. Nobody thinks mind transfer robots are immortal."

"They don't have to be. The piece of metal that killed Nanca would not have killed Norum. It took the full blast of the bomb to do that. People will think about it, and remember that Norum seemed very human before he was killed. They'll have duplicate brain recordings made of themselves and eventually they'll start buying superaide bodies."

"I suppose you're right, Adam, but sometimes I think the biofundamentalism preached by your great grandfather Wal-

116

ton has permeated all of us in the family, whether we like it or not."

Not far away, Burtland Smythe sat in shadow, munching food cubes while the underground river flowed darkly past him. He smiled to himself at his own cleverness and he felt quite safe. Remembering the story of Adam Durant's birth in the old subway had inspired him to use it as a place to hide until he finished getting all of his equipment ready.

It had been easy to leave Federation Spome immediately after the assassination. No one had yet programmed the identicheck at the transporter so there was no alarm, no barrier as he entered it. No police waited for him when he arrived at the transport terminal nearest Manhattan. Soon someone would think of his possible escape routes, and then, when asked, the computers would tell where he had gone, but now he was free and could do what he wanted.

What he wanted was revenge. In his warped little mind something had broken. Muttering "Nanca" over and over, he promised her that he would take revenge on everyone responsible for her death. He had forgotten it was himself.

In one of the seedier sections of Manhattan was a small shop, with a larger back room known only to special customers like Smythe. The owner had been glad to sell him the necessary equipment, as in the past he had provided the Breen family with illegal mind controllers or minibombs.

When Smythe had explained that the Breen family needed protection after the assassination by what he called an unknown assailant, the shop owner nodded. There had already been a call out for information on Burtland Smythe, with a reward offered. The shop owner looked forward to the reward.

Smythe killed him and stole a collection of false identidisks. They wouldn't fool a computer because Smythe's retinal pattern wouldn't match those stored in the disks, but he was only counting on fooling humans, temporarily.

In the subway tunnel, Smythe finished the food cube,

117

brushed himself off, and went out to get an airtaxi. In addition to the false identidisk, he wore a mustache and the shop owner's best clothes. Arriving at transport terminal, he went directly to the section for Centauria, where bored guards stood in case any Centaurian dignitaries arrived for the funeral. None had come—Adam Durant didn't count—and none would, for President Deno had said he would never visit the Terran solar system again, and no other member of his government felt like going to Earth.

The guards were not interested in anyone traveling from the Terran solar system to Centauria. Who would want to go there except wealthy tourists curious about a spome in another solar system, or emigrant scientists who couldn't get along with the Feds? The news had made it clear that the assassin was a well-known bioeffer who would undoubtedly wish to stay and hide on Earth, the only place where any human could disappear and perhaps never be found.

Smythe waved his identidisk at the guards, a scowl of impatience and a flourish of briefcase indicating that he was a Centaurian businessman eager to get home. He was passed through the identicheck before the computers could indicate that anything was wrong, and another bored operator touched a button to start automatic transport as soon as Smythe entered the chamber.

Once inside the transporter, Smythe confirmed the start procedure by touching another switch, just as the alarms went off outside. He had not passed the computer identicheck, but it was too late because the transporter had already activated.

His molecules, sent by hycom waves through hyperspace, reassembled in the Centaurian transporter where he killed the human operators before they could react to the duplicate alarm. He locked the doors of the transporter office and made a call.

"Tully? This is Burtland Smythe. I've killed Norum and

118

proved to the Federation that mind transfer robots are vulnerable and dangerous. But Nanca is dead and I wish to give myself up for punishment here in Centauria. I'll give myself up to you, and only you, although you can have a police squad to guard you if you think you can't trust me."

Matt hurried to the transporter station at Centauria's port end, accompanied by five armed policemen, one of whom was Hank Deno, who kept in touch with his father, the president, by intercom. The police wore shields to protect against stun blasts and minibombs, and insisted that Matt wear one too.

"Hello, Matt." Smythe stood in the doorway of the transporter. His hands held no obvious weapons, but the right was closed into a fist. "Nanca is dead. My Nanca."

"You killed her, Smythe."

"Oh, no. She died in the cause." Sweat dripped from Smythe's nose and he didn't wipe it off. "You can try to seduce humans into believing mind transfer is good. Even I believed it for a while—and Nanca—but she's dead, isn't she? Death is the finish of human life. Intelligence is biological. Human. Nanca is human. Was human. Never robot. Robot monsters pretending to be human—"

"Come on, Burt," said Matt. "We'll help you get treated."

Smythe opened his right hand as the police started for him. "I've fixed a little surprise for Tully Robotics and this place of hell called Centauria." Hank Deno grabbed his arm, but Smythe's thumb closed on the detonator and the large bomb inside the transporter went off.

CHAPTER•19

"Damage report," said Horace Deno, his face a taut mask of sorrow. "How many killed—besides Matthew Tully and my son?"

"Fifty-eight dead, one hundred and five injured, Mr. President. The transporter terminal is totally demolished and with it the hycom transmitter, which used the same—"

"Yes, yes. But is the hull intact?"

"Perfectly. Repair robots and human engineers have inspected it thoroughly and there are no cracks. The power supply to the port end has been restored. We have full use of all our sublight vstations, so communication within the spome and to our satellites is intact."

Deno nodded. "Good. Proceed with repairs. After the cremations we will have one state funeral for all."

What could be found of Matt Tully was cremated and, after the funeral, scattered in Wildpark. Since he'd always put off having a brain recording made, there could not be a mind transfer robot named Matthew Tully.

Tully Robotics started preparing the few superaide robot bodies available for mind transfer of those among the dead who had recordings in storage. Hank Deno was one of them.

Within a week the engineers reported that they could not build another hycom without parts from Federation factories, and without a transporter, those factories might just as well have been in another universe.

President Deno made another speech to the citizens of the new, independent nation of Centauria. "We cannot go to the Federation for help. We cannot even tell them that we are alive. Our engineers say that we can build factories to make hycom and transporter parts, but first we must make machinery for refining minerals which must be mined in the aster-oids of this solar system which contain them. This will all take years to accomplish.

"Fellow Centaurians, let us not be paralyzed by our tragedy. The assassin intended to blow up not only Dr. Tully but Centauria itself. Nevertheless our hull is intact and our at-mosphere safe.

"We now can't retreat to Earth if our spome fails us. We will see to it that it never fails. Our farm and manufacturing satellites will make it possible for us to survive alone, and we will build more.

"Our buildings are safe because they are extensions of the spome's hull, but it is imperative that some of them—begin-ning with the hospital—be converted to self-contained units able to seal themselves off in case the spome's air ever escapes.

"So far our spome has not failed us. It is our nation. We are no longer part of the Terran Federation. We can do without them, and if contact is resumed, it is Centauria that will be particular about allowing them to visit us! I say cheers for Centauria—and to hell with the Federation!"

Bess, working with the injured in the hospital, did not cheer along with her patients.

"You've got to rest," said Meg. "You haven't slept at all."

"I must keep going."

"Here comes Seven. I sent for him."

Protesting, Bess finally let Seven lead her out of the ward to her own office, while the high-tec robomeds and the other human doctors kept going. Meg followed Seven.

Bess leaned against her desk but would not sit. "Now don't tell me the hospital has plenty of other doctors and help. We've never had an emergency like this before."

"Doctors tired from not sleeping and racked by grief should rest occasionally," said Seven. He brought up a chair for Bess but she paid no attention.

121

"What about Adam?" Bess said. "He doesn't know whether or not Centauria is intact. He doesn't know Matt is dead. I won't be able to talk to him for years. I won't be able to see him for many years after that if we can't build a transporter and have to wait for the Feds to arrive with one. I can't bear this—losing both Matt and Adam."

"Adam isn't lost," said Meg. "We know where he is even if he doesn't know about us. And I'm sure the Feds will send out another robot ship, with another transporter, just in case someone's alive in the Centauri solar system. Ships can go almost at light speeds these days if people don't go along. It shouldn't take more than ten years, everyone says, and maybe we'll have a transporter built before that."

"Oh, go away," said Bess. "Nobody understands."

Seven picked up Bess as if she weighed nothing and carried her into a small room at the back of her office. He shut the door behind them and then put her on a narrow cot that was almost all the room could hold.

"Bess, you are now going to take a nap. I understand. I loved Matt. I love Adam—I even delivered him, remember? My experience of knowing you and Matt and Adam cemented me to humanness and saved my sanity. I shall miss Adam but I'm going to see to it that his mother takes good care of herself. I will wake you in one hour."

"Promise?"

"I promise."

She went to sleep at once and he walked softly back out to the office, closing the door without a sound. Meg was waiting.

"Seven, I'm ashamed to tell you, but I'm no good working in a hospital with wounded bodies and frightened minds and blood and death. And I'm ashamed of the self-pity I feel because no one feels sorry for me, cut off from my mother and from my home—and Adam. I feel lost here."

Seven glanced at the picture on Bess's wall. Unlike the live holov picture of Alpha Centauri A in his own office, this was of Earth, an ocean with a mass of water unimaginable for

122

anyone born in Centauria. The ocean seemed endless and compelling, as if one could plunge into the dark water and forget everything.

"You should plunge into work, Meg. But doctoring isn't your cup of tea. You're Matt's child and I believe you'll be just as inventive. You and Jonwon."

"Two supposed geniuses that seem to know alot but have not yet shown any signs of genuine creativity." Meg sighed.

"I have complete faith in you and Jonwon," said Seven. "I think the two of you might invent something terribly useful."

"Even if we invented a better transport, how could we make it when Centauria can't even repair the one that's blown up?"

"Try thinking about it. Go back to the lab and ponder on Centauria's situation. When Bess wakes up, I'll help her in the hospital for a while so she can go back to the twins as soon as possible. They're upset, too."

"You don't mind . . . hospitals?"

"Oddly enough, I enjoy everything that's biological."

Her face pinched and gray, Meg started for the door, then stopped. "Seven, can't you tell me what I should try to invent? With Jonwon, that is."

"A magic carpet, perhaps?"

"Seven! You know that hyperdrive is impossible. Of course, if a hyperdrive engine *could* be made small enough to fit into a ship—but the best theoreticians have never been able to work out even the theory of such a drive."

"I thought you and Jonwon were the best theoreticians around. I happen to know that when Norum was going to persuade the Feds to fund hyperdrive research, he had you and Jonwon in mind. Don't you want to see Adam before the arrival of the sublight ship the Feds will undoubtedly send out to see if any of us are still alive? That will take—"

"Years. I know. But all of us scientists have been told over and over that a hyperdrive is impossible."

"Think about it, Meg."

123

CHAPTER • 20

The Terran Solar Federation voted funds for the latest space-ship to be converted to total robot operation. It was stripped of all excess weight, including toilets for the humans who would transport to the ship from time to time to check on things. Humans in suits could visit (with their own excretory bags) because the latest transporters were small enough to be carried in operating condition.

A month passed before the ship left, and during that month there was complete hycom silence from Centauria. Dinah cried frequently, certain that Centauria had been blown up because before he left Manhattan, Burt Smythe had mailed a letter to her stating his intention. Adam had insisted that the letter not be made public.

"People might start believing that there's no one alive in Centauria, and the ship might turn back," he said. "I'm sure there are people alive, and even if Centauria itself blew up, the farm and manufacturing satellites would stay intact."

He did not add that there might be robots alive, even in Centauria. Seven and Jonwon.

"I've lost my daughter," wailed Dinah.

I've lost everybody, thought Adam. Maybe not Jonwon. I bet he's still alive. But Seven's body isn't as shielded. He might be dead too. The thoughts went round and round and always made him feel hopeless. He couldn't talk to Dinah about them, but sometimes he talked to One-O.

"Perhaps you should live your life as if it were certain that you will see your family again. That will be better for you and for them, Master Adam," said One-O.

Adam gaped. He had never known that One-O was capable of a speech that long and that intelligent. "I'll try, One-O, but

I wish you wouldn't call me 'Master.' You're not a Terran aide robot."

"Perhaps it would be safer if I seemed to be only an aide," said One-O. "If I always call you Master Adam there will be no mistake."

Adam went back to his efforts at cheering up Dinah, with no success. Then one day he was thinking about his twin sisters and suddenly started to cry, unable to stop before Dinah caught him at it. "It's just that they haven't had much chance to live, and I feel so helpless about my family."

Meg's mother brightened at once. She enjoyed cheering up other people, forgetting her own sorrow and anxiety in the process. "In my happily misspent life, Adam, I've found out that helplessness is best conquered by doing spectacular things."

"I'm not brainy or talented enough to be spectacular."

"I didn't say 'be.' Adam, you can do something spectacular. Anybody can. The trick is to find out what, and the process of finding that out is often lots of fun."

"But I don't know . . ."

"In the meantime you will go to school here in Manhattan and find out what you're good at."

He didn't argue. He went to a good school and studied hard, discovering that while no genius, he wasn't stupid compared to Terran kids. In fact, Centaurian education was so advanced that he was ahead of his age group.

Another month passed; the rescue ship was moving out of the solar system and gaining speed, and Dinah's new play was a hit. She had money and looked tired but radiant each night when she returned to the penthouse.

Usually Adam was asleep, but one night he waited for her by the big window in the living room, watching the lighted towers of Manhattan above the broad darkness of Central Park.

There were a few ancient street lamps visible among the

125

trees, and occasionally an aircar strayed through the warning signal that protected the park's boundaries, but amid the twenty-four hour bustle and brilliance of Manhattan, the dark wooded space seemed primordial as if dumped out of a time machine into the heart of the city.

Yet it's not primordial, thought Adam. Dinah says it was planned and planted back in the nineteenth century. There must be good in people after all.

"Hi, Adam. You're up, so what's up?"

"I wanted to talk to you about my future. I can't go back to Centauria until the ship gets there, and that'll take practically ten years. I have to have a career and earn a living, but . . ." He stopped and hoped he wouldn't cry.

"You don't have to earn a living yet, dear. I'm filthy rich, thanks to Mother's will, and so is Meg if she's alive. As to a career, you're almost ready for a university so just select the best one in the city."

"I'll be seventeen soon and I'm already doing college work. My father Jonathan went to Harvard and I'd like to finish college there if they'll have me."

Dinah leaned back on her cream-colored sofa. Recently she had abandoned roles suitable for thin and effervescent girls. The resultant spread into maturity—literally and figuratively—did not make Dinah look fat, but she was certainly more voluptuous. Critics thought she was now a better actress, but Adam saw under the lush surface a tense woman who felt fulfilled only on stage.

"Harvard," said Dinah, meditatively. "A long time ago I was working summer stock near Boston and I took a Shakespeare course at Harvard. One of the professors of the medical school was in it too and it was absolutely fascinating, or rather Paul was—that was the doctor, not the Shakespeare prof—and he, I mean Paul, said doctors should study Shakespeare to keep their human perspective in high gear and . . . where was I, dear?"

126

"Being fascinated by somebody named Paul."

"Oh, yes. Paul Hirson. Teaches at Harvard Medical School. It was such a long time ago, and we didn't really date or anything because he was married at the time, but we conversed after class—it was a wonderful little tea shoppe, so transplanted British and all that—"

"Dinah—"

"Adam, I think you'll be a good doctor, and if I'm wrong, well, I'm hardly ever wrong about people except some of the idiots I've married, but you might find it useful to consult Paul Hirson about the whole problem of your career. . . ." She paused, yawned, and then grinned at him. "Unless you're determined to be a roboticist. Hardly your best role, Adam."

"Why not?" he asked defensively, although he'd been wondering the same thing himself.

"You're alot like your biological father. He once told me he should have been a physician instead of a roboticist because while he liked making robots, he really just wanted to be useful to people."

Useful. Someone had told him—was it Matt?—that soon after being activated, Seven had remarked that he wanted to go through existence doing as little harm as possible. Adam asked Seven about it.

"Oh, yes. I said that. A coward's way out."

"Of what?"

"A way out of the responsibility."

"But what responsibility?" Adam had asked. "It wasn't your fault that you were born—I mean, activated."

"True, but once into existence, we owe ourselves and others something."

"What?"

"Something. Maybe just to be useful. To help, and always with compassion."

There in Dinah's beautiful room, Adam remembered Nanca's question to Jonwon. What is the purpose of your exis-

127

tence? In many conversations with Meg, they'd argued about it. She always said it was to uncover the secrets of the universe, and Adam could never think of anything as grand as that.

Compassionate helping. It didn't sound spectacular, but it was certainly an interesting new addition to the universe. Perhaps a key to something more?

"Dinah, I'm not sure . . ."

"Adam, from the expression on your face, you'd think I'd suggested that you take up the profession of algae farming or worse, growing clone steaks and chicken breasts and what-not. You know, dear, you're the only family I've got left now, and I want you to consider yourself my son. I'll pay for the best education you can get wherever and whatever you choose."

"Thanks, Dinah. I only meant that I'm not the best . . ."

"And you don't have to go to medical school if you don't want to, but you do remind me of Paul Hirson in some ways, big and sort of quiet, most unlike the men I unfortunately married, including of course your stepfather Matt, who I loved but I assure you your mother is much better for him. Paul—I was talking about Paul, I believe—used to say that although medicine may be hi-tech these days, human intuition and rapport are still important. Surely you believe that? Your mother is such a wonderful doctor."

While Dinah took a breath, Adam said, "I'll apply at Harvard at once. And see Paul Hirson as soon as I can. I'm sorry I've been so depressed about Centauria . . ."

"Honey, try to remember that life is to be lived. Not that I've ever been good at living it respectably but I've made alot of people happy and I've had alot of fun. I think I'm going to enjoy having a son in college and maybe medical school. I may even reform."

One-O sat with Adam while he studied, and soon Adam

128

was aware that the robot was studying too. One-O didn't always understand, but he always remembered, and could question Adam and help prepare him for the entrance examinations. When the Harvard acceptance arrived, Adam had his first quarrel with Dinah, over One-O.

"He's the only interesting robot I've ever had in the house and I don't want him to go with you to Harvard." Dinah's red hair seemed alive with dangerous electricity. "Besides, I have a feeling that you'll never believe you accomplished it if you don't finish college and medical school by yourself."

In the end it was One-O who decided. "Master Adam, Seven told me that you felt inferior to Meg and Jonwon. Perhaps your cousin Dinah is correct. You need to find out—alone— the ways in which you are intelligent."

"Blast it, One-O. You sound just like Seven."

"Inaccurate but flattering, Master Adam. I have been studying Seven for my entire existence. I am not as intelligent but I have learned to use what I have."

Adam reddened. "Which is what I should do. All right, I'll go alone."

"Bravo, Adam," said Dinah, hugging him.

Before he left, Adam walked through Central Park to the ancient museum he always tried to visit when he came to Earth. He headed straight for the dinosaur exhibits, remembering the one time he and Jonwon went to the Centaurian museum that showed everything from the history of the spome and the astronomy of her stellar neighborhood, to the Terran culture and natural history the Centaurians had left behind.

There was even a Tyrannosaurus rex skeleton that many people said occupied too much space. It was Adam's favorite.

"Look at it, Jonwon. When I was small I used to imagine I could climb inside its bony chest to look out at the world from high up, the way a boy did in one of my books. I love this old dinosaur, don't you?"

129

"No, Adam. It is nothing but a collection of dead bones. It was never intelligent. It's worse than a robot aide or taxi."

"You've never seen a robot taxi. They have them only on Earth."

"I've read about them. I understand how all robots work, from taxis to Computer Prime in the Federation, or the Centaurian A.I. that keeps the spome operating properly. I'm going to design marvelous robots, not aides nearly as stupid as a dinosaur."

"Dinosaurs may have been stupid but they enjoyed life and before they became extinct they existed for many millions of years—more than humans or robots have."

"Extinction is symbolic. It makes no difference how long they existed as a species. They died off."

"I suppose you're hinting that humans will eventually become extinct too." Adam expected Jonwon to hear the sarcasm and deny the accusation.

The robot stared up at the dinosaur. "Humans can't become extinct as long as intelligent robots exist."

Remembering this uneasy conversation, Adam stared up at the terrible teeth of an even bigger tyrannosaurus looming over his head.

I never asked Jonwon what he meant, thought Adam. Did he mean that intelligent robots would save humanity from extinction or that humanity would survive as mind transfer robots or—or that untransferred superaide robots will become what humanity had once been?

"As I told your cousin when she called, I do indeed remember her." Paul Hirson pulled at his short brown beard and grinned at Adam as if he were thoroughly enjoying the memory. "I'm surprised that she remembers me at all."

"She does," said Adam comfortably. It didn't take long to feel comfortable with Paul Hirson.

"I read about her now and then. I gather she's divorced. I

130

am, too. No children. I don't consider it obligatory to pass on my genes but I would like a baby of my own before I become too far advanced into what this era calls extended middle age. Anybody trained in biology and believing that biology is fundamental should find children interesting."

Remembering the twins, Adam chuckled and agreed. It hadn't taken him long to find out that there was more than one kind of biofundamentalist, and that Paul Hirson was the best. Paul even liked the idea of robots who could think as well as a human, and seemed fascinated by Adam's description of the child Jonwon had once been. Paul's biofundamentalism was reverence for life, not hatred of anything.

"Paul, I want to tell you about my three fathers. I need to share that with you, and when you and Dinah are married—"

"Do Centaurian seventeen year olds always arrange the lives of their elders, especially elders who haven't met each other for many years?" But he said it with a twinkle, and listened quietly while Adam told him that he and Dinah would be good for each other, and even more quietly as Adam explained about the three fathers.

"I see what Seven means to you. Perhaps it's better that the mind transfer partially failed in his case, since he may be the only being in the universe with memories he knows belong to someone else, yet who has found a center of stability and has let go of his specialness. That's hard to do."

"I'm worried about Jonwon, who can't let go of his specialness as the only untransferred superaide. He's likely to stay the only one. If Centauria is alive, of course."

Paul nodded. Adam always put in that sentence.

Adam suddenly found himself crying. "Sorry. I've done alot of crying alone, but not usually in public."

"This isn't public. Cry away."

He did. After blowing his nose, Adam said, "Waiting ten, maybe fifteen years to find out if the people you love are alive or dead . . ."

131

"Is horrible. Let's assume some are alive. Shall we say definitely Seven, who in spite of his vulnerable body sounds like a survivor? That's the trick of existence in this crazy universe of ours."

"Seven said the trick is to survive to be of use."

"I hope I can meet your Seven some day. Because I think he probably knows the other secret, too."

"What's that?"

"Being able to let go."

But Adam didn't understand that one.

CHAPTER • 21

"Jonwon, I want to talk to you alone."

"We are alone, Meg. Seven has gone to help the twins with their harpsichord lessons until Bess gets home from work."

Meg looked around wearily. In spite of Seven's advice, she had not been inside Tully Robotics since her father's death and even now she kept expecting him to walk in, his wide smile crinkling his cheeks at the sight of her. She sat down and said nothing.

"I'm glad you've come," said Jonwon, breaking the silence Meg so often wrapped around herself, even when she said she wanted to talk. "It's lonely here without Matt. I even miss One-O. He was so reliable and hardworking, and so pleasantly unemotional."

Meg bridled. "Unlike us humans, I suppose."

"What's the matter, Meg?"

"Matter? My father is dead, the boy I love probably thinks I'm dead, and it will be ten or fifteen years before he finds out I'm not—"

"You're assuming the hycom won't be fixed until the transporter arrives from the Feds. With the factories in full operation, we might have a workable hycom years before that."

"By the time Adam finds out I'm alive he'll probably be married, and in the meantime, I'm trapped here in this tiny fake world with my two half sisters my only relatives—I'm certainly not going to pretend you're a brother, as Adam did."

"We are all part of Bess's family."

"Jonwon, only Adam could ever persuade me it was great to be human, and he's not here. If some of the explosion victims make successful mind transfers, I want to do the same."

With an unbreakable grip, Jonwon pulled her by the wrist

133

out of his lab and through the underground passage to the Tully house. She yelled and kicked at him, but it did no good.

"Seven, we have to consult you," said Jonwon, still holding an angrily crying, disheveled Meg.

Seven closed the harpsichord and stood up. So did the twins, eyes wide. "First I have something to say to the twins. Agnes, stick to the flute, because you're terrible at keyboard instruments. Amy, keep up your harpsichord practicing and you'll be an excellent musical partner for Agnes. That is all I have to say on the subject of musical careers for eleven year olds, but if you don't practice hard I'll say alot more."

Meg followed the two robots into the garden and sat down on a shaded bench. "Why should the twins try to be musicians when robots play better? Besides, computer-generated electronic music is perfect, isn't it?"

"That's the trouble with it," said Jonwon. "I'd rather hear humans play on old instruments anytime."

"Are we here to discuss music?" asked Seven mildly.

"Meg wants to transfer to a robot."

Meg sobbed, while Seven slowly sat down beside her and put his arm around her. "And you brought her to me, Jonwon?"

"I think she wants to forget Adam, but she's his girl and he's my brother. And she's too young to transfer."

"Jonwon just doesn't want to have another robot roboticist around as competition," said Meg.

"That's unkind," said Jonwon. "I've been waiting for you to come to work with us in the labs. You're even smarter than Matt, and you've got a doctorate already, and you certainly don't need to be a robot to be a better scientist than any of us."

"But I've been too depressed to work," said Meg. "I hate the human body, vulnerable to emotions, to death . . ."

"It may be harder to kill robots, but they can die. Norum died. And all superaides have emotive fields, whether full of

134

human brain patterns or not," said Jonwon bitterly. "I'm sorry you hate being human, but humans made me capable of emotion and I hate it. And no one can help me because no one understands. I'm the only completely untransferred superaide."

Seven held up his hand. "I'm suddenly tired of hearing you two self-pitying rivals for the 'I am not understood' award. Meg, you will always be irrevocably human whether you are biological or MT, and you have to come to terms with it just as Jonwon must come to terms with being all robot yet taught by humans to be human."

Suddenly Meg laughed for the first time since her father's death. "I thought that somehow I could achieve anything if I were a robot. I've believed that once Jonwon started work on the magic carpet he'd succeed. Have you discussed hyperdrive with him, Seven?"

"No, I was waiting for you to tell him."

"But hyperdrive is impossible," said Jonwon.

This time both Meg and Seven laughed.

"We know hyperspace exists because the hycom and the transporter both use it," said Jonwon, "but there's just no theory that makes the damn thing usable by a *ship*."

"There was no theory of universal gravitation until Isaac Newton thought of it, either," said Seven.

"Jonwon, we must try!" said Meg, her eyes shining. "And then we'll be able to meet the Feds as they lumber through normal space to bring us a transporter."

"But it's going to take us years to get even the raw materials for the transporter, much less a hyperdrive engine," said Jonwon. "Even if we work out the theory."

Seven leaned over to touch a rose petal. "I suspect that hyperdrive may not need huge engines and exotic raw materials. Perhaps it's a matter of different concepts, thinking more in computer terms, which is what you're good at."

135

"If you have it partly worked out, why don't you present it to the Centaurian government yourself?" asked Meg.

"Because I haven't worked it out at all and never will. What I've told you is almost all I've got, except for a few bits of math and some computer run-throughs that don't mean much. I'm counting on the two of you to solve the problem, as soon as possible."

"That sounds like an order," said Jonwon.

"A plea," said Seven.

"I want to do it," said Meg, "and I will, if I can become a robot and work around the clock like you two."

"Seven! You haven't convinced Meg to stay human!"

Humming to itself, a bee landed on a fat yellow rose next to Seven. He turned to look at it as if he had never seen a bee before. He watched as the bee lumbered into the heart of the rose, pollen dusting its legs.

"So convenient to know the purpose of one's existence," said Seven. "I, too, think about that terrible question Nanca asked you, Jonwon. I don't know the answer completely—no one ever does—but I sure as hell know that one purpose is to find out the purpose."

"But Seven . . ." Meg began.

"I have the brain patterns, the memories of an old man stashed away in my otherwise robot brain, and I often feel as if you in the younger generation are abysmally lazy, wanting to know instead of finding out, wanting to have instead of to be, to get answers instead of asking questions—but I think I already said that."

"I didn't bring Meg here so you could lecture us, Seven." said Jonwon. "Why aren't you just helping her accept and enjoy being human?"

"I thought I was." Seven paused, and smiled at the bee. "Why should Meg create purpose for herself as a human when you haven't stopped complaining about being a robot long enough to get some fun out of creating your own purpose in existing."

"Hah, got you, Jonwon," chortled Meg. "I guess you and I aren't that different, after all. Why don't we accept his challenge, even if you have trouble accepting robothood and I have trouble being human? Let's invent hyperdrive."

"It will be a lot of work," said Jonwon.

"This family likes work," said Bess, standing in the doorway. "Come on, Seven. The twins are driving me crazy."

Seven went inside with Bess, while Jonwon and Meg stayed in the garden, each rehearing Bess's assertion that they were part of her family.

The scent of the roses was strong, and Meg took a deep breath. "Umm—wonderful. I'm sorry you can't smell them, Jonwon."

"So am I," he said, and smiled. Then he laughed, a rare event. "Does Adam smell good to you?"

"Yes—" The word was out before she could stop herself. "Okay. You win. I enjoy being human. At least, I enjoy the more primitive aspects of it. I guess I can wait—to be a robot."

CHAPTER • 22

As the weeks and months went by, Meg and Jonwon were still reviewing each theoretical step of the hyperdrive problem, and getting nowhere. They snapped at each other, and Meg could not conceal her envy of Jonwon's ability to work without having to stop for food and only rarely, now, to rest his mind.

One day Meg stamped into Seven's office and sat down, an angry spot of pink on each cheek. "Why—*why* is it so difficult finding a way to make a ship escape from normal space and just be in hyperspace, which is there all the time anyway?"

"A spaceship not only has to escape the patterns of normal space, but be able to go where it wants to by using hyperspace, where the speed of light limit doesn't count, and then the ship has to emerge back into normal space intact—"

"Any minute now I'm going to scream," said Meg. "Jonwon and I can't think of anything anymore. Why was it so easy for people to invent matter transporters and hycom transmitters, both using hyperspace, and so difficult for us—"

"I was trying to explain that it wasn't easy," said Seven. "Crucial inventions are never easy, not when you take into account the long history that led up to them. May I remind you that it took humans several thousand years to invent the wheel, and some primitive cultures never did?"

"But I'm so *motivated*! I *want* hyperdrive, because it will take too many years for Centauria to rebuild the transporter, if ever, and I want to see my mother and Adam, and I want to go to Earth, where there's a big planet safely beneath me instead of a metal hull around me, with stupid artificial gravity—Seven! That's it!"

"Stupidity?"

"The antigrav aspect of hyperdrive! If a ship has to move

138

from three dimensions to dimensionlessness, then antigrav, which of course doesn't involve hycom or transporters except in the weight of particles changed to—"

"Meg, you're losing me. Better tell Jonwon."

She ran off and Seven went to see Bess.

"Meg has a new idea. Maybe there's hope." Seven came closer. "You look tired, Bess."

"Discouraged. I wish Hank Deno's most recent recordings had transferred successfully, because the one taken when he was eight makes a poor mind transfer robot. Prepubertal brain recordings will probably always transfer badly."

"I know. The new Hank Deno is not the eighteen year old who died, nor the eight year old who was. He's more robot than human, with no more personality than a bright aide."

"Maybe a pet would help humanize him," said Bess. She shrugged, winced, and began rubbing the back of her neck.

Seven massaged it for her. "You're working too hard, to keep from thinking, I suppose. I know you miss Matt and Adam, and I miss them too. But remember you have a pet robot in me, and I'll help—" Her fist slammed into his arm. "That didn't hurt me but I bet it hurt you."

Bess rubbed her knuckles. "Not as much as your words. I don't need a pet—anything—to humanize me. I'm human, and you know that you're mostly human, and dammit, don't we need each other?"

"Need? Oh, Bess, how I love you!"

"Then shut up and hold me, will you, Seven?"

In the lab, Meg stood awkwardly holding out a closed wicker basket to the robot Hank Deno.

"I don't want it," said Hank in a flat voice. "I just want to watch Jonwon work."

Meg opened the basket and took out a fat brown-and-white rabbit. "Bess says she's pregnant, and you could make money

139

breeding rabbits because we can't import pets from Earth now."

Hank took the rabbit into his arms. "Soft. Pretty. Maybe I'll keep her." He wandered off without saying thanks.

"I'm glad the other mind transfers aren't like him," said Meg. "How are you doing on our main problem? Maybe if you weren't so damn competitive and shared more with me we'd get further instead of both being bogged down."

"Go away, Meg. I'd rather have Hank with me. He's more restful and doesn't interrupt my thinking."

"Damn you! I give up! You never get tired and you'll never give up. Just don't speak to me again."

Jonwon didn't even look back as she ran out.

That night Meg woke after four hours of restless sleep. Except for the faint hum of Centauria itself, the house was silent while Bess and the twins slept and the robot aides stood waiting for daytime, when their activities would not disturb humans. Seven had gone to repair a faulty computer in one of the agricultural satellites, and Jonwon was at the lab.

Through the branches of the apple tree that leaned against the house, Meg could see the faint glow of the central bubbles along the core of Centauria, and beyond the clouds was the dim presence of the other side of the spome that surrounded her.

"I want to see the moon from Earth," she whispered, and remembered that she had dreamt something about the moon. Luna City, where her father had been born? No. Something else. A vision of moon—moonlight—disappearing, appearing. Shapes that lift because they had to lift because there was no reason not to. . . . Meg dressed and ran to the lab.

Jonwon looked up in surprise because it was so late for a human. He watched as Meg silently turned on the holoscreen, taking a long time to select what she wanted to show him.

The image that flicked into shape was a black sky filled with puffy clouds drifting across the face of Earth's moon,

140

which seemed to hide inside the cloud and then emerge trailing white patterns against the black.

"Look, Jonwon. The moon isn't actually in the clouds, but it seems to be. To the eye, it's all in the same field, a pattern of images related to each other. That's what hyperspace and normal space are—patterns, and the spaceship has to have a field around it that slides in with the patterns because those of hyperspace have a nondimension without the distance factors of normal space—oh, blast, I'm not explaining it properly at all!"

"Wait, Meg. Let me think."

Fifteen minutes later, after Meg thought her leg muscles would cramp, Jonwon broke the silence. "The field around the ship would be like an object in a transporter room, converted to transmissible energy. It would slide away from the pattern of the ordinary universe, and only dimensionless hyperspace would be left. And the ship would go with it."

Meg laughed with delight. "Yes! Yes!"

"Have I ever told you how I envy the primitive human talent for thinking in primitive images and then integrating them into creative inspiration?"

"My fellow genius and friend robot, you now have the onerous task of putting my primitive work of art into practical reality. I envy you your capacity to do it. I'm sure you will."

Jonwon's handsome, solemn face changed. He smiled—and said, "Thank you."

141

CHAPTER • 23

Adam felt more like Machiavelli than Cupid when it was announced that the well-known actress Dinah Breen would marry Professor Paul Hirson, M.D. By the time the marriage had lasted two years and produced Rufus Lorimer Hirson, Adam was distinctly pleased with himself.

"You're a genius, Adam," said Dinah, as she nursed Rusty. Her beautiful face looked as if it would never again wear an expression of discontent.

"Hardly. I'm getting through med school, but I have to work very hard—"

"You knew that Paul and I were perfect for each other, something I suspected those many years ago in Shakespeare class, but didn't have the nerve to admit to myself or even think might come to pass. I've been deliriously in love before—ah, many times before—but never with this strange feeling of being settled. Of being—I don't know . . ."

"Contented?"

"That's it. Contented to be his wife and Rusty's mother and at the same time Dinah Breen. Paul seems to think I should juggle all three roles, but first I'll nurse Rusty for a full three months."

She nursed happily for six, but managed to be at home to visiting celebrities and dignitaries, academic or otherwise. Adam tried to get away from studying once or twice a week to visit his new family—and One-O.

"Master Adam, you have done well," said One-O. "I am sure that Seven and your parents will be pleased that you have entered medical school."

One-O followed the unwritten rule in the Hirson house: do

not add "if they are still alive" to any sentence about anyone in Centauria.

Adam was well aware that his love for One-O frequently spilled over in compliments that a robot was not supposed to need, but Adam believed that One-O both needed and appreciated positive feedback. "One-O, I'm not as smart as the smartest humans, and you always say you're not as smart as the superaides, but you have a practical talent. You wait to see how things develop and then you modify your actions. That takes skill in observing and judging."

"I am not aware of judging," said One-O. "I do what I do because that is the way I am. Seven once said to me that when he designed my brain he was annoyed with trying so hard to perfect the superaide brain, and wanted to make a brain that was practical instead of being brilliant and innovative and one step ahead of humans."

Oho, thought Adam, I've just learned one of Seven's secrets. The superaide brain was meant to be a step ahead of humans if it was not used for mind transfer. I wonder if Matt knew Seven was doing that? But perhaps Matt, who wanted to make superintelligent, unprogrammed robots, did know and hoped he'd be able to make many Jonwons.

"Do I miss Jonwon?" He said it out loud to himself one night. He felt responsible for Jonwon, and worried about him, but did he really like him?

"Not the way I like One-O. I love One-O, and Seven. Not Jonwon." Moonlight from Earth's mammoth natural satellite was lying across his bed. He sat up suddenly and saw his face in the mirror on his half-opened closet door. "Jonwon is better looking than I am." That was a fact. Jonwon was also smarter. Much smarter.

"Do I envy Jonwon?" The Adam in the mirror looked ashamed, because he knew for the first time that he did not envy the robot. Jonwon could have his genius, and his potential immortality. Adam would take biology instead.

143

And in the meantime One-O was not one step ahead, like Jonwon. He was just himself, just . . . there. And more and more people met One-O and wanted the Federation to build similar robots.

When Paul Hirson, a recognized biofundamentalist, talked to the Federation about making One-O–type robots, they listened and the plans went forward. Roboticists studied One-O and aide factories began production of the new, practical, more intelligent aide. It was not widely known that it was One-O himself who helped the roboticists get the factories going.

While this quiet revolution was going on in what Matt always called the bioeffing Federation, there were increasing murmurs about mind transfer. People remembered that robot Norum had seemed quite human, and had even been killed along with humans. Why not try for the chance of a second life in a robot body?

Everyone had brain recordings made and filed away for the day when the Federation ship reached Centauria and its robot factories, where the secret of the superaide brain was known.

Once when One-O walked him back to the medical school, Adam said, "I've been wondering whether the secret of the superaide brain is securely in Centauria. If the Federation scientists asked you for it, could you give it to them?"

"Yes, Master Adam, but they only asked if I knew how to make a brain like my own. I said I knew enough to program the factory computers, but that I did not understand it. That was a true statement. Then they never asked if I knew how to make superaide brains."

"And if they do ask some day?"

One-O thought. "I will try to avoid answering. I think I will tell them I do not understand the superaide brain. That is a true statement."

"I hope it works, One-O. I don't want the Feds to make

144

superaide brains yet. They're a long way from treating robots as equals."

"I agree, Master Adam. After the assassination of the MT Delegate Norum, I deduced that biofundamentalist fanatics might continue to destroy other mind transfer robots. By the laws of robotics that were given to me, I cannot take responsibility for giving the Federation any information that would make other mind transfer deaths likely."

"The laws of robotics are meant to save human life when possible. Mind transfer gives humans the chance to live after biological death. The Federation might condemn you for deciding, after the death of only one MT robot, to keep the secret of MT immortality from all humans."

"Master Adam, Norum died. I cannot judge the statistical chance of success if the Federation manufactures superaide brains, if those brains are used for mind transfer, and if someone wishes to destroy them. I had to decide on the basis of the only statistic I know. Norum is dead."

"I see," said Adam, although he was not sure he did. "Anyway, after what they did to Centauria, let them wait until they have to buy from Tully Robotics. If—you know."

"I know, Master Adam."

When Rusty was four the Hirsons went to Dinah's Manhattan penthouse on the occasions when she starred in a holov play, and sometimes Adam, now a young doctor, got a few days vacation from hospital work to visit them.

He took Rusty and One-O to see the dinosaurs in the museum. The little boy and the robot stared solemnly up at Tyrannosaurus together. Then Rusty gave the crowing laugh that indicated particular pleasure.

"What do you think of it, One-O?" asked Adam.

"If I have emotive circuits, and that has never been clear to me, I like the dinosaur, Master Adam. It is interesting to look

145

at, both in its shape and as a specimen of evolutionary engineering that after successful millennia went wrong."

"It sure went wrong," said Rusty. "All those big teeth, and now it's extinct."

Rusty, Adam reflected, was as precocious as Meg had been. He had a spasm of feeling inadequate and then glanced at the calm face of One-O, also not a genius but who seemed to enjoy his own thinking about things, including dinosaurs. Jonwon had reacted so differently to Tyrannosaurus rex.

"One-O, do you have any thoughts about extinction?"

After a longish pause—expeditions with Rusty always caused heavy thinking in both Adam and the robot—One-O spoke much slower than usual. "Seven used to say that extinction is perhaps inevitable. Certainly all life will probably die when the universe stops expanding and collapses."

"But do you think humans will become extinct before the universe stops expanding?" As soon as he had asked the question, Adam regretted it. Rusty was sitting on his shoulders and he felt the boy tense up and bend forward to listen to One-O's answer, which seemed to be taking longer than ever.

Finally One-O spoke, rather rapidly. "No, Master Adam. I do not believe humans will ever become extinct. Unlike dinosaurs, humans are capable of change."

"Into robots? Do you think that's how we'll evade extinction?" It was one of the favorite points of discussion between Adam and Paul.

"I don't want to be a robot." Rusty pulled Adam's hair. "I love One-O but he's got to be him and I've got to be me."

"One-O and I are merely having a theoretical discussion."

"Crazy," said Rusty, which meant that he didn't understand what was just said. Adam was relieved to find that there were some words a bright four year old didn't know.

"Theoretical discussions are hard for me," said One-O, with what Adam suspected was a glimmer of humor. "But to

146

answer your question, Master Adam, I think that mind transfer will be used, but perhaps it is not the only way of change.
Biological life remains more adaptable than anything else. I
wonder if perhaps there will be a joining."

Suddenly Adam had an inward vision of a new dimension
to existence produced by the joining of biological life and
robot life beyond mind transfer—but he lost it as Rusty began
impatiently swinging his feet against Adam's middle.

Then Adam noticed that One-O was looking down, either
at his robot feet or at the tip of the dinosaur's bony tail just
beyond. The museum had curved the tail so that the tip lay
directly under the huge head. One-O seemed graver than
usual.

"I would like to see what happens in the future," said One-
O. "Is it wrong for a robot to want that?"

"Certainly not. I'd even like to see to the end of time, but I
won't last that long, and you might."

"Robots will not last until the end of the universe," said
One-O. "We must evolve too. We must help humans through
the end of all things."

"Thanks, One-O." Adam didn't want the robot to see the
tears in his eyes, so he tilted his head back to look at the
huge dinosaur looming over them.

I don't want to climb inside it anymore, thought Adam. I
want to be worthy of One-O's respect, and the help that One-
O intends to give humans no matter how stupid we are.

He was still looking at Tyrannosaurus rex when shouting
people ran through the corridors of the museum. "There's a
ship from Centauria out by Pluto! Centauria is alive!"

"I am Jonwon Tully, speaking to you from the Pluto spome's
hycom station. Centauria didn't have time to manufacture a
hycom while we were inventing hyperdrive, but we did the
best we could to get here as soon as possible. Please give me
the present coordinates of your rescue ship and I will try to

147

transfer your new transporter to my own vessel, to be taken immediately to Centauria so that the link to the Federation will be reestablished. We will, of course, release all the data on the hyperdrive engine to the Federation so that you will have the benefits . . ."

Adam listened sardonically. Centauria was being polite, but with a distinct air of talking to the Federation as an equal—no, as if the Federation were not quite up to Centaurian achievements, as indeed it was not. Jonwon had also not revealed the fact that he was a robot. Were there really humans alive in Centauria?

Then Jonwon detailed just what Burtland Smythe had done to Centauria, with a list of who had died. And those who lived again, as mind transfer robots.

Grieving for Matt, Adam had no sympathy for the stunned Federation, confronted by a newly powerful ex-colony capable of traveling in hyperspace and giving its dead citizens second lives in robot bodies.

But the guilt of the Federation, festering for six years, was lifted. Centauria was intact and although people had died, some of them lived again—only ten, to be sure, but that didn't matter. What mattered was that a fanatical Federation bioeffer had tried to destroy Centauria, had killed humans—and the roboticists had come to the rescue.

CHAPTER • 24

Centauria was wary, and even Adam Durant had to pass a security check before he could go home to a spome that was very much a world to itself, politically and philosophically independent of the Federation.

Home! Yet even as Adam embraced his family he realized that he now had several homes. He decided not to tell anyone in Centauria that he had come to love the planet Earth.

Meg was shy at first, but she seemed glad that Adam wanted to get married as soon as possible. "I've had girls, Meg, but I always stayed in love with you. I hope you still love me."

"I do, but I'll probably be a terrible wife. I've been immersed in robotics and hyperdrive for so long that—"

She stopped abruptly, and he worried. "Meg, are you sure you want to get married? Maybe we·should live together for a while. Or maybe there's someone else. You worked so long with Jonwon . . . is it . . . did he—Meg, you don't still want to be with robots all the time? Or—become a robot?"

"I think about mind transfer alot, but Bess says I don't know much about living as a human. I need you, Adam. I need you to teach me that. Please put up with me."

Adam wanted to hold her and stroke her but he had to ask one more question. "Does Jonwon want you to stay as you are, working with him . . ."

Meg laughed. "Oh, no! Once hyperdrive was invented, he started to ignore me as much as possible. He's retreated into robothood with a vengeance, working on secret inventions he won't tell anyone about. He's horrible, and I certainly don't want to be that kind of robot. Maybe I don't want to be a robot at all, yet. Please make love to me, Adam."

* * *

According to Seven, Jonwon didn't work all the time in the lab or in the small factory satellite given him by Centauria when it was clear that he was getting somewhere on the hyperdrive problem.

"He works constantly, and listens to music constantly," said Seven. "Especially human music, and especially that played by the twins. Perhaps Jonwon yearns for the diversity of human experience, and finds some of it in human music."

"Oh, Seven, it's so good to be able to talk to you again."

Seven had a new, shielded body and head, with a face like his old one but more expressive. He looked worried. "We are all so glad to have you back, Adam. Are you certain you don't mind that I've married Bess?"

"I haven't become that kind of bioeffer," said Adam. "Besides, the marriage was appropriate. You've always been my father."

The twins had boyfriends, but seemed more absorbed in their burgeoning careers as musicians. "Adam, stop complaining that Jonwon hasn't come to see you," said Amy. "He's out there in his satellite, and only comes into Centauria at rare intervals now. It's annoying when he does come back because he's got this thing against electronic music, which Agnes and I use a great deal."

"He's a pill," said Agnes. "Electronic music may have inescapable predictability to a genius robot, but that's why we humans like it. The predictability is soothing, like the complexities of Bach that are nevertheless very logical. Humans can forget themselves when listening to perfect electronic music because we don't have to be aware of any humans making it. In the days before electronics, humans could lose themselves in ordinary music because they didn't know the freedom from human influence and variation."

Adam disliked electronic music because he enjoyed watching live musicians play and hearing the many variations a

150

human orchestra could give to the same piece. he did not argue with the twins. Nobody—except possibly Jonwon—ever won any argument with the twins about music.

Paul and Dinah and Rusty came by transporter for Meg and Adam's wedding, and nobody made any negative comments about the fact that the person who gave Meg away was a robot. To Adam's delight, Paul and Seven hit it off well from the start, and were soon having deep discussions.

One day Adam was with them and found himself complaining again that his adoptive brother Jonwon had not even shown up for his wedding. Worse, Adam blurted out that Jonwon's behavior was enough to make any human agree that superaides should be used only for mind transfer.

"I understand the fears of biofundamentalists about intelligent, unprogrammed robots," said Paul. "I don't agree with them, but I do wonder whether the prejudice against even mind transfer robots will return once it is clear that those few who make it into the second, robot life are living on and on, while biological humans die."

"There won't be just a few," said Seven. "The robotics factories in the Federation are converting to superaides, so there ought to be enough bodies to go around eventually, and when mind transfer fails, there will be many brain recordings with which the experts can try again."

"And when everyone expects a second life as a robot, will that kill the Frankenstein's monster idea?" Paul shook his head. "I wonder."

"Well it won't change anyone's prejudice against untransferred superaides," said Adam. Then he remembered that he was responsible for Jonwon's existence. Perhaps Jonwon was obnoxious because he had not been trained properly by the young boy Adam had once been. Guiltily, Adam added, "Humans think of superaides as inhuman, almost alien robots,

151

but Jonwon didn't seem to be like that at first. Perhaps he doesn't have to be now. What can I do to help him?"

"I don't know," said Seven. "Ever since the hyperdrive engine really worked and took him away from Centauria for the first time in his life, Jonwon's seemed disturbed. He goes to that orbital factory in his little ship and no one is allowed to be there with him."

"Little ship?" asked Adam. "I thought the hyperdrive ship was only one prototype, given to the Feds so they can make others in their big factories."

"I meant the small conventional drive ferry Jonwon uses to get to the factory," said Seven. "Paul, has Adam taken you to Wildpark yet?"

Adam thought about it all the way into Wildpark. A ferry?

"Something on your mind, Adam?"

"Yes, Paul. I'm worried about Jonwon."

"Because you like him or because you're afraid of him?"

Surprised, Adam leaned against a pine tree and wished a puma would show up to distract the conversation. On second thought, no puma. Rog had died of old age and his successor was not with Adam on this trip.

"Adam?"

"I think it's both, Paul."

Jonwon had always been an extremely careful genius. It would be most unlike him to make only one of anything.

Suppose Jonwon possessed a second hyperdrive engine that he'd never told anyone about. What was he doing with it?

CHAPTER • 25

Meg said that Jonwon tuned into all Centaurian broadcasts and must know about Adam's return and the wedding, but he didn't acknowledge the news or the invitation they sent.

"Don't expect anything from Jonwon, Adam. I suppose he can't help the way he is. Just be glad he was willing to exercise his genius to invent hyperdrive."

"I've heard that the invention is yours, Meg."

She looked sad. "I just got us out of a theoretical bog. I couldn't have produced the actual hyperdrive myself."

Adam kissed her and wished he were not so glad that Jonwon stayed away.

After Meg became pregnant, Adam sent an old-fashioned letter to the silent, isolated Jonwon, and told Seven.

"Be prepared for rejection, Adam. Especially now that Meg is pregnant. Jonwon has problems with the biological. You'll understand when you see the movie he once made. It's an ardent sermon on why intelligence must leave biological life behind."

"He wants everyone to mind transfer?"

"I don't think so. He disapproves of mind transfer."

Adam took a deep breath. "Blast! That means he wants the universe to be inherited by robots who have no biological memories. Does the movie explain this?"

"Not exactly. Let me show it to you."

The movie had evidently been pieced together from many others, most of them taken on Earth. It began with a cheetah running across a yellow plain in pursuit of a gazelle, each a marvel of biological grace in form and movement.

"How beautiful," said Adam.

The cheetah broke the gazelle's neck with a swift movement and light died in the large brown eyes. The cheetah ate, jaws dripping red, and when it was through hyenas, jackals, and vultures came, until a pride of lions chased away the orthodox scavengers in order to have an easy feast.

"I know that killing is ugly," said Adam, "yet I find myself fascinated by absolutely anything biological. Eating and being eaten is the way of the universe, I guess."

"Watch," said Seven.

The movie seemed to go faster and faster, animals and plants being eaten, and then the predators and scavengers themselves dying to become food for worms and insects, which were also eaten by others, down to molds and microorganisms.

The eating and being eaten, the killing and dying, the birth and growing that ended only in another cycle of killing and dying—it never stopped, and went on everywhere, from humans at mealtime to tube worms dining on bacteria in the ocean depths, from voracious microscopic creatures in the sea under Callistan ice to the fauna inside the plumbing of spomes orbiting Sol, or Alpha Centauri A.

"Everything has to eat something that was alive," said Adam, suddenly ashamed. "Everything except the most primitive organisms that eat chemicals in the environment."

"Primitive organisms and robots," said Seven. "But that doesn't make me feel superior the way it does Jonwon."

The movie went inexorably on and on. "He's overdoing it!" cried Adam. "Spelling it out over and over!"

"Poor Jonwon thinks the biological universe overdoes it," said Seven. "But to my more or less human mind, the diversity, the exaggerated overdoing is the poignant and promising way the universe has organized itself. One should remember that out of the biologicality has come extraordinary beauty and intelligence. Adam, stop looking sick."

"My stomach is rumbling. Here I sit, assaulted by the

154

horrors of having to live on other life, and my body is cheerfully telling me that it's time for lunch!"

"*Your* lunch is either grown in algae tanks to be processed
and flavored, or it's grown in flesh clone farms. You eat only
simple cells, and have not caused the death of organized
creatures with intelligence of any kind."

"Seven, you may have memories of eating, but I have to do
it, and those algae die. You robots live by a power source
similar to what keeps stars going, and you don't have to kill
anything in order to survive. Right now I envy robots."

"I suppose that's the purpose of Jonwon's movie," said
Seven.

Meg was six months pregnant before Jonwon returned, so
quietly that only the family knew he was back. He stayed in
his lab, cool and remote if anyone visited him.

One night, after Meg was asleep, Adam dressed and tiptoed
into the main hall. He was about to walk down to the tunnel
that led to Tully Robotics, but the door to the guest wing
opened and Adam, not knowing why, shrank back into
shadow.

Bess and Seven had moved to the guest wing after Adam's
marriage, but Adam had not thought about their way of life.

Seven came out humming what sounded like Bach. He was
going back to work, because while a human wife had to sleep,
a robot husband had only to rest his mind occasionally.

Instead of taking the short way through the tunnel, Seven
walked out into the pale darkness of the Centaurian night.
Bess once told Adam that Jonathan Durant had loved to walk
at night.

Hurrying downstairs, Adam entered the tunnel and ran to
the lab, hoping to corner Jonwon and have it out with him
before Seven arrived, but no one was there, not even One-O.
Adam wandered around, bemused by the evidences of high-

155

powered robotics theory being put in action, but understood nothing.

Uneasy because Meg understood everything here and he did not, Adam wished someone, anyone would come in. He began to feel that even the simple microbubble computers were eerily alive and thinking dire thoughts about biological intruders. They seemed totally alien to a man who worked with humans all day. Adam felt ashamed that he did not even understand the medical computers and had to depend on the medi-tech-robots to use them.

Opening from Jonwon's room was a large storage closet full of equipment that Adam was examining in a bored way when he heard a noise outside. Peering around the corner, he saw that Jonwon's old table—the one his superaide body had been on when it was supposed to take Norum's mind transfer—was placed in a dark corner, its legs removed. As Adam watched, it slowly moved aside. He ducked back into the closet.

The scraping sound continued, and then there was an odd sort of buzzing noise, interrupted by the sound of footsteps entering the room from the door, and then other footsteps joining these from the corner of the lab. They seemed to meet somewhere in the middle.

"How did you get in here, Seven?"

"You left your door unlocked, Jonwon, but even if it were locked it wouldn't keep me out. I found your escape hatch a long time ago. I've been waiting for the right time to talk to you about it. Perhaps this is it."

"There's no need to talk if you've cracked the code for my escape hatch."

"I've only managed to get inside this room and find out what that tabletop covers. I haven't been able to use it, and even if I found out how, I wouldn't do so without your permission. I wanted to investigate, not intrude."

156

"So very noble of you, Seven. How many people have you told about my private transporter?"

"No one, but if someone else finds it you'll get in trouble. Matter transporters are supposed to be the property of the government, even those that are, presumably, improved experimental models in the possession of the designer."

"I need this transporter," said Jonwon. "You know I can't bring my ship into the ferry terminal here. It's not like other ferries. I use this transporter to go back and forth to the ship, which I keep at a concealed dock in my factory satellite. Now that the Feds have their own minitransporter, they don't need to know about mine."

"Perhaps not. But what are you doing in your factory satellite—or do you stay there at all? Where do you go in that hyperdrive ship?"

"Away—from everyone. I'm not like any of you. I'm pure robot, raised by humans to be like them but never equal to them, not the way even a botched-up mind transfer like you can be equal. I will never know what it is to be human, never remember what it was like. Why did you push Adam Durant to bring me to life to satisfy your blasted curiosity? Why did you let them try to raise me as human?"

"I've never been sure why I did it, Jonwon. And in spite of your hatred of life and my anguish for you, I have never been sorry. I still think it was important to create intelligence not based on biology, an intelligence that might ultimately understand the universe better, go further . . ."

"How far can I go, how much can I understand when I am constantly struggling to find out the purpose of my existence?" Jonwon's voice was harsh and loud, and Adam felt like crying.

"Can't you forget that Nanca baited you with that question when you were too new to tackle it? Perhaps the purpose of existence is to live it."

"You're a damn bioeffer hedonist at worst."

157

Seven laughed. "And so I am. But any intelligent being has a right to fret about the purpose of existence if he wants to. He might even come up with something interesting, although I suspect that the struggle to find out is itself one answer."

"That doesn't make any sense at all. That will never satisfy me. And your attitude is one of the reasons why I must go away. You and your human family will contaminate my work."

"Which is?"

"That's my business."

"But you are my business, and the business of the family, who love you."

"Love has no place in the real universe, the one uncontaminated by biological life. I belong there. I will not be just a disgusting imitation of homo sap."

"Fascinating how you use the ancient word 'disgusting' as if you could smell and taste. The word really means 'negative taste' in Latin. Face it, Jonwon, your mind is considerably human, as you will find if you bother to plumb its depths, explore your full identity, discover your assets—oh."

"Oh, what?"

"I just reheard in my mind what you said. You meant me. I am a disgusting human imitation, as far as you're concerned."

"How could you marry Bess—and sleep with her!"

"I love her. I satisfy her, and I find that I, too, am satisfied. I have integrated the person who was Jonathan Durant into the person who is robot Seven. I'm happy, and I'll be damned if I'll let you do anything that will hurt Bess and those dear to her."

"Why should I hurt any human? I've been taught the laws, and I obey them far better than many humans do. I simply want to get away from human influence, and if you tell me that will hurt those who love me, then so be it."

"You say all that with a frozen face, Jonwon, no matter how

158

uncontrollably loud your voice gets at times. Since when have you tried to be so frozen and neuter?"

A brief, nasty barking sound indicated that Jonwon had cut off his own laughter. "I learned the principle from you, remember? You told me it was discovered long ago that the expression on one's face not only affects others but alters one's own thinking, even in robots who don't have the added turmoil from neurological and glandular hormones. It is very useful to be, as you call it, frozen and neuter. I intend to explore the principle much further, far away from humanity—organic or mind transferred—and its chains of love."

"Love is the best product of the evolution of our universe, and don't tell me that biological evolution was accomplished through the horror of eating and being eaten, of death and more death. Jonwon, at your worst you remind me of the literalness of the giant computers, and of the pathetic human desire for the universe to be an entity bestowing approval or disapproval, the ultimate father, the personified machine to end all machines who will tell you the purpose of your existence so you won't have to work it out for yourself."

In the ensuing silence, Adam felt sweat trickling down his arms and forehead, and he was thankful that robots can't smell. He only hoped their superior hearing would not pick up the sound of a human heart pounding anxiously inside the closet.

Finally Jonwon replied. "I remember when you taught me that the universe just is, that it doesn't have a built-in mind or purpose. I hated hearing it. I don't know what to do or be in such a universe."

"Accept being a useful part of a universe that's developing intelligence, compassion, and purpose. Try enjoying it."

"Is that all you care about, Seven? Enjoyment?"

"Blast it, Jonwon, you know damn well that the struggle to develop purposes and to understand is enjoyable too."

"It's hard, agonizing work and I don't enjoy it but I'm going

159

away until I can accomplish something. Tell Adam and Meg and the others I'm sorry I didn't say good-bye, but I have some important exploring to do."

"All right, Jonwon."

There was another scraping sound, and Jonwon spoke again. "You see, it's not enough for me to assume that daily existence is a good thing, and that human science plods steadily on accumulating knowledge and understanding. I can't wait. I have to believe that there are other intelligences out in the universe who are beyond us, not embedded in biology like humans and mind transfer robots. I am free of biology and I'm finally free of my jealousy of Adam and Meg, of their instinctual knowledge of who they are, part of the web of life, their place in the universe. I have no place yet."

"There's an old zen saying that when one thinks too much the only remedy is to laugh."

"That's so . . . human. I can't laugh anymore. The universe isn't funny. It's terrible and I've got to understand . . . everything."

"I wish you luck," said Seven, and went back to Bess.

Adam waited, for Jonwon seemed to be there still. He hoped he wouldn't sneeze and could stay immobile until Jonwon left. It seemed terribly important not to reveal that he had listened to an intensely private conversation.

But he did sneeze, and Jonwon found him.

"Sorry. I didn't intend to listen, but I didn't see how I could get out once I'd started to listen and, well, I'm sorry."

Jonwon was expressionless, but it seemed to be that it cost him something. "It's all right, Adam. Maybe now you'll understand why I have to leave, and maybe someday you'll forgive me."

"I forgive you, even if I can't understand. Just please forgive—I was going to say 'me,' but I think I mean 'us humans.' "

There was almost an echo of a smile on Jonwon's mouth.

"It just doesn't matter anymore. Please wait here in the storage closet until I've gone. And say good-bye to Meg for me."

Adam nodded, and Jonwon went back into the other room, closing the closet door. There was another scraping sound, and then the peculiar buzzing noise.

When Adam emerged from the closet the room was empty.

CHAPTER • 26

Adam told Seven what he'd overheard. "Do you think Jonwon should be left alone to work out his destiny?"

"I don't know. Maybe I'll go after him one of these days, but right now Jonwon's problems seem beyond me, and besides, I'm too busy—mind transfer business is picking up."

"So are the difficulties. I hope the counseling clinic we're setting up takes care of some of them. I hear that some visiting Terran psychiatrists want one for the Federation, too. And Bess says that Lee Teleg is going to become our first transfer psychiatrist."

Adam felt himself reddening as he remembered meeting Lee in the hospital corridor when he was visiting Bess. At first he didn't recognize her.

"You look familiar," Adam had said.

"I used to be a cop," said the girl. She was dressed in whites with the hospital's Insignia for doctors on her lapel. "I'm Lee Teleg."

"Then you're—" Adam gulped.

"That's right. I'm an MT." Lee said it with *an*, as if the word were *empty*.

"You and Hank Deno were rookies together," said Adam.

"My first transfer took—his didn't. Then I decided to go to the medical school your mother established here. Somebody had to become the first MT physician."

"Seven," asked Adam, "why don't the MTs mind the way people say it, as if it were the word *empty*?"

"They say it's true—mind transfers do occupy an empty superaide brain, and they think it's funny. I understand. I know that every MT feels so full."

In spite of the problems—like the high divorce rate of mind

162

transfers—there were more and more of them. The numbers began to swell in the Federation when a dying fundamentalist preacher had a brain recording made and was, as he put it, resurrected in a robot body.

As time went on, the Federation overturned centuries of restrictive laws to permit robots—MTs—equal rights with biologicals. But intelligent, untransferred robots were still prohibited, and even in Centauria, none were made, especially since the superaide bodies were wanted for mind transfer. Now, instead of talking about biofundamentalist belief in staying biological and mortal, people said there would be a different kind of population problem if the Tully hyperdrive were not used to find habitable planets in other solar systems.

The search intensified once more hyperdrive ships were built, and eventually, in the third solar system investigated, a planet with a thin but breathable atmosphere was found. It was rocky and cold, but plans were made for domed cities even more splendid than those on Mars, and gardens that could grow and add to that precious air.

But there were other planets found, ones that only MTs could use until the environment was engineered to accommodate biological humans. There are plenty of planets, everyone said, worlds for everyone, worlds for fragile humans and for those in their strong second lives as robots.

The good news slid quietly over the fact that hyperdrive was tricky. Ships often foundered and crews had to return by transporter before they got to the new solar system. Once there, of course, the transporter they carried would keep them in safe contact with home, but only the hyperdrive ship could get them through the gray nothingness of hyperspace to a star system that might or might not have planets, or even suitable orbits for spomes.

In the meantime, Meg had a son they named Walt, and as Adam held him he felt the anxiety of any parent—what if my child should die? For it had been decided that mind transfer

163

of children was forbidden. All attempts had been disastrous; either the superaide brain deactivated, or the subsequent child robot became psychotic. Hank Deno was, so far, the only child transfer who was not psychotic, unless lack of humanness could be considered its equivalent.

"I'm glad Hank shows no interest in my baby," Adam said one day when he was lunching with Bess. "I wouldn't want Walt to know him."

"What's going to happen to poor Hank?" asked Bess.

"He seems to be waiting for Jonwon to come back. He hangs around the robotics factory, but he's never learned much. The nicest thing about him is that he raises a few rabbits to sell. Odd that he still likes rabbits."

"Perhaps humanness dies hard. I hope."

When Walt was five years old Jonwon returned one night, unannounced. One-O was alone in the main lab and heard sounds in Jonwon's room. Seven had taught him how to open the lock, and he found Jonwon. The superaide was wearing an oddly metallic, straight tunic that came to his knees and left his arms bare. His frozen expression seemed to harden at the sight of One-O.

"Hello, Jonwon. You are back."

"I want to see Hank Deno. Where is he?"

"Down the hall in the room we gave him. He is feeding his rabbits. He is going to give one to Walt Durant."

"Walt?"

"Adam and Meg's son. Five years old tomorrow."

Jonwon stared straight ahead for a long minute and then said, "Get Hank. Tell him to give all the rabbits to Walt. I have no room for pets in my ship, and I want Hank to join me."

"I must consult with Seven."

"No—but of course you will. I forget what you're like, One-O. Stay here and I will get Hank myself."

"Jonwon, I know about the superaide brains and the equip-

164

ment you stole when you went away before. Seven and Meg know, too, but we have not reported it. Why did you steal?"

"Centauria owed me something for the work I did, so I took what I wanted. Why I took it is no one's business." Jonwon went to find Hank, and when they came back, One-O was gone.

"Hurry up, Hank. Get on the transporter. We must leave before One-O returns with Seven."

Seven and One-O arrived too late. There were no other robots in the room, but a cage of rabbits was on the floor.

Walt's birthday party was a success, thanks to Hank's rabbits. Bio, the mother, was a long-haired, long-lived breed popular in Centauria. Adam thought it was amazing that to go with Jonwon Hank had given up the only creature he loved. That night Adam couldn't sleep and decided to visit Bubble theatre to get poor, inhuman Hank off his mind.

At first he didn't care for the new light and sound show with electronic music, shifting color, and rhythmic bounding of the hammockwebs, but gradually the patterns seemed to sink into his brain until he felt as if his concrete form dissolved into the ever-changing, vibrating parts of a universal field.

But that's what everything is anyway, he thought, even a lost child like Hank or smart superaides who invent private transporter codes. He remembered a conversation he'd had with Jonwon soon after the robot had learned enough to go past Adam in standard education.

"Explain humanness, Adam. What is it like to be human?"

Adam had been reading Shakespeare in an effort to stay ahead of Jonwon, who was more interested in robotics, and to his own surprise knew hunks of it. " 'One man in his time plays many parts, his acts being seven ages . . .' "

"I know all of Shakespeare. Is that supposed to be an answer?"

165

"I don't know. I haven't had the seven ages yet. Humans aren't built to retain early memories, so I can't remember the mewling and puking much. And I haven't been a whining schoolboy because I love school. I suppose I'll always love Meg and sigh like a furnace my entire life, but I don't know too much about it yet, or the other stages. My mother says they all overlap, and mix into each other, especially the miseries. Is that an answer to your question?"

Jonwon shook his head. "Misery. Pain."

"What's the matter?"

"Matt told me that superaide bodies like mine have to be designed to experience painful feedback sensations in response to potentially damaging stimuli. I thought it was a stupid idea, but once the twins were playing with a candle and teased me to hold my hand over it. I could do so longer than they could, but soon the sensation was unpleasant and I stopped before my synthoskin was damaged. Then I discovered that there are different kinds of pain."

"What do you mean?"

"The twins felt guilty about teasing me and they cried. I felt unhappy, a different kind of pain. Both kinds in rapid succession, but the first was easier to take. If I had known my actions would frighten the twins, I would not have experimented with the candle, but I did not know. From that day I began to be afraid when I was with them—afraid to make them unhappy."

"Because you love them."

"Don't say that! I don't understand it! All I know is that intelligence and the capacity for emotion makes one regret the past and worry about the future. If that's the human condition, then I don't like it."

Adam remembered being flippant and competitive. There was one other poet he could quote a little. "That's human, Jonwon, knowing that 'forward, tho I canna see, I guess an' fear.' "

"I don't want to guess," said Jonwon.

Early one morning, when everyone else was asleep, Walt Durant sat on the grass in the backyard and stroked Bio's still silky black ears while she munched a lettuce leaf. Her two latest offspring were almost old enough to be given to Walt's best friends, as promised, but they had a tendency to wander off and eat half the garden in youthful haste. Bio preferred to be fed by a devoted owner.

A shadow fell across the boy's hands, and he looked up at someone he had never seen before. He smiled because he was now six and no longer afraid of strangers.

"How's Bio?" said the man, who looked young but with a sort of frozen face. He was carrying a square box.

"She's fine," said Walt.

"May I hold her a minute? I raised her myself."

"You mean she belongs to you?"

"Yes." The man lifted Bio to his chest, holding her gently. At first she struggled, but when he stroked her, she relaxed as if she knew him.

"Are you going to take her away?" asked Walt, his lips trembling.

"I need her," said the stranger, putting the rabbit in his box and locking the perforated lid.

"You don't! Give her back—she's mine now!"

"No."

Walt hit the man's legs and it hurt his fists. The man raised Bio higher and stepped back. He didn't even blink.

"You're an MT! An empty MT!" shouted Walt, running after the man, who walked into the house so fast that Walt couldn't keep up.

Before the rest of the house woke up to Walt's yells, One-O came from the study, where he'd been at the teaching machine.

167

"A nasty MT said Bio belongs to him and he went into the tunnel with her."

One-O ran.

"I am sorry I could not stop Hank Deno," said One-O when the family met for a conference about Bio. "He'd left by the time I arrived at Jonwon's transporter."

"You see what it means," said Meg. "There's breathable air where Bio is going. Do you suppose Jonwon's ship has an atmosphere now, just for Bio's sake?"

"It was a cruel thing to do," said Bess. "I thought Jonwon had learned the laws of robotics."

"But Hank Deno hasn't," said Seven.

PART • IV
DEATH

CHAPTER • 27

For her thirty-fifth birthday, Meg asked Adam for a tour of the Federation's four colony planets. Two vaguely Earthlike planets had human emigrants still in their first lives, but the other two could accommodate humans only under domes and seemed to be filling up with MTs who didn't mind an atmosphere too rich in carbon dioxide. The MTs were, however, planting vegetation that would ultimately make those planets easier on humans.

Adam could take a long vacation from his clinic job now that there were more doctors in Centauria, and he traveled with Meg, hoping the trip would help her be less restless.

For over a year, he'd found himself asking Meg if she were still happy in the marriage. She always said yes. "The problem is work, Adam. I've nothing interesting to do."

The new planets bored both of them. "The mostly MT planets are too busy trying to prove they can catch up to the technology of Earth and Centauria, and the human planets are too artsy-craftsy pioneer when it's not necessary," said Meg.

"The pioneer stuff is attractive to tourists," said Adam.

"Not to me. Let's go home."

No matter how far away in the galaxy the colony was, home was just a short transporter trip away. It did not seem to Adam that they had had a vacation at all. They had not left their problems behind or come to any new frame of mind that would help solve them.

Finally Adam had a talk with Seven. Not Bess (although Seven would undoubtedly tell her) because Meg had become envious of her mother-in-law's happiness in her profession.

171

Perhaps Meg, who seemed to be aging faster than normal, also resented the fact that Bess still looked young and lovely.

"Let's see, Walt's ten now, isn't he?" asked Seven, who knew quite well exactly how old Walt was.

"Yes, and more interested in school and his friends than in his family. Meg doesn't feel needed as a mother."

Seven's eyes turned to the familiar picture of Alpha Centauri A. He was obviously not going to remind Adam that Meg had been only half a mother to Walt, leaving the rest for Bess.

"And although her improvements in superaide design have been successful, she feels like a failure," said Adam. "I don't know what she does here at the lab—"

"I do. She sits in Jonwon's old room, staring at the transporter. You shouldn't have told her about it."

"I don't keep secrets from my wife. Has she cracked the locking code?"

"No, and neither have I. Jonwon was quite determined that no one would be able to follow him."

"But Meg wants to."

"It looks like it. Better talk to her, Adam."

Meg was furious. "It's ridiculous of you to be jealous! I don't want to live with Jonwon. I want to find him so I can work with him again. He must be doing fascinating things . . ."

"He's been gone so long that he's probably dead."

"Jonwon will never die."

"Is that what bothers you? He's a virtually immortal robot and you are a thirty-five year old human who for idiotic reasons feels old and tired?"

"I'm a has-been, Adam. I've been a has-been ever since the hyperdrive engine was completed. I've done nothing truly innovative since. Jonwon stimulates my thinking."

"Sorry you have a husband inadequate to the task."

"Don't be sarcastic. I love you. You're my consolation and

172

my refuge and you put up with my inadequacies as wife and mother. I know I've been making you unhappy lately, and I'm very sorry, but I'm so tired of being human."

She started to cry and he put his arms around her. "Meg, my darling, once you asked me to keep you human."

"I know. I enjoy—I enjoyed it. Sometimes I still do, but mostly I worry about time passing . . ."

"Great galaxy, Meg, you're only thirty-five! In an age when biological humans live full productive lives well over their hundredth birthday, how can you worry so about time?"

"I remember once when I was visiting Centauria and Seven took us to the top of Starboard mountain to see the pumas. We went the safe way, up the inside tunnel to the visitors' pen."

Adam had almost forgotten. He'd been only six. "There were two young ones, with their mother. I remember."

"But you've probably forgotten the rabbit she brought them. It was hanging so limp from her jaws, and bloody."

Seven and Adam had never shown Jonwon's movie to anyone else. Adam did not remember the rabbit, but he suddenly saw it through Meg's eyes. "What happened?"

"They ate it. You thought it was great but I threw up my lunch, and Seven talked to us. Bet you can't remember that, either." When Adam nodded miserably, she put her arms around him and said, "You're such a dear, Adam. You think being alive is wonderful, and you love all living things."

"What did Seven talk about that I can't remember?"

"I don't know the exact words, but it was something like this—'The fragile, short lives of biological beings appear in the vast anonymity of the universe like brilliantly colored blossoms, making a pattern that's ever changing because no part of it lasts long. That's all death is—part of the pattern.' "

"That's beautiful."

"Is it, Adam? I suppose it is, to biofundamentalists."

"Am I one?"

173

"Anyone who loves the nitty-gritty of biological life the way you do must be a bioeffer at heart."

They grinned at each other and Adam's heart lifted, only to sink again when Meg said, "I want more than that pattern. I want meaningful work that lasts. If Jonwon's found it, I want to find him."

"What about me, and Walt?"

"I think I could persuade Jonwon to come back to Centauria and do his work here."

But Adam knew he would never do that. And Meg knew it, too. Some day she would unlock the transporter and go to Jonwon's hyperdrive ship. Would she come back? Could she?

When Meg's annual visit to her mother came around, he decided not to go with her, much as he wanted to see Paul and Rusty, who was a more likeable teenager than most, already in Harvard and planning to be an exobiologist (the new planets had primitive flora and fauna needing intensive study).

Perhaps Meg needed to be without him. Perhaps Dinah, still in love with her final venture into domesticity, would help Meg be happier with life as it is.

"Are you happy with life as it is?" asked Bess, when Adam told her his reasons for not going.

"Of course."

"Are you?"

He stared at his mother. He'd never really thought about it before. "I assume you don't mean life with its current problems. Are you asking if I have any of Meg's desire to explore the unknown?"

"All doctors should have some of that. The biological universe and the human body in particular are still very mysterious. Are you content to stay with those mysteries?"

"I think I am."

"Perhaps." Bess's still-unlined brown skin seemed to glow with health and her own happiness, in contrast to the sallow,

174

faded look of Meg's face. "But I noticed that you were much more interested in the native organisms of the new planets than Meg was, and you enjoy arguing about whether or not alien life should be left alone to develop its own way."

"Sure. I'm pro alien biology, but I suspect that once life becomes intelligent it starts to contaminate the universe."

"Now you sound alot like Jonwon."

Adam's fist clenched, and then relaxed. "All right, Mother, you win. You asked if I were happy with life as it is, and I guess I'm not. I condemn Meg's curiosity about Jonwon, but I'm just as curious—and blast it, I want to find him first! I must know what he's doing!"

Bess said nothing for a moment. She turned to look at her picture of Earth's ocean—Adam couldn't remember which one it was. Did she have tears in her eyes? Strong, calm Bess?

"Adam, I can't tell you not to try to find him. Seven still thinks Jonwon is worth saving, and perhaps he is, but—I don't know. Seven has promised not to go to Jonwon even if he cracks the transporter code."

"Then he won't. He'll tell me the code and I'll go, before Meg does."

"I know you will, Adam. Perhaps it's necessary, but all the same, I hope nobody cracks the code."

Adam was lonely without Meg. Lee Teleg tried to interest him in the latest MT problem, Bess told him to take a vacation with Matt's relatives in Luna City, and Seven suggested that he go to the Jupiter spome, where the twins were putting on an electronic and live music concert.

Adam stayed home. When Meg called to say she was staying a week longer, he moped. When Walt went off to school the next morning as if errant mothers were not important, Adam took the day off.

What passed for spring in Centauria was in full bloom, and there was a bunch of red-striped tulips in a glass vase on the

175

dining room table. Adam ate a bowl of horribly healthful cereal and stared at them.

"Master Adam,"—One-O still called him that—"is there anything I can do to help you?"

"Why aren't you at the lab?"

"There is nothing for me to do there at the moment. Nothing important. I have already done my regular chores. I came back to the house because you seem so unhappy, and we have not talked together for a long time."

"No, we haven't. I miss it. How are you, One-O?"

"I am in good working order as usual, Master Adam. I am sorry that Horace Deno is not."

"What's this?"

"Seven told me early this morning that during the night President Deno had a stroke. He is not expected to recover, since the damage is too severe for microsurgery. Seven is preparing for mind transfer of the previous recording."

"Seven should have told me. I'm not Horace's doctor, but I would have liked to know."

"Dr. Bess will no doubt tell you about it when she gets home from work. There is nothing you can do now."

"Poor Horace, losing his son and getting a robot like Hank. This must be hard on Mrs. Deno."

"Seven is concerned about her. She wants Hank to return."

"Impossible. We don't even know where he is."

"But I know how to find him, Master Adam."

"What!"

"I have not told Seven, because Seven would insist on going himself because of the possible danger, and he has promised your mother that he would not."

"One-O, are you going to ask my permission to let you find Jonwon and Hank?"

"Yes, Master Adam. For so long, you were the one who gave me orders. I still think of you as the logical person to ask."

"But how can you find them?"

176

"When Hank stole Bio and I chased him back to Jonwon's transporter, I saw the code setting before it was erased electronically. I decided not to tell anyone."

"And now, for the sake of Caroline Deno, you want to use it and try to find Hank."

"Yes, Master Adam. May I go?"

"How will you keep Seven from knowing what you're doing?"

"Seven is spending the day in one of the orbital factories that makes superaide brains."

Adam stood up, stretched, and was astonished at how good he suddenly felt. There was something exciting and interesting ahead. Bess was right. He was as curious about the unknown as Meg. And because he was biologically minded, he was curious about the environment Jonwon provided for rabbits.

"I'll go over to the lab with you," said Adam.

The space suit that was supposed to be his size felt reasonably comfortable, although he had never worn one before. There were suits of all sizes hanging in every building in Centauria nowadays, just in case.

"Master Adam," said One-O for the umpteenth time. "Please do not come with me. It might be dangerous for you."

"I'm in a suit, and Bio is there so even without a suit I should be okay. Stop worrying, One-O."

"I will not activate the transporter until we can consult with Seven."

"He'll stop me and you know it." Adam held the suit's helmet. "Help me put this on. I'm responsible for bringing Jonwon to life. It's my business to find them, more than anyone else's. I order you to start up the transporter."

"Yes, Master Adam, but . . ."

"No buts, One-O. Please let me have one adventure in my terribly ordinary life."

177

CHAPTER • 28

The sensors of Adam's suit indicated that there was air in the control room of Jonwon's ship, but Adam did not remove his helmet. He did not have time.

Jonwon and Hank were not there, but three strange robots were. They were short, streamlined, and had no eyes, only a band of dark material circling the head. There was no mouth, but words floated into the receiver of Adam's suit. It was impossible to tell which robot was speaking.

"The ship's sensors indicate that you are a human being inside a space suit. Why have you and that robot come here?"

"I am Adam Durant. I have come to see Jonwon and Hank. Please let them know that One-O and I are here."

"We are doing so." As the words entered Adam's helmet, Jonwon's robots seized One-O with arms that seemed to be too big and powerful in comparison with their bodies. "Do not struggle, robot called One-O. Permanent instructions command us to seize all unknown robots for Jonwon's inspection."

"Why aren't you holding me?" asked Adam.

"We have no instructions about humans, although there is a cabin in the ship made ready for a human named Meg. You are not that human. Stand there until Jonwon arrives."

"Master Adam, I think you should step back on the transporter plate and go to Centauria at once."

"No," said the robots. "We have blocked outward use of the transporter until further instructions."

The transporter buzzed, and as Jonwon materialized Adam began to feel the onset of claustrophobia inside the space suit, where sweat was making his clothes damp in spite of the supposedly efficient environment the micromachinery provided.

178

"Hello, Adam. Sorry I wasn't here to give you a more hospitable greeting. My robots have never seen a human before. Take off your helmet—the air here and below is quite breathable by humans, although it might smell odd to you."

When Adam removed the helmet and put it on the floor, his first breath told him that the air smelled faintly like a rabbit pen, but before he could ask about Bio or why One-O had to be seized, Jonwon activated the viewscreen.

Adam gasped. He was looking at a planet with an atmosphere full of patches and streaks of cloud, but not so full that the surface could not be glimpsed between them. It was a dark, sparkling green until Jonwon touched something else on the control board and the ship moved to a lower orbit.

"The lighter green is the highest part of the planet, still under the ocean but shallow enough for robots to build on it, as I have done. Would you like to look at the start of my city, Adam?"

"Sure. Does anything live in the ocean?"

Jonwon laughed. "It's a planetary ocean with nothing higher than microscopic plants in it, something like algae that mat together to form a floating scum on the surface, hence the startling green color."

"Like seaweed in Earth's oceans?"

"Not that complicated. This planet has no moon, hardly any exciting weather except for gentle rain showers. Nothing to foster rapid evolution. The scum cells photosynthesize, eat the minerals in the sea, and the dead bodies of each other."

"But since they are microscopic, you don't have to be aware of all that eating and being eaten. I've seen your movie, Jonwon."

"Did you—or perhaps One-O—break my transporter code and find my ship merely so you could discuss with me a movie that you biologicals probably enjoy?"

"I'm here to ask Hank to come back to Centauria. His father is dying and his mother wants to see Hank."

179

Jonwon shrugged, and Adam remembered when the robot had studied the child Adam in order to learn how to do it. "You can ask Hank, for all the good it will do. You and I will transport to my headquarters, without One-O. He must remain here. I can not permit other robots on Far."

"Far?"

"Hank named the planet."

There was only one building on Far. Its transporter plate was in a dark storage room on the ground floor, at sea level. As Adam walked upstairs, for there was no lift, Jonwon seemed to hurry him past the second floor and up to the roof, surrounded by a waist-high wall. There was a ship's landing cradle along one side, and in the open section of the rest of the roof was an open rabbit hutch containing Bio. The outside air smelled almost like a good salad.

Jonwon pointed out to the dark green sea. "That's Far. Hank will be up soon. He's working with my two other robots on equipment we're going to try using for communication with any alien visitors we hope to get."

Adam didn't pay enough attention to Jonwon's last sentence because Bio hopped out of the open hutch onto the roof. Her nose quivered and her silky fur seemed healthy enough. Adam bent down, took off one glove, and stroked her ears.

"We distill water for her, she eats rabbit food I stole from a Centaurian farm satellite, and we're growing vegetables in hydroponic tanks. There's now air in the ship for her, so you can tell your son that Bio is well cared for."

The roof panel opened again and Hank stepped out onto the roof, expressionless as ever. "It is unfortunate that my father is dying, but I must stay here, away from human influence."

"Don't look puzzled, Adam. I've already told Hank your news." Jonwon pointed to a buttonlike device fixed on his head. "I've invented a mental intercom, so we can speak mind

180

to mind. All my robots have it built in, and they don't need air for communication. It's very convenient."

"Hank, your mother is very unhappy and wants you to come back before your father dies. He will mind transfer but she wants you to see the biological Horace Deno once more."

"No. I must avoid contact with humans. I must be all robot. I must not contaminate the new superaides."

"Those eyeless wonders?"

"Adam," said Jonwon, "I did not ask you to come here, or to give me your opinions about my robots. They are alive and intelligent and will some day create a true civilization of robots on Far."

"And is that supposed to be the answer to your search for the purpose of your existence?"

"I don't know, but I hope that my robots will find the answer, after we leave the planet to them. Hank was once human and I was raised by humans to think too much like you, so it will be better for the new superaides to have us live in the ship, available for consultation."

"Maybe they'll start praying to you like a god."

"That was unkind. Not like the Adam I knew."

"I'm sorry if I sound annoyed, but if a cabin has been made for Meg, you can't expect me not to be angry at the idea that you've planned all along to take my wife with you some day. Have you promised her you'd return and carry her off like one of the Olympian gods, stealing a mortal?"

"I've planned nothing about Meg. I'm just ready. She wanted to work with me, and I thought that perhaps she would come some day. It makes no difference."

Was Jonwon lying? Or was he as confused about Meg as she was about him? "Jonwon, humans could build here, too. It's selfish of you not to report it. Are you going to hog the whole planet for your blasted robots?"

"I found it myself, built, set up solar plates to supplement

181

fusion packs, and my robots have the right to a planet uncontaminated by humans, or any advanced biological life."

"You didn't choose an airless planet, dammit! You found one where Hank could have a pet—a mammal that's not bright but compared to that scum, she's certainly a sample of advanced biological life! Are you so certain that your super-aides won't grow to love her as much as Hank does—and my son did?"

Hank picked up Bio, stroked her, and put her on the broad top of the wall. "Bio is mine. You can't take her back."

"Be careful," said Adam, putting his glove back on. "She might get frightened and hop off the wall in the wrong direction, drown and end up as fertilizer for the algae."

After Hank put Bio back down on the roof, Adam saw that three of her small turds had been left behind.

Adam laughed and said, "Don't tell me you've already fertilized that alien ocean with Bio's feces!"

"No," said Jonwon. "We've been using them for the hydroponics. We tried the scum water undistilled, but no Terran plant would grow in it, so Bio fertilizes her own food."

"Oh well," said Adam, "if the scum inhibits our plants, then I guess you might as well keep the planet for your robots. Federation planetary engineers would have to kill off the scum and start the planet's ecosystem with Terran specimens."

Jonwon seemed to be listening to something other then Adam's voice, for he suddenly wheeled and ran downstairs. Adam followed, and found him in the first room on the second floor, staring at a viewscreen with two blank-faced robots beside him.

"You might as well look, Adam. This is the other reason why I haven't told the Federation about Far. My long range sensors have picked up a change of movement in—that."

It must have been far away, magnified by the sensors to show in the viewscreen, for clouds swirled around the object, a pyramid shape that bulged at the bottom and shone silver in the sunlight.

"An alien artifact?" asked Adam. "When did it come?"

"I don't know. It was here in orbit around Far when my ship came out of hyperdrive to find a G-type sun and a habitable planet in this area. I've tried to investigate the thing but when I took the ship close enough to touch it, we all got a severe electric shock. It protects itself. And now it's moved closer to the surface, perhaps to investigate you, Adam."

"But where in the galaxy is the creature that could make an object like that?"

"The galaxy? Adam, Far isn't even in the Milky Way galaxy of home, but in the sister galaxy Terrans call M31, in the constellation of Andromeda. No one from the Terran worlds has explored this galaxy but me."

Adam was stunned, and frightened. It was all very well to step into a transporter and whisk off to another planet or spome or transporter-carrying ship, but to be this far from human civilization—no wonder Hank had given the planet that name. "I want to go home, Jonwon. I'm sorry if my presence has upset you or your robots in any way."

"Upset? I am beyond human emotions, Adam."

"Then I'll go away. You robots and your alien visitor can play games together, pretending there are no humans in any galaxy, but first I'll try Hank once more. He used to be human."

Hank met them with his hand outstretched. In the open palm were two of Bio's turds. "I'm going to put these in the hydroponics tank, Jonwon."

Forgetting any last minute appeal to the boy he had once played with, Adam said spitefully, "You missed a turd. It's still on the wall. I thought robots were more careful."

"Forget it, Hank," said Jonwon. "Bio produces enough feces for the hydroponics."

Hank wavered, but went back for the turd. Just as he

183

reached for it Bio hopped toward Adam, and Hank turned suddenly, knocking the turd off the far side of the wall. There was an immediate sound of hissing, and then an ominous bubbling noise.

Adam ran to the wall and looked down. "There's a big black patch in the green scum, and it's frothing. It also smells horrible. I think Bio's turd is killing the scum."

"There's a terrible noise!" said Jonwon. "What is it?"

Adam could hear only a faint, high-pitched vibrating sound but the robots seemed to be stricken by it. Hank held his hands to his head, and Jonwon was shaking his.

The two superaides erupted out of the staircase, walking fast and deliberately toward the edge of the roof.

"Go back!" yelled Jonwon. "The sound may deactivate you!"

Without stopping, one of the superaides picked up a quivering Bio and threw her into the ocean.

"But it wasn't her fault!" screamed Hank.

Adam saw Bio's body literally fall apart in the frothing scum, the pieces dissolving and blending into oily blackness spreading as far as he could see.

The two superaides climbed onto the wall and before Jonwon could grab them, jumped into the ocean. They instantly sank under waves that rose higher and higher every minute.

"They've deactivated," said Jonwon. "I could hear them die through the intercom. And they had sent for the ship. I've told it not to come but—damn—there it is!"

"Let's get in the ship and go home!" cried Hank. "I want to go home, Jonwon!"

But the ship did not hover on antigrav long. As if it meant to stay, it settled into the landing cradle that was already creaking, the girders attaching it to the roof perceptibly vibrating from the turbulence in the ocean.

While Hank was running toward the ship a large crack opened up in the roof and he tripped on it, rolling under the landing cradle. Jonwon ran after him but stopped when the ship's airlock opened and the last three superaides came down the ramp dragging One-O by the legs.

One-O was carrying Adam's helmet and threw it to him. "I cannot break their grip, Master Adam. They say they must jump into the ocean and take me with them. I have failed to protect you. Please put on your helmet before you are affected by the sound, too."

When Adam couldn't drag One-O away from the superaides who were trying to pull him over the wall, One-O begged him to put on the helmet. Adam did so, and then shook Jonwon, who was standing in front of the ship holding his head.

"Jonwon! Help me get One-O away from your robots. They're going to drag him into the ocean with them. I'm not strong enough, but you are. What's the matter with you?"

"Noise—vibration—paralyzing robot minds—get me into the ship—must get away. . . ." Jonwon lurched toward the ship but at the ramp he fell, rolling onto his back with his legs under the ship.

One-O was trying to hold onto a metal bar at the inside base of the wall, but the superaides had the rest of his body onto the surface. "Master Adam, I must say good-bye, for the vibration is affecting me and I will not be able to hold on much longer."

Adam knelt next to Jonwon, turning up his suit receiver to hear better. The sound of Far was like a blow, and for a moment he thought he would faint. Then he yelled as loud as he could through his helmet's mike.

"I need a weapon, Jonwon."

The answer was faint. "Airlock. Right side."

In the airlock Adam took a gun from the wall brackets and holding it, ran down the ramp shouting, "Stop! Don't jump!"

The superaides paid no attention, and pulled One-O away

185

from the metal bar. Before they could drag him over the wall Adam shot them, once in each superaide head.

Adam had thought the gun was a form of stun weapon that might penetrate shielded robot brains, but it was a laser gun, and Jonwon's robots fell back to the roof, dead.

CHAPTER • 29

Horrified, Adam pulled the three dead superaides off One-O's body. "I had to do it, One-O. You're safe now."

But One-O was silent and motionless. His eyes were open but did not turn toward Adam.

"One-O! Did the laser beam—did I kill you, too?"

There was no reply. Then Adam noticed that each of the dead superaides had a neat hole through the skull. Carefully, he inspected One-O's head and body, but there was no hole.

Adam didn't know much about laser guns, but he thought that there wasn't any spread of radiation from the tight beam that destroyed everything in its path. One-O must be paralyzed from the vibration of Far's ocean scum.

When One-O proved to be too heavy to drag to the landing ramp, Adam yelled to Jonwon. "Help me get One-O into the ship. He can't move—Jonwon?"

Above the roar of the ocean, there was a high metallic sound as if someone were screaming. Jonwon was still on his back by the landing cradle, but Adam could see him move his hands on his head. Further under the cradle was Hank, lying prone and kicking his feet up and down like a child in torment.

The ocean's vibration was changing, the sound deepening to an almost unbearable roar mixed with the thundering crash of waves upon the building. Adam found that each time he tried to move his body ached, either from the vibration itself or from the shaking of the building. It was impossible to walk upright so he began to crawl toward Jonwon.

Then, drowning out the scream, came a terrifying metallic tearing sound. The ship swayed on the landing cradle as if it had come to life.

187

"Jonwon! Hank! Get out!"

With a final piercing screech of torn metal, the girders of the metal landing cradle collapsed. The small ship plunged to the concrete roof of Jonwon's solitary building on Far.

Adam crawled through the rubble and found Jonwon's body cut in two by a fallen girder, the lower half smashed beyond repair. All he could see of Hank was the torn half of his head, and beyond it parts of a superaide brain spilling out.

He turned back to Jonwon, and saw the robot's eyes move. It didn't seem possible that Jonwon could be alive, until Adam remembered that although the main power source was in a robot's pelvis, there was an emergency power pack at the base of the skull, lasting—two hours? Three?

"Jonwon, are you in pain?"

"No, except from the torn edges of my synthoskin. Is Hank badly damaged?"

"Skull crushed and broken in two. He must be dead."

"Damn. What about One-O and my robots?"

Fighting nausea, Adam explained. "I'm sorry, Jonwon. I didn't mean to kill them but they were taking One-O . . ."

"I understand. They were not paralyzed by the sound like One-O. They were drawn toward it. I think I know why, because I feel as if the noise might stop hurting my mind if I could get inside the sound. I don't know what that means, and I'm afraid. Don't let me jump into that ocean."

Adam did not mention that unless Jonwon hauled himself by his arms, he could not walk to the edge to jump into the ocean.

"I'll drag you into the ship, Jonwon. The airlock's open and the ship looks intact, if tilted. Perhaps we'll be safer there. And if you can tell me how to open the transporter, we'll go home to Centauria—"

"Can't. As my robots left the ship they told me—mind to mind—that they had blocked the transporter mechanism."

188

"I'll prop you up to the control board so you can put the ship into hyperdrive and we'll go home."

"To get from M31 to the Milky Way galaxy through hyperspace takes many hours of actual time. My power pack will run out. It will be quicker to use the transporter on the first floor. Drag me there, Adam, before the sound drives me crazy or deactivates me."

Adam, carrying what was left of Jonwon, was almost to the ground floor when suddenly all the lights went out. "Jonwon, is there another power supply for the transporter?"

"Yes. Perhaps it will still work."

Adam took another two steps in the dark and felt the soles of his boots slide on wetness. Encased in his heavy suit, and carrying an even heavier robot, he couldn't keep his balance, but before he fell he managed to turn, shoving Jonwon onto a landing. Then he crashed onto the stairs and plummeted down into water, hitting his right leg on something sharp at the bottom. He groped for the stairs and hauled himself out of the water and up to the landing.

"Jonwon, the building must have cracked and let in high waves. The transporter's under water. We'll have to try the one in the ship." He carried Jonwon upstairs and into the control room of the ship, propping the torso up so Jonwon could use his hands.

But the robot's eyes were closed.

"Jonwon! Don't deactivate!"

"I wish I could. There's a heavy wrench in the storage cabin—get it quickly."

When Adam brought it back, Jonwon said, "One blow, Adam. Make it just one. I think if you hit hard enough you'll crush my brain. I want to die— I don't want to go insane. I think the mental intercom may be increasing the vibration in my head, but it can't be turned off."

Adam picked up the wrench. "Close your eyes, Jonwon."

"Why Adam, aren't you going to say good-bye to me?"

189

"Shut up."

With a powerful twist of the wrench, Adam tore the inter-com from Jonwon's head. "Did that hurt? Did I damage your brain?"

"No. It's better. I didn't think of that. But the sound is getting louder and louder so I'll probably deactivate anyway. Is that what happened to One-O?"

"I don't know. Why didn't your robots deactivate before they jumped into the ocean?"

"The only explanation I can think of is that they were not really individuals, since they had a version of a hive mind. But once in the ocean their brains died. I don't understand how the blasted scum could have changed so much, or be so lethal."

The turbulence was worse than ever. Each wave that crashed against the building and showered the roof seemed to be coated with a black substance that bubbled and writhed by itself.

Watching it in the viewscreen, Adam became aware of a cold sensation in his right leg. He looked down and saw a small rip in his space suit. Inside, his foot was wet.

"Are you all right inside that suit, Adam? Through the faceplate you look as if you're sweating."

"Of course I am—it's hard work dragging around the heavy upper half of my brother. But I'm all right. Let's try to unblock the ship's transporter mechanism."

After a few minutes, Jonwon stopped. "No use. Either the superaides messed it up too much, or my mind simply isn't functioning enough. In another hour I'll be dead."

Adam was staring hopelessly into the darkest corner of the control room when he saw something on the floor and went to investigate. It was one of the food pellets for Bio.

"Jonwon, was this ship filled with air when Hank brought Bio to it?"

"Adam, I'm getting worse. It feels as if my sanity is dissolv-

190

ing in that sound. I can hear it, feel it even inside the ship. Please kill me before—"

"If there wasn't air in the ship, Hank had to use something for Bio. He brought a box when he came to get her. What was it?"

"Stasis . . . box . . . Adam, kill me . . ."

Adam found it in the storage cabin. He went outside the ship to find the laser gun, and took them both to the control room. Grasping Jonwon's head with one hand, he severed the neck from the torso with the gun and put the head inside the stasis box. Jonwon stared up at him.

"You'll sleep, Jonwon. Ever since Matt found out that Seven could think in the old-fashioned stasis, it's been improved so that any MT superaide brain will be unconscious in stasis. It hasn't been tried on untransferred superaides because there was only you, but it should work just as well. Close your eyes and think how delighted Meg will be to put your head on a new body. You'll be all right. You're not going to go insane or die."

Jonwon smiled. Adam shut the box, turned it on, and sat back, exhausted.

He must have fallen asleep. He got up, dizzy, his eyesight fogged, and he couldn't rub his eyes. He wanted to take off the helmet but was afraid. Why was it so quiet?

He went down the ramp to the roof, and through the suit's receiver heard only a deep, rumbling sound that had lost the horrible high notes. Even the ocean was calmer, no waves spraying upon the roof, and the color changed to a purple-blue that looked like a storm cloud on Earth. Had the algae died?

When he looked away from the ocean to the figure of One-O, he still thought he saw purple, spots of it. They did not go away. Horror filled his mind and he tried to take off his helmet. At first the lock seemed stuck, but finally it opened

191

and he could breathe outside air again. It smelled strange, but better than the air in the suit.

He was still seeing purple spots, but as he leaned against the wall next to One-O's body, staring at a clear space of the roof so the spots would show, they changed gradually to a vibrant gold color, sparkling so much he was almost blinded.

Taking a deep breath, he took off the suit and rolled up his right pants leg, slightly torn. There were long streaks of purple running up the leg, and as he watched they faded to gold. His knees gave way and he sat down on the roof, shuddering. Now his hands and arms were discolored, too.

I'm infected with an alien organism that can't possibly live in my body, he thought. The question is, will my body kill it or will it kill me?

The roof was sopping wet, but the water was draining off through screened slits at the base of the wall, and while Adam sat there wondering what to do the puddle around him became streaked with gold, frothing up as if it were coming to a boil. Adam stood up and kicked at the puddle, but the froth bubbled between his toes and he saw that his feet were bright gold. So were his hands. He took off his clothes—his body was completely gold, not the color of jaundice but a rich red-gold that obscured his natural color.

Into the terror came a moment of wonder, for the gold seemed to start in his body and stream into the puddle, and then out in long rays like a primitive picture of a sun. The rays fed down through the drainage slits and after a while Adam saw them journeying out across the ocean.

The sound changed again to something pulsing and powerful, not unbearable, but suddenly Adam thought he knew what the robots had felt. It was as if only drowning in it would stop the mind from coming apart.

"I won't go crazy!" he shouted aloud. "I'm here alone and I'm infected but I won't let my mind give way . . . I'll . . . I'll

192

. . . but what can I do? Stop the damn noise, you're driving me crazy . . . crazy . . . like Jonwon—I could jump—I won't!"

There was a screaming sound in the noise, and he realized it came from himself. "I've got to calm myself. I'm sick and I feel rotten but I can take a deep breath and let it out and think . . . pretend . . ."

That was it. He could pretend the noise was music, an orchestra of countless algae cells contaminated by alien molecules from Bio and Adam Durant. He closed his eyes and the sparkling gold spots were almost gone. He tried to visualize his mother singing as Seven played the harpsichord, the twins joining in. And Jonwon loved music, human music, not this alien sound . . .

"No! I won't give in! I must believe that it is beautiful music and won't harm me."

He hummed to himself, keeping time to pulsations caused by the vibrations of countless millions of one-celled ocean plants, changed because two biological creatures from another galaxy had invaded their planet.

Still humming, Adam watched the purple-blue of the ocean scum change to the color of gold. As the water left on the roof dried a yellow powder remained. He picked up a pinch of it and put it in one of the puddles. Immediately, the tiny grains dissolved and the puddle frothed, its gold color intensifying.

Spores? Had the spray entered the ship? Then he looked at his body and saw that the gold of his skin was fading but he was covered with a fine yellow powder as if he had dusted himself with it. He walked to the airlock and looked in without entering. Dust—everywhere, no doubt from the water he had tracked in when he took Jonwon to the control room.

The dust was a source of infection from the alien scum of Far. Even if he managed to control the ship, he did not dare bring it home to Centauria, or anyplace where biologicals might get sick or robots deactivate.

Adam's chest hurt. His heart seemed to be skipping beats

193

and his breathing was labored. Fighting panic, he went to the control room and studied the mechanism that ran the ship. There was the usual provision for manual control if the ship's small brain of a computer were not functioning. He tried to get the computer to respond but it seemed dead.

All Centaurians know how to control a small ferry manually, for the knowledge might save their lives if the spome were damaged. Jonwon's ship was only a ferry modified for hyperdrive, and Adam knew how to run it on space-normal.

But there was no place to go, not at space-normal speed. Adam found the cabin saved for Meg, used the bathroom and drank some water. Then he went back outside, where at first he wondered what was happening to his eyesight until he realized that the blaze of color in the sky meant that the sun of Far was setting. Soon he would see the stars of M31.

He was hot and tired but the sound no longer bothered him. Soft, sweet, and everywhere, the music seemed part of him, not alien. He lay down in a dry patch of roof, facing upward so he wouldn't see Jonwon's lower body or the still form of One-O.

"I think I'll sleep a little. Goodnight, Far."

Just before his eyelids shut, he thought he glimpsed a flash of dying sunlight reflected from a silver surface overhead, but he was asleep before he could think about it.

CHAPTER • 30

He woke to what seemed like total darkness. He felt depleted of energy and unable to move, until he became aware of a faint sheen in front of his eyes. It was when he tried to reach up to touch it that he found his arms were tied down.

So were his legs, and his head felt as if hard wires circled it. He could turn his neck just enough to see some night sky between the roof wall and the thing that pinned him down. The sky was pricked with more stars than were ever seen from Earth. He was still on Far.

Panic surged in his mind and his overworked adrenals poured out hormones that brought him quickly to full waking.

"I'm on the rooftop of Jonwon's building, on the planet Far," he said aloud, slowly and distinctly. "Jonwon's head is in the stasis box, One-O is here on the roof, perhaps deactivated, and all the other robots are dead. Something metal has tied me down with wires and is"—he tried to focus on the object directly over his body—"sharp-edged, square with a bulge at this bottom side, and shines like silver."

The alien artifact had evidently decided to inspect him. It hovered above his body on obvious antigrav, wire tentacles reaching down to imprison him. Then Adam realized that one of the wires on his forehead seemed to have a particular pressure, as if it ended in a flat surface pressed against his skin.

"Well, are you reading what's left of my mind, damn you?"

There was, of course, no answer.

"I wonder what you got from my sleeping brain. Jumbles of bad dreams? All the information I ever knew? I'm not from this galaxy—are you? Why are you here? What are you going to do with me?"

He wanted water inside his mouth and outside his bladder, but there was no use struggling to get free. Calming his mind, he tried to think reasonably.

"You're an alien artifact, either a mindless object with the capacity to inspect things, or something with a brain, even if you don't seem communicative. Chances are you're something of a robot, in our terms, with enough of a brain to know what to do in many situations. Perhaps you've been told, or been programmed with instructions about what information to get from the brains of alien critters you inspect. If you have what you want from me, please let me go because I need to piss."

Adam hadn't really expected a response, but the sound of his own voice made him feel less completely isolated in an alien place.

"Well, let's postulate that you haven't gotten everything you want from me. In which case, what is it you want? Do you report to biological creatures or to others like yourself, or robots once made by biological creatures?"

Adam remembered that he was naked, and decided that the pressure from his bladder was the worst physiological problem, easily relieved. His bladder sphincter did not agree.

"Damn it! Let go! So I have to undo years of civilized training! So I get a little wet! I can take a shower later."

The sphincter relaxed and warm liquid ran over his thigh to puddle beneath him, but the night air of Far was not even remarkably cool, so he didn't feel uncomfortably wet.

"That's done. Now I wonder if the creatures who made you came from this galaxy or evolved someplace else. Yet it doesn't really matter where you came from or even where I came from because all life, organic or not, and all intelligence— well, they're all one, aren't they? All part of the universe?"

Suddenly he felt very happy. "I'm going to imagine that you've understood me, and that you're happy too. But I hope

196

you'll let me go by dawn because I have to figure out how to get home. . . ." He was back asleep.

When he woke again, the sun of Far was just rising above an ocean that glittered gold, but was as placid as Adam had seen it when he first arrived—only yesterday? And he was free; the alien artifact was gone. The softer noise of Far still penetrated but it no longer bothered him. Pretending it was music seemed to make alot of difference to his own brain.

He entered the ship, drank, showered, and examined himself carefully. He was no longer yellow, but a pale version of his normal light brown. He pulled down his lower eyelids and confirmed the diagnosis of anemia, for the conjunctivae were pale. Since he hadn't lost blood from a wound, the cells must have been destroyed.

"Okay, so I need a transfusion. I feel weak and dizzy and it's a little difficult to breathe normally, but aside from loss of red blood corpuscles and hypoglycemia from lack of food, I'm probably all right." This time his voice didn't sound reassuring. Adam Durant the patient was not convinced by the bedside manner of Adam Durant the physician.

He found Bio's food, but even after he poured water on it, he gagged when he tried to eat. He gave up and sat in the control room to think, but the golden dust everywhere discouraged him.

If he and the ship were dangerous to any place where air and water and sunlight could start the spores growing, he might still take the ship to a Centaurian satellite. Perhaps robot medics could tend him and bring him food—but how could he learn to use Jonwon's hyperdrive?

The ship's computer did not respond verbally, so its cognitive functions were out, yet something had to be working in it or there wouldn't be lights, plumbing, a viewscreen, and a few other basic signs of computer operation on a low level.

He studied the control board and decided that he could certainly raise her on antigrav. But that wouldn't get him

197

home. And if he did go home, could he be certain that a robot medic might not carry back a single spore. . . .

No one else should die because of him. "I killed three robots, but Bio's turd might have contaminated Far's ocean at any time—yet somehow it was I who brought destruction and death." He retched, but nothing came up.

"I can't figure out anything. I'm not bright like Meg and Jonwon. When I was six Meg scolded me because I couldn't read yet—she read at three—and I was so ashamed I ran to Seven who said I could probably master it if I tried."

So master this situation. The words were Adam's thoughts, but it felt almost as if Seven were speaking to him.

Could spores survive in space? His memory disgorged the name spirogyra, which formed spores thickwalled and resistant to external conditions. Far's spores might survive, but on the other hand he had nothing to lose, as Seven would say, in trying to clean the ship.

As the ship lifted on antigrav from the fallen girders, Adam, shut up once more in his space suit, fought down his claustrophobia and turned on the ship's receivers. Nothing came in but the sound of Far, growing fainter as the ship rose through the atmosphere. Adam found himself turning up the volume so he could still hear what he now thought of as Far's music. He wondered if he were hooked on it, and remembered Jonwon's first two superaides, jumping into the ocean with Bio as if a pied piper were calling them.

The noise suddenly disappeared, at any volume, and Adam saw in the viewscreen that he was above the atmosphere. He put the ship into orbit and discovered that he was sweating and trembling. He went through the ship and tied down anything that looked loose, and put Jonwon's stasis box into a cabinet he could lock. Then he went to open the airlock. He could fasten himself to the railing and be safe inside his suit while the ship's air escaped, or he could open his suit and go out with it. And die quickly.

He was shaking so much that he had to sit down on the floor right by the airlock, in the golden dust . . . not golden. Brown. Dusty brown. Adam picked up a handful and ran to the bathroom in what he thought of as Meg's cabin. He poured water on it and absolutely nothing happened.

The spores were dead. All of them. He removed his space suit and found that spores lodged in the inside crevices were also brown and dead. Perhaps the mutated microorganic scum of Far could not survive separated from itself, or from the vibrations the ocean now made.

Unless his own body was somehow infectious, it would be safe to take the ship home if he could turn on the hyperdrive. He went to the control room and there in the viewscreen was the planet Far, a cloud-spangled golden ball.

But not a simple, shining gold. Between the clouds the ocean seemed to be criss-crossed by curved lines as if there were faint indentations in the surface scum, which bellied outward slightly between the lines. It reminded him of something but he couldn't remember what.

In the terrible silence of the control room, free from the planet's vibration, Adam stared at Far, wanting to go back. He touched a switch. "I'll just descend a little and hear the sound—might as well make sure it doesn't bring the spores back to life. . . ."

"Descending to planet. Computer control of ship possible only above atmosphere."

"Computer! You're alive!"

"I am operational."

"But—you weren't. Are you all right now?"

"Sentence not applicable to computer. Inactivation of central processing unit within atmosphere a proven fact."

"Stop descent!" Adam wished the looming planet would disappear, to be replaced by his own man-made world of Centauria. "Computer, did you sustain any permanent damage from your inactivation by the planet's noise?"

199

"Data indicate no damage."

"But you'll be inactivated as soon as we hit the atmosphere of Far?"

"Yes."

"But what is it in the sound that causes the paralysis?"

"Unknown. Sequences of sound meaningless according to comparison with all data in memory banks."

"Computer, I want the ship to descend under manual control, to pick up something from the surface. Can you show me which controls I must use to do this?"

"Controls shown by indicator light. Descending."

It was an emotionless, not very bright computer, and Adam was relieved that it did not react to the necessity of returning to a condition of paralysis. It merely obeyed.

One-O, picked up by the ship's grapple and brought through the airlock, was inert, and remained so until the ship went beyond the atmosphere. Then, to Adam's relief, he stood up and began apologizing for his inadequacies.

"Stop that, One-O. In reaction to the vibration you and the ship's computer both went into temporary inactivation. You didn't want to jump into the ocean with Jonwon's robots, and you didn't go crazy. I am so pleased to have you back, especially since I may not be able to leave the ship if we get to Centauria. You're not infected, but I am."

"Then we must go home so that you may be cured. Do you know how to put the ship into hyperdrive?"

"No, but the ship's computer does. I just have to order it to do so."

There was a long pause, while Adam watched Far in the viewscreen, lost in a wordless memory of sound from one-celled organisms that formed a deadly scum on a planet's ocean.

"Master Adam, I have little emotional capacity, but what I have is affecting me at this moment. I am frightened. I can discover no change in my capacities, but in my memory

200

banks there is a strong addition—sound of no recognizable meaning, stored in more microbubbles of my brain than ordinary auditory sensation would be."

"Perhaps that's because the scum produces vibrations not only heard as sound, but also felt throughout our sensory receptors, affecting cognitive aspects of the brain—you know, One-O, I think this ought to be studied, and perhaps if we took the ship back down—"

"Master Adam! Lock into the coordinates of Centauria! Command the ship's computer to take us there at once on hyperdrive. I also have the longing to go back to Far. We must leave at once, while we still can."

CHAPTER • 31

"Bess, are you certain?" Seven stood beside her desk, one hand on her bowed shoulders. She seemed older and for the first time, frail.

"Yes. Lee Teleg and the robot medics have gone over Adam thoroughly in Jonwon's ship. They've fed the data into our best hospital computers. He's had permanent cell damage. The nervous system was more resistant and will stay alive longer but everything else will die slowly because there's no repair. We have to replace the heart at once, and then the kidneys. Eventually clone organ replacements won't be enough, and Adam must mind transfer."

"How soon?"

She swallowed, and put her hand up to rest on his. "He's been told he has maybe six months of organic life."

As she cried, Seven picked her out of her chair and held her in his arms, staring over her head at the picture of a Terran ocean, rough and dangerous, but friendly compared to the alien ocean that had doomed Adam.

"He's too young, Seven!"

"Not a child. He'll be a good transfer robot." But she went on crying, and he wished he could cry, too.

No tears came to Meg's eyes but she looked like a stricken statue, with pale lips that seemed to be chiseled in stone.

"He's not infectious, Meg," said Seven, wishing she would stir. Her lab was too quiet, as if everything had been turned off. "He's being transferred to the hospital for surgery."

"Will they let me see him there? So far he hasn't seen anyone but robots and mind transfers like Dr. Teleg."

"The alien organism is dead, and all the tests show that Adam cannot pass it on to anyone."

"It's killed him. That damn planet killed my Adam!"

"Not yet. And when he's an MT he'll still be Adam."

"Go away, Seven. You don't understand."

"I think I do."

"No. It should have been me. I was going to find Jonwon, find that lethal planet. I wouldn't mind being an MT and Adam will. It's all Jonwon's fault."

"Adam blames himself for going to Far with One-O, who should have gone alone to tell Hank that Horace was dying."

"Seven, from what Adam has told us about Far, One-O would not have come back. If it hadn't been for Adam, perhaps all the robots would be deactivated, but I wouldn't have cared as long as Adam was home, safe and still biological. He went with One-O because Jonwon tantalized all of us with the bloody mystery of his existence, and Adam likes to solve mysteries."

"Meg, I believe that Adam wanted to find Jonwon first, so he could come back to share it with you, instead of . . ."

"Well? Instead of what?"

"Perhaps Adam was afraid that if his wife found Jonwon, she would not come back."

President Cavister had worked for Tully Robotics before going into politics, and succeeded to the presidency of Centauria when Horace Deno resigned. Cavister was arguing with his science council about Far.

"The news has already leaked to the Feds, who insist they should explore Far, but Adam Durant won't give them—or us—the hyperdrive coordinates, or the transporter code. He says the planet must be under permanent quarantine."

"He's right," said Seven. "If even one spore managed to survive a rapid trip to Earth, their oceans might fill with the lethal organism."

203

"Centaurian MTs," said one of them, "could safely explore Far and make it our colony. M31 will be *our* galaxy."

"Not if the vibrations paralyze robot brains," said Seven. "Besides, the question is academic. Adam will not tell."

"There's still the brain of the robot Jonwon," said Cavister. "If sane, Jonwon should remember both coordinates."

The fresh scar on Adam's chest itched. "Thanks, Seven. I'm glad you didn't tell anyone about the alien artifact. It's the other thing I told the computer to wipe out of memory. I guess both governments are furious but after what happened to Bio and me, and to the minds of the robots, I had to make it harder for anyone to go there. Jonwon must not tell, either."

"How about One-O? Doesn't he know them?"

"Only the transporter coordinates to the ship. I've discussed the matter with One-O, and he certainly won't tell. These politicians, Centaurian or Fed, don't realize how dangerous Far is. And what gives them the right to go to another galaxy and wipe a planet clean of alien life, however simple and unpleasant?"

"I suppose they've been seduced by the fact that Far has a better climate than any Earthlike planet found so far."

"Seven, even the alien artifact left Far alone!"

The restored Jonwon sat up so abruptly that the observer from the Federation, who was sitting up front to be the first to ask for the coordinates, drew back as if a monster had come to life. Meg and Adam grinned at each other.

Jonwon ignored the sudden flood of questions and looked directly at Adam, who shook his head slightly—in a "no."

"Thanks, Adam. You saved my life."

"I'm sorry about the superaides, and that I couldn't save Hank. One-O is all right."

"Good. How did you pick up One-O?"

It was a crucial question, and before anyone could object,

Adam spoke rapidly. "The ship's computer was operational above the atmosphere, so I had it set things on manual and we went back down to pick up One-O with the ship's grapple. Then I wiped the transporter and hyperdrive coordinates from the computer's memory banks."

"Now just a minute," said the Fed. "We want to ask this robot for the—"

"This Federation security cop, and President Cavister over there, both want the coordinates of Far, either by ship or by transporter, because they want to kill the ocean scum and terra-form it for themselves."

"Indeed," said Jonwon, smiling at the Fed and Cavister.

Cavister stood up, bigger than anyone else in the room. "Far is obviously suitable as living space for humans and robots once the lethal organism is removed. Colonization of the planet will open up the entire Andromeda galaxy to us since there is no evidence of other intelligent life . . ."

Adam's left eyelid went down halfway, then snapped up.

". . . and you, Jonwon, as a Centaurian-built robot, owe it to your own nation to give us the coordinates."

"See here, Cavister!" yelled the Fed.

"Wait," said Jonwon. "Adam looks okay, so why should the organism harm anyone except robots?"

"Adam is dying," said Meg softly.

Seven nodded. "The organism entered through a tear in his suit and injured his cells enough so that he will not live longer than a few months. Preparations for mind transfer are under way."

"It's not your fault, Jonwon," said Adam, for Jonwon's face showed an anguish he'd never seen on it before.

The Fed stood up, since Cavister had not sat down. "Any human will be safe as long as the space suit remains intact, and once the planet is cleaned, that won't be necessary."

"I see," said Jonwon. "I want to talk to Adam alone."

"First give us the coordinates," said the Fed.

205

"And if I don't?"

"You will be guarded until you do."

"Not allowed to speak to my family alone?"

"No," said Cavister. "I'm sorry, but your personal wishes, even the needs of Tully Robotics, must come second to the needs of humanity. You have, of course, been taught the laws of robotics?"

"Yes. If you come to my lab with me I will show you how to get to Far by means of my private transporter, which has the coordinates on it. I do not bother memorizing numbers handled by the computers built into transporters."

They all trudged down the hall, Jonwon leading the way like a sun god, blond and tall, followed by the bulk of Cavister and the rotundity of the Fed. Adam, Meg, and Seven walked silently behind them, united in hatred for politicians.

Jonwon opened his transporter. "Adam, why did you stay sane on Far even when you were infected?"

"Get on with it!" yelled the Fed.

"Shut up," said Meg. "Let them talk."

"I might have gone crazy," said Adam, "but I pretended the noise was music, and after a while I could bear it. In fact, I began to believe it actually was music. I suppose any sound, however horrible to one intelligence, might be music to the ears of another."

"Fascinating," said Jonwon. "There's alot out in the universe that nobody understands. Adam, I apologize for letting Hank take Bio to Far. Everything bad that happened is my fault. I thought a biological phenomenon like the ocean scum was not worth investigating, so precautions against contaminating it were not taken. I'm sorry you were infected."

"I went to find you of my own free will," said Adam.

Cavister grunted. "You two can review your respective guilts at some other time. We want to know the coordinates."

"Certainly you do," said Jonwon. "You humans taught me the laws of robotics—protection of human life is paramount.

Long ago I decided that I would never be able to protect humans from myself, because I am as fallible, as pigheadedly stupid as they are, so I went away to find my own destiny. I failed, but I'm not going to negate what's good about the laws of robotics now that you want to take up where I left off. I will not help humans get to Far. I must protect you from your worst danger."

"But we told you we can avoid the contamination—"

Jonwon held up his hand and the Fed shut up. "You misunderstand me, sir. The worst danger to human beings is their own lack of reverence for life. Good-bye."

Before anyone could move, Jonwon stepped on the transporter plate and dissolved into nothingness.

Cavister, who could read transporter coordinates better than most politicians, raced to the control panel. "Damn him! He set it to erase the coordinates immediately. We'll try to get them out of the computer memory, but they probably aren't there now."

The Federation official's intercom beeped and he listened with an earphone. "The guards outside Jonwon's ship say that it has vanished from the ferry hangar."

"Then he didn't go to Far—he went to his ship," said Cavister. "Where is he going in it—back to Far?"

"There's never any point in asking where Jonwon's going or why," said Meg.

CHAPTER • 32

Bone marrow transplants every month. New kidneys after two, new liver after four months. At six months Adam was still functioning but transferred his patients to other doctors so they wouldn't be upset by his physical deterioration. He also wanted to live as fully as possible every minute left to him in his failing body, but most of the time he didn't know how.

He hung around Tully Robotics, watching Meg and Seven and the manufacturing computers create his new body. "Are you sure that's what I look like?"

"You at your best," said Meg. "As an MT you'll never look too young or too middle-aged. You'll enjoy the erect-at-will penis—"

"You mean you'll enjoy it," he said, patting her behind.

"Both of you will," said Seven, "thanks to the humanness of the new superaide body. Furthermore, the MT's empathy with the human partner's climax creates one for the MT."

"You can't be serious," said Adam.

"I also believe that it's more than empathy. The emotional component is real. Primitive reaction in the human mind goes way back. A biological human or an MT who's never seen a snake will have a primate startle response when unexpectedly encountering one. No ordinary robot startles at snakes, and I bet Jonwon doesn't either. Although . . ." Seven paused, with a faint smile.

"Although what?" asked Adam. "Something about Jonwon and sex?" He didn't dare look at Meg.

"Not exactly. Jonwon seems to respond to music with an almost orgastic concentration and unification of mind and body. Perhaps there's a primitive experience built into all

208

organized matter, emerging from patterns that form in the basic particle fields of the universe. Jonwon may receive it from music."

Adam grinned. "Somehow I suspect you of postulating that orgasm is built into the universe!"

Meg giggled, but Seven seemed to put on an excessively serious expression. "Why, Adam, I may very well have been talking simply about profound experience. It's so human of you to think in terms of sex."

Adam turned red. "Well, at least I won't blush as an MT."

It was one of the few times of happiness for Adam, for usually he could think of little except how sick he felt, physically, mentally, and emotionally. His body deteriorated slower than expected, but just as inexorably, and sometimes he wished it would be faster. He had a brain recording done soon after he came back to Centauria, but refused to make another until he was near death.

"I want to go into robot life knowing as much as possible about myself, about how I was when I approached death. Please, Seven, let me do it that way." Meg was on his side, and Seven gave in, although Bess kept nagging him to take many recordings in case several failed.

"Don't worry, Mother, I won't wait until I'm terminal. The act of dying must be my own private biological experience, not to be passed on to a robot self. I feel too jealous already of that robot I'll become. I don't want him to share in my death, my final unique identification with the biological universe."

"Robots can die," Bess reminded him.

He'd told no one that three of Jonwon's superaides died because he shot them. "I know they can, but biological dying is different. Or perhaps I'm just clinging to a typical bioeffer idea so that I'll believe my own dying is superior."

Bess did not smile.

* * *

209

Adam did not feel superior. The MTs were prone to call him up to give him cheery encouragement about his future life that only made the present existence more intolerable. The biological humans, other than his own family, tended to avoid him, for he walked around Centauria with doom in his eyes.

One day when he forgot to eat he collapsed in a crowded shopping mall. The nearby biological humans seemed to move away from him, but he didn't need their help because One-O was not far behind and ran to pick him up.

Later Adam asked Seven if One-O had been specifically programmed for helpfulness. "If I'm not actually with someone One-O knows and trusts, he's behind me all the time. I've come to count on him. Did you tell him to follow me?"

"No to both questions. I think he enjoys being helpful. His brain isn't as complex as a superaide's, but he probably has some sensation of emotion. It certainly seems to give him much satisfaction to follow the laws of robotics in his own style."

"I've even seen him smiling a little," said Adam. "I'm glad he's not like those eyeless, smileless robots of Jonwon's, with hive minds and less personality than an aide."

"Yes. One-O's ability to smile probably makes him capable of emotion, and thus more human. As you and I have often discussed, facial expression alters the emotions processed or produced in the brain almost more than vice versa."

Adam squirmed with self-consciousness, sure that Seven was obliquely referring to the fact that he went around looking grim and haunted most of the time. Dammit, I am haunted, he thought. Can a murderer under death sentence look happy?

For once they were alone in Seven's office, for Meg was fussing over the new robot's hair and One-O was helping her.

"It's not just your illness or your anxiety about mind transfer that's bothering you, Adam. Want to talk about it?"

210

"Yes. I killed three of Jonwon's superaides. I've never know-ingly killed anything before." Adam explained, and added, "If I hadn't been so stupid I'd have noticed it was a laser gun and shot at their arms so they'd drop One-O but could still jump into the ocean if that's what they wanted to do. They were such inhuman robots, yet they were alive, and I killed them. I think about it all the time."

"You will, for a while. On Earth, I killed two humans. Bess and Matt called it an accident because I didn't know my own strength when I threw Eliot's guards, but they died and I have never forgotten it or forgiven myself. I have lived my life trying to atone."

Adam cried, and when he could speak he said, "Thank you, Seven. Thanks for telling me. I will atone, also."

As the days passed and he grew weaker, he wandered restlessly through Centauria, thinking of himself as a ghost that could not be laid to rest. Meg seemed absorbed in the new robot, and Walt, knowing his father was going to die, had already started to withdraw from him.

One afternoon, Bess told Adam she was taking several hours off and wanted to walk with him in Wildpark. He was upset. His mother was so intensely biological, so dedicated to helping the human body survive. As a doctor, he had always been more interested in the problems of MTs than she was.

She strode along effortlessly while he tried to conceal his labored breathing, but she soon noticed it and slowed down.

"Walt says you don't help him with the rabbits anymore."

"I thought Walt didn't want a sick father around."

"Is that the real reason?"

"No, Mother. I hate rabbits. They remind me of Bio."

"I think you're full of hate. And scared, having to walk around grieving for your own death before it happens."

It was August, the woods in full leaf, the ground dappled with their patterns as the light from Alpha Centauri A filtered

211

through the mirror system. He had never felt so alienated from life, and from the people he loved.

When he didn't answer, Bess said, "Perhaps it would have been easier for you to die quickly, as Lee Teleg did, waking up as a robot, but I'm selfishly glad you have these extra months as my biological child."

She wiped her eyes and patted the hand he placed on her shoulder. "You don't have to comfort me, dear. I thought I was trying to comfort you. My marriage to Seven gives me hope that you'll be happy as an MT. Each life has a pattern of its own as an aspect of the universe."

"Oh, Mother, the universe is horrible."

"Haven't you learned yet that you are the universe, one small part of it that knows itself?"

"You always taught me the universe just exists, that it isn't consciously alive and caring even if we'd like it to be that way, especially when we're sick."

Bess chirruped to a squirrel and fed it a nut that magically appeared in her palm. Animals always came to her.

"That's true, Adam, but I believe the most important thing about the universe is that some parts of it are alive and caring—like you. If there were enough parts, or patterns, maybe the universe would turn into something else. Or maybe it wouldn't. Maybe it doesn't matter as long as you are part of whatever changes take place."

"Have you ever seen Jonwon's movie, Mother?"

"So that's what you're brooding about—the alien organisms killing you and Bio? The Terran-evolved organisms that will eventually eat your dead body?"

Somehow Bess's bluntness made it all right. "Eating and being eaten isn't so horrible, I guess."

"It does seem to be a big way that the universe changes."

"Thanks, Mother. Remind me from time to time that I was always in favor of change."

* * *

Lee Teleg said she wanted to tell him the truth about being an MT. His supposedly new heart kicked up a storm of extrasystoles and he had to take a pill, but he listened.

"The first group of us MTs had to learn from scratch, but now there's a good support system to help you with anything you don't understand or you need to learn. Everyone says mind transfer is easier on males, who can be sexual athletes at will, but human males sometimes find it hard to make love to a robot wife who doesn't have warm skin or smell like a human female. But there's a worse problem, Adam."

"Being able to live longer than biologicals?"

"The age difference doesn't matter much in this first generation of MTs, but soon biologicals will resent us, and I'm afraid that biofundamentalism will become fanatical again."

"I wonder. My friend Paul Hirson tells me that there are only a few bioeffer idiots eager to sign a pledge never to MT because they think a robot can't contain the so-called soul."

The corners of Lee's full mouth twitched upward, exactly as if she were still biological. "Do you think I have one?"

"I don't think anyone does," said Adam. "But I'd like it if you told me what it's really like to be a robot."

"At first I hated not being able to smell or taste, but it's nice not having to worry about my weight, or having to sleep so much. I'm not going to detail everything I miss, or find enjoyable, because you won't understand until you're there. Don't worry, Adam. There are more and more MTs every day and we'll help you. You won't be alone."

The conversation should have been encouraging, but like all the other talks he'd had with family and friends, Adam always reverted to feeling alienated.

It became harder to make love to Meg, although when he did it momentarily freed him from fears that poisoned every day, including the notion that Meg disliked a sick husband and was longing for the robot Adam.

By late summer, he was suddenly much sicker, his body a

213

terrible weight, difficult to drag around. He refused a medi-chair and shuffled slowly along, hating his disability and the people who observed it. He spent most of his time in Wild-park, where no one could see him.

Except One-O. Adam tripped over a rock and fell one morning. His knee hurt and he began to cry helplessly. When One-O tried to help him up Adam yelled, "Stop it! Let me get up by myself one more time."

"I would like to help you, Master Adam."

"Oh, don't bother. I'm sorry I yelled at you. It's just that I'm suffering—more in mind than in body."

"As you choose, Master Adam."

As I choose? He thought about it all the way back to the house, walking angrily and without One-O's help so he arrived breathless, on the verge of collapse.

He leaned against the hall closet door, which closed all the way and upset his balance so he fell again. He started to sob, and then he heard a small voice from inside the closet.

Opening the door he found his son huddled under Adam's old coat. Walt was now a gangly boy who usually tried to act older than his age, but at this moment looked pathetically young.

Adam saw a book on rabbit care lying beside Walt and asked, "Something wrong with the rabbits, son? I'm sorry I lost interest in them recently."

"The rabbits are okay. I was just tired."

"I guess the closet can be a snug place sometimes. Mind if I sit here with you? I'm a little tired and upset myself."

They both sat under the coat, and Adam put his arm on the boy's shoulders, as thin as Meg's had been when she was young. Adam's breathing quieted, and he began to sing one of Walt's favorite songs about the glory of Centauria. They sang it together and went on to other songs until the closet door opened wider and Amy peered in.

214

"Agnes and I just transported in for concert rehearsals. Want to come or are you both in the closet for being bad?"

"We'll come," said Walt. "Dad—will you . . ."

"Sure, now that I'm over my temper tantrum about things."

Amy's eyes widened. "I guess you're allowed, considering."

"No I'm not! One-O is right."

"About what?" asked Walt.

"Choosing."

CHAPTER • 33

The burst of bloom in late summer faded into September, but in Centauria there was no crisp chill of fall to color the leaves and Adam was homesick for the triumphal brightness of a northeast American autumn. As his own strength faded, those brilliant leaves seemed to represent a final flourish of biological courage.

And he desperately needed courage—to say good-bye to all things, to smile acceptingly in the coming confrontation with death. Suddenly he knew that he wanted to go back to Earth, and to die near his father's grave.

First he had to make the final brain recording. He asked Seven to take it when they were alone in the lab. "I don't want anyone here but you," Adam said. "I don't want anyone else to know how frightened I am. Lately I've been obsessed by memories of Jonwon's movie, and I'm becoming terrified by biological death."

"Then you'll either be worse or better after you see my movie," said Seven, touching a switch. The room darkened and a section of ceiling lit up in holov. "Lie down on the mind transfer table while I prepare the apparatus. Just look up at the ceiling and think whatever you have to think."

The holov ceiling became the blackness of space, and in it a spiral galaxy turned slowly. It seemed crystal clean because he was too far away to see interstellar dust and debris, much less the output of that professional dirtier, organic life.

He felt as if he were swimming in space with the galaxy, his impending death only a microscopic flicker in the majesty of things as they are. He felt proud of the thought, and yet suddenly furious.

"We can't help eating and being eaten, messing up that

clean grandeur, being small and dirty! Life is still important!" His involuntary shout died away when the movie changed, and he seemed to be falling into the galaxy.

Stars were born in violence, raging in nuclear fusion to stay alive, exploding or collapsing or burning out, dying in more violence or subsiding in a colder death. New stars bloomed in the debris, and many of these had planets.

He was closer, witness to life beginning and evolving, eating and being eaten. This time he was not frightened or nauseated. The pettiness of life's violence and tragedy was nothing compared to what was going on in the rest of the universe. He laughed out loud.

Then he was moving away, back and back, until he saw not just one galaxy but many systems of stars, spiral and globular and any shape or size. The galaxies were rushing away from each other, but slowly they stopped, and came rushing back, faster and faster, colliding with each other, collapsing together—and for a long moment there was silence and something that might have been either very dark or very bright.

"Is this picture computer-generated?"

"It would be difficult to take it live, Adam."

The picture captured him again, and he seemed to be watching the same blasted business of eat and be eaten, until he realized that these were inorganic molecules combining and changing in energy transformations.

"Okay, you've made your point," he said. "Eating and being eaten is just another style of energy transformation that the whole universe indulges in. But dammit, galaxies aren't conscious and I am."

"Wait, Adam."

The picture changed and he was deeper into the structure of matter. So deep that it was no longer matter but energy, and then no longer energy but patterns. He was about to sit up and complain when he looked again at the ceiling, and saw that it was a garden.

217

There was One-O, solemnly planting bulbs with the help of a small boy. Walt? The boy turned and Adam saw himself.

Now he became aware that all along there'd been music. The counterpoint of Bach, seemingly independent melodies growing joyously and separately and yet together. Two harpsichords, one certainly played by Seven and the other . . .

"Who are you playing harpsichord duets with?"

"One of the more advanced music computers. I thought it would make an interesting combination for my movie, in which nothing is clean and sane and free from the violence of energy transformation."

On the ceiling the images of boy and robot faded. As the room returned to its normal lighting, Adam looked at the quiet face of Seven, ready for him.

"Everything dies. Is that the point?"

"No, Adam. Unlike Jonwon's movie, mine ends with a simple little boy and a simpler robot planting flowers, a nonviolent method of energy transformation indeed."

"And the music. I'll think about it. I'll have alot of time for thinking when I'm a robot. I guess the real point is that I've got alot to learn. Thanks for bullying me into admitting it."

"Me? A bully?"

"I love you, Seven." Adam closed his eyes and visualized the violent beauty of a galaxy full of dust and planets, and a quirky by-product called life that claimed it had a right to be there in many forms, including idiotic human beings or their less idiotic creations, robots. Or scum vibrating on an ocean. Many ways for life to live.

As the recording started he drifted into the most peaceful sleep he had known since he left Far.

Within a month his condition had deteriorated to the point where he had to spend most of his time in a medichair. Meg made the arrangements and they were to leave for Earth in the morning, accompanied by One-O. Adam had refused all farewell parties and said he wanted to spend the evening in Seven's office. Everyone argued, and even Seven was annoyed, but Adam insisted.

"I think I know what you want and I'm not going to do it."

"Seven, do this one favor for me. I know it's against MT rules, but I need it. Maybe he needs it."

"Meg should be here."

"No! I don't want him to have her even for a second while I'm still alive. Please, Seven, I know that my last brain recording was successfully transferred. Take the robot out of stasis and let me talk to him."

At last Seven gave in. One-O wheeled Adam into the room and left him there, alone. The transparent stasis bubble lifted and at first Adam thought the transfer had failed, for the robot did not move.

"Adam?"

The robot sat up and swung himself around so easily that Adam grimaced with the pain he would have felt trying to do it himself.

"Hello, Adam," said the robot, who was not surprised. After all, they'd been thinking about it for a long time.

Adam leaned forward, conscious of his legs trembling under the discreetly adjusted blanket of the medichair. "How do you feel in that body?"

"All right."

"I mean, are you—one person, or do you have my memories and your own consciousness?"

"I'm conscious of myself as Adam Durant, no one else."

Pain seemed to crush Adam's chest until the chair injected medicine. "I shouldn't have awakened you. I leave tomorrow for Earth, and I want you to go back into stasis until I am not just gone from Centauria but dead and buried. Do you mind?"

"No. There's complete oblivion in that stasis chamber."

"Like death, I suppose. I also hope you don't mind that I'm planning to end my life myself. Had I—"

219

"You thought of it all along."

"I'm much sicker now than I was when your brain record-ing was made. Perhaps my appearance revolts you."

"No. Are you in pain?"

Adam hated the look of pity on the robot's face. "The chair takes care of that. I must end things while I'm still able to. My achievements in life have been so mediocre, and my illness the result of my own blundering stupidity, so I want to have some control over the way it ends. . . . I keep forgetting that you know all this."

"How long has it been since the recording was made?"

"One month. Everything gave out at once, so the terminal stage arrived quickly. You will never experience it." Had the robot caught the superiority in that?

The robot nodded. "I am glad to be alive and in no danger of illness, but please know that I'm also envious. You're having a biological experience that I'm denied."

Adam managed to laugh at that, promptly lost his breath, and waited while the chair took care of him. "Forgive my smug bioeffer superiority—it's about all I have left. And I think I finally understand those bioeffers, and people like Matt who wouldn't have a brain recording made. You see, I know you are revolted by me, but I am horrified at you becoming Meg's husband and Walt's father. Sorry, but that's the way it is."

The robot didn't move. Only the false eyelids slid half way over the false eyes that were looking at the floor, or perhaps at Adam's feet twitching on the foot rest of the wheelchair. "I'll try to stay human," said the robot.

Stay human. Not *be* human. He thinks of himself as hu-man! Adam tried to grasp this and failed. "Although it hasn't been long since we parted ways, in that time I've learned more than you ever can about biological existence, and soon you'll know more about robot life than I'll ever know. You are

220

not the self I am now. We have become two mysteries to each other."

The robot grinned. "But we like mysteries, don't we? As long as they have a beginning, middle, and end with everything satisfactorily explained. Unfortunately life is different."

"Yes," Adam said impatiently, "except that in my case I know the end of the story. I'm leaving the stage and other players—you—will continue, but it will be another story, not mine."

"Thank you, Adam, for allowing me to continue."

Looking at his robot self, Adam felt an astonishing rush of gratitude that warmed his feeble body and made him less annoyed with how the medichair had to deal with his precious and unreliable biologicality. "Seven taught us that nothing lasts forever, not even the universe."

"He likes mysteries too," said the robot. "Unlike Jonwon. Remember when Seven said that the uncertainty in the universe gives the universe potential to develop into whatever it can become? And Jonwon said, 'I won't put up with uncertainty!'"

"How the hell can you remember the exact words?"

"I don't know. This new brain seems to have the ability to find stored memories better than I could before."

"Damn you."

"I'm sorry. Please put me back in stasis. This interview is obviously bad for you, and you must stay alive to get back to Earth."

"Stop being so damn considerate about the proper closure to the mystery of my life!" When the robot didn't respond, Adam's shame deepened, and he tried to clear his mind. He closed his eyes and said, "Odd. I feel years older than you, not just a few weeks. As if you were more my son than my other self. Let me think a minute about mysteries."

It was very quiet in the stasis room. Adam's hearing was not what it was, and he could no longer detect the ever-

221

present faint vibration of the machines that kept Centauria alive. He supposed the robot's hearing—but it didn't matter. Nothing mattered except ending this foolish meeting. And dying.

He tried to smile at the robot. "I've been doing alot of thinking about the future that I'll miss and you won't. About the mysteries that are waiting to be solved. Like how to help Jonwon, or what's going to happen to Far, or where that alien artifact came from."

"I'll try to explore those mysteries for you."

"But there's something I'm finding out. I think that no mystery is ever solved completely. We only uncover one after another, because the solution to one opens up other puzzles. That's part of the fun of being alive and intelligent. Please stay alive. Stay curious. You and I—well, I know I'm not terribly intelligent, but there must be something important to do, some significant mystery to solve . . ."

"I'll try."

"Don't just live through whatever's happening. Choose. Although I'm a lousy example, doing nothing except living through the process of dying."

"That's not true. You made the choice to talk to me. To help me stay human. And perhaps to find out for yourself that you've arrived at some sort of contentment you never had before. Is that true?"

"Ridiculous! Blast you . . ." Then the fury subsided without drugs, replaced by a sense of peace colored by mirth.

"You're right! I've stopped wanting to know what happens next. I've handed over the burden of living, content to let everything go and sink back into what is. Who was it who said it was important to be able to let go?"

"Paul Hirson."

With enormous effort, Adam held out his hand to the robot who took it gently in smooth, cool fingers. The hands clasped.

"Good luck," said Adam. "I'm a little tired, so if you'll press that switch, Seven and One-O will return."

As One-O wheeled him out, he heard the other Adam say, "Good-bye, and thank you."

The faint hum of Centauria was obvious even in the insulated stasis room. "Are you ready?" asked Seven.

"No. I must write him a letter. You'll read it, and if you think it's a good idea for him to have it, give it to him as he's leaving for Earth."

"Come to my office. There's paper in my desk."

"I don't want to leave this room, or even this table. The temptation to stay out will be too much. Please bring the paper and pen to me here."

"Yes, Adam."

"I'm not Adam. Not yet."

"You are both Adam. There are many ways in which life can be lived."

CHAPTER • 34

He said good-bye to his mother and Seven. Bess had been crying but he felt certain that those two could take care of each other. It was different with Meg. She was going with him to Earth, and her thin body and taut face daily tormented him with his inability to help her.

Just as he was about to enter the transporter, Bess bent over his medichair and kissed his forehead. For the last time he inhaled the fresh odor of her hair and skin, and was almost overwhelmed by hideous regret, but the chair persuaded his heart and lungs to function and he was able to smile.

"Be good to . . . me. The other me."

Bess nodded, and beyond her shoulder he saw Seven raise one eyebrow quizzically. Adam laughed and wondered if robot Adam would be able to learn that trick. "Okay, One-O—wheel me inside."

Carefully, One-O guided the chair into the transporter, and Meg followed without a word.

The difficult trip to Earth was not as horrible as he had expected because Paul and Rusty Hirson met them. Adam and Meg were whisked to Dinah's vacation home, where Adam spent several days in the warmth of the late October garden before One-O handed him a letter addressed to him in his own handwriting.

"I don't want to read this!"

"It is from the other Adam, Master Adam."

"I know that, dammit! Go into the house and get Meg—she's taking a nap."

"Seven told me to give it to you when you were alone. He said it would be better for the other Adam to know that you received his message. I have not read it but apparently it contains things he could not say to you."

He wanted Meg. He wanted her to say that she loved him, that she didn't care about the problems of a robot, even one with Adam's face. "Blast it, One-O. Everyone acts as if I'm still responsible, still part of their universe."

"Adam needs you to read this," repeated One-O.

It felt like a final betrayal. "He's your Adam, now?"

"No, you are. After you die he will be Master Adam. I think this is what you wish, is it not?"

"I suppose it is, One-O."

Meg opened the terrace door and ran to him through the garden path, her long black hair flying out behind her and shining in the sunlight. "I couldn't sleep and I heard your voice. You sounded angry."

"I have a right, don't I?"

She looked stricken. "Yes. Yes, you do."

"I'm sorry, Meg. I have to read something I don't want to read. I'm supposed to read it alone."

"I'll go back in the house and make afternoon tea. Mother says you used to like it when you were here."

"I'd love some. Weak tea, darling."

Meg went back without kissing him, for the first time since they arrived on Earth. He'd noticed that even a separation of a few minutes seemed to compel her to kiss him and murmur she loved him, as if she didn't want him to die without the last words being those of love. Yet this time she hadn't done it. It was robot Adam's fault.

The hand holding the letter trembled with rage, but a leaf from the apple tree drifted down upon it and he looked up through the branches to the blue sky of Earth, cleaner and bluer than it had been for long centuries.

"Listen!" said One-O.

At last he heard it, and then he saw them. A great V of

225

geese were honking overhead, passing to the south. All time was passing. He opened the letter.

"Dear Adam,

"Please don't try to answer this. If you have anything you want me to know that you haven't already told me, tell One-O, who will let me know it when you are safely dead.

"I use the word 'safely' not because I feel safe, but because you will have achieved the safety of death where nothing more can happen to anyone. When you woke me for that interview, I couldn't bring myself to tell you that I felt slightly resentful at having to go on coping with the universe in a body not my own.

"Yet I don't want yours, the body that betrayed me. You were right. The person I am now has never been as sick as you seemed to be. I choose to live as a robot rather than die as a human, but is that because my thoughts and feelings are no longer completely human? I will never know.

"After One-O wheeled you out, I thought about deactivating myself so that Adam Durant's life would only be the one you lived, the one you will end. Then, aside from my—our—eternal wish to please Seven, I decided that my suicide would be a betrayal of you. The things you said made me more conscious than ever of my failure to accomplish anything of worth, of my stupidity in going to Far to find Jonwon, an act that killed me biologically and has sent Jonwon away again, perhaps forever.

"Jonwon is not your responsibility now. Someday I'll have to do something about him. He needs help, but I don't know what kind. And then there's the blasted mystery of Far, and what intelligent aliens were observing it, and . . . but I am the Adam who's stuck with the problems.

"Go ahead and laugh at me, Adam. I'm yourself, and it's always worth while laughing at oneself, even a synthetic

226

duplicate who's scared of the responsibility to do better. But please be assured that I will try.

"I hope it won't hurt you if I tell you that I wanted to cry when I saw how the disease has ravaged your body, and then I was egotistically angry because I am deprived of the biological release of crying. Somehow I had expected that if I saw you before you died, you would seem more myself than any holoimage, but—don't be shocked—you were a total stranger. Perhaps it is good for you to know this because I suspect that I seemed that way to you. You are Adam Durant, and a stranger. So am I. The stranger dies, and another goes on. It's a lonely business, isn't it?

"Seven will put me back into stasis now. I wish you a death that isn't too difficult, whatever the hell that means. I promise to continue your life for you the best I can. Fellow stranger, please know that I love you."

"He's me! Really me! I'm not going to die! One-O, when you get back to Centauria, tell him I approve of him." Adam put the letter in the pocket of his tunic. "Now go get Meg."

She brought the tea, with his favorite cookies, and while they ate he felt a secret glee because he knew he could go on loving her even after the useless biological Adam died.

Finally he said, "The day is so beautiful, and tomorrow it may rain, taking the rest of the leaves off the trees. Let's visit my father's grave."

In the woods gold tapers seemed alight among the dark green of the hemlocks and sometimes a maple flamed red and orange in a clearing. There were purple asters growing around Jonathan Durant's grave. Adam held Meg's hand for a while, and then he sighed with contentment.

"Kiss me once more, Meg, and then leave me here."

"Not now! It's too soon!"

"Now. I'm happy. I want to die while I'm happy."

She fell to her knees beside the medichair and began

227

sobbing wildly. "Maybe at the last minute they'll find a cure! You must stay alive until then, and you must not leave me!"

"I'm waiting for you in Centauria."

"No! I'm sorry to upset you, but I'm afraid. I didn't think I'd mind having you be a robot, especially since I always wanted to be one myself, but he'll never be like you. Never."

She rose and kissed him passionately, then nuzzled her face into his neck, mumbling words he could barely make out. "He won't have your flesh or your warmth or the delicious smell of your skin, even now when you're sick it's still there, and I can't do without it, I love you so much. Stay with me."

He tried to push her away but she clung to him like a frightened child. "Meg, let go. You must let me go."

"No, you're going to live. I want you to live. Don't leave me. I want you, not a robot." She kissed him again, licked his lips and cheeks, pressed her face against his.

For a moment he felt a surge of strength, and even a partial erection. Her warmth seemed to be increasing his; her vitality flooding him with new life.

"Meg, my darling." He put his hands on her breasts and kissed her lips with the fire that burned in him, but as he did so, the strength ebbed from his body, the cold seeping back.

"That's our last kiss, Meg. Please go now. I must do this thing, while I still can. Don't let me get to a state of helplessness neither of us could stand. Let me go. That will be your last gift to me."

Finally she drew back, trembling. "You were going to have a painless injection. Later, much later."

"I've changed my mind. I'm happy and contented with my life right now, in this beautiful place, in love with my beautiful wife. I'm going to turn off the chair."

"Adam! You can't! It might be painful. I won't go!"

"It will be a natural death." He managed to grin. "And right now I feel very much a part of good old nature. Please go, Meg. The other Adam needs you. Don't do this to him."

228

She didn't leave, but stayed beside his chair, crying. He pulled out the letter and thrust it into her hands. "Don't cry anymore, Meg. Read this when you get back in the house. I think you'll realize that, in Centauria, I'm still alive." She looked at the handwriting and then up at him, startled. "Meg, thank you for being my love, and if you still love me, let me do what I must." He managed to lean over and kiss the silken top of her head.

"Adam, will you—will he—still love me?"

"I will always love you."

Then she was gone, running through the trees as if she could not say it back to him this time.

For a moment he felt so bereft that he wanted to call to her, but he heard One-O step closer to the chair, and then there was only the soft noise of wind in the trees, and the high warbling twitter of the chickadees. He settled back in the chair. Meg was now the other Adam's problem. He hoped they would love one another, but he could do nothing about it.

"One-O, I feel such a deep contentment. I once read that the present moment is eternity and contains all the mystery of the universe. I've never understood it. I still don't, but I have a feeling about it that makes everything seem good. I don't suppose that's very clear, is it?"

"No, Master Adam."

"Are you interested in mysteries, One-O?"

There was rather a long moment of silence until the robot answered. "I am interested. I do not have the capacity to solve mysteries, but I can help those who do."

"Go on helping. Remember that, One-O."

"I will, Master Adam."

"Now please walk away, back into the trees where you can still see me but I can't see you. I'm going to turn off this chair now."

The robot didn't move.

"I gave you an order, One-O. Obey it."

229

"Seven guessed you would die this way, but I think you should receive a drug to make you unconscious first."

"What did Seven tell you to do if I chose this way?"

"To let you do it, Master Adam."

"My friend One-O, it was you who reminded me that I always have a choice, even about suffering. This is what I choose."

"I will obey, Master Adam. Will you shake hands—for good-bye?" One-O held out his hand.

Astonished, Adam shook hands and watched One-O walk into the woods, circling so that he would be out of sight when Adam turned around in his chair. Relaxing again, Adam savored the smell of the woods, the murmur of the wind in the hemlocks, the birdsong, and above all, the warmth of sunlight.

But shadows were growing longer. Planet Earth continued to spin and soon the garden, the particular place on one particular continent that contained Adam Durant, would be out of the sunlight.

Darkness was coming, but right now . . .

Adam smiled to himself and then cleared his throat so that he could speak out loud. He wanted One-O to hear.

"Everything changes, yet this changing moment is eternity."

He turned off the chair and waited, letting go of life easily.

PART • V
ROBOT

CHAPTER • 35

Two weeks later One-O clumped out of the cottage, through the garden, and into the clearing in the woods beyond. He came to a halt in front of Meg and bowed stiffly.

"Why the dutiful servant routine, One-O?"

"I am a servant and dutiful but I may have exceeded my duty. I have sent for your mother. She and her family are due to arrive at any moment—"

"I want peace and quiet!" Meg's too-thin body jerked upright in the folding chair beside Adam's grave. "I want to be left alone!"

"Seven called me on hycom. He says you should return home to Centauria."

"This is as much my home as Centauria. More, in fact. My husband is buried here."

"Master Adam is still in stasis, awaiting your return. You should release your thoughts from his biological self."

"Go away, One-O." Meg began to cry. "Adam is here."

"The biological Adam's molecules, as well as those of his father and his ancestors, have gone back into the ocean of existence. They are free."

Meg stood up and stared at One-O. "Where'd you get that?"

The robot started to speak and then stopped. His hands moved out, palms upward, in the human gesture of supplication. "I cannot explain how I think such thoughts. My brain seems to be slightly different since I went to Far. I have thoughts that seem right to me although I do not always understand them completely. I have also read every book in Master Adam's library, and there is one sentence that might help you."

"Out with it, One-O."

233

"Long ago a poet gave a farewell to another poet, who had just died. He said 'Good-bye—back to the universe, my friend, and thanks.'" The corners of One-O's mouth lifted in the faint smile he could achieve with effort. "Is it right?"

"Quite right."

"I hear the arrival of your family. Shall I tell them you are here?"

"Yes. Thank you, One-O."

As the robot marched stolidly away, Meg looked down at Adam's grave. She put her fingers to her lips and blew him a kiss. "Thanks," she whispered.

Then she heard Rusty galloping toward her. His fiery hair was redder than the maples as he skidded to a stop in front of her. "Can I go with you to Centauria, to wake up Adam? I miss him alot, and I want him back in whatever form that's possible. Don't you?"

"Yes," said Meg.

Adam paced up and down Seven's lab. "This blasted heal-itself brain certainly has emotive circuits, or whatever you and Matt think you put in it."

"Your father, Jon, and Matt created the basic design," said Seven. "I'm proof of that. I merely improved on it."

"There's too damn much capacity for emotion! Now I know why Jonwon was so angry about having this kind of brain, and why he made one for his robots that reduced their capacity for feeling emotions."

"But from what you tell me, Jonwon's robots were less emotional at the expense of individual self-awareness. They were nothing more than mobile parts of a radio-linked computer."

"I suppose so, but it seems abnormal to be emotionally upset without bodily signs of anxiety. I keep thinking my heart must be pounding and then I remember that I don't have one. I wish Meg hadn't told you to take me out of stasis

234

before she arrived. I'm scared stiff—hah! An idiotic human remark unsuitable to robots who are stiff anyway . . ."

"Adam, sit down. The language is full of words that don't fit your present condition, but it soon won't matter. When a blind human says that he sees what someone means, people may feel embarrassed but the blind man doesn't. You have been awake all of two hours, and you're obviously the Adam Durant I helped raise. Stop worrying."

"I've looked in a mirror, Seven. I don't look myself to me. While this body was being made I'd wonder if I'd feel it was a trap. It is, and I can't escape."

"My grandmother—I mean Jon's grandmother—used to say that one shouldn't dwell on bad thoughts because they might come true if you let them. Instead of feeling trapped, how about trying to accept that the functioning of your brain has been freed from the vicissitudes of biological existence. Think of this body as a suit of armor protecting you."

"I don't want to be like Hank, fixated on being a robot, hiding inside his safe robot body."

Seven's laughter reverberated in the room, as if his emotions had upped the volume. "My dear son, you have absolutely no chance of being anything but a very human MT, as your present anxiety about meeting your wife should tell you. Perhaps it would help if you'd remember that she's the one who needs you. Don't get smug about how safe you are in your new body, stronger, doing with less sleep, living longer than any human—"

"Seven!"

"I just wanted to show you what all mind transfers have to fight against. Start now. I'm glad I was a partially failed mind transfer, because my early days of being a robot were so horrible that it was remembering my human side that saved me from insanity. Your birth helped. You and Bess. I love your mother very much, Adam. Listen—can't you hear One-O's footsteps? He's never been light on his feet."

235

The door opened and Meg walked in, followed by Walt and Rusty and One-O. Walt and Rusty were enthusiastic and couldn't seem to stop talking, but after what Adam was sure were hours and hours, Seven led the boys out.

"Master Adam," said One-O firmly, "I believe that you two will want to talk alone." He shut the door behind him.

Meg sighed. "One-O is very persistent these days. Very bossy about what he thinks is the right thing. I might have stayed sunk in grief for much longer on Earth if he hadn't sent for Mother and Rusty, both of whom believed that I still had a husband. Mother was particularly impossible, telling me I'm too thin—"

"You are. You should take better care of yourself."

"Don't doctor me."

"I am a doctor. And your husband. Shut up and let me hold your skinny body in my arms."

Her eyes reddened, a tear rolled down one cheek, and she had to sniff back a leaking nose, but she seemed like the most precious jewel in the universe, every palpable rib of her. He stroked her hair and she leaned against him.

"Adam, I wanted him—you—in the flesh. I'm afraid."

"So am I. Look." He held up her hand, higher than her heart. The veins collapsed as the blood drained down in the pseudogravity of Centauria, the pale flesh less streaked with blue. His own hand remained exactly the same. "I'm fake, Meg. But this ingenious body you helped make for me is not so completely phony that I can't still feel human. Even now the feedback of touching your skin is—not exactly as it was, but so familiar, darling."

Meg's tears stopped and she nodded, suddenly a proud roboticist. "That's a damn good body of yours, Adam. Soon the humanness of your transferred brain patterns will take over and the sensations generated by your new body will feel like your old human ones."

236

She leaned toward him, pressing her lips on his. "How's that sensation?"

He was intensely surprised. "It was pleasurable! You witch! You've put magic into this body!"

After six months of what he couldn't help thinking of as connubial bliss, he decided to discuss sex with Seven.

"I know I'm making a better than average adjustment to mind transfer, but still it's the primitive things that bother me, like not being able to smell anything, especially Meg's body. I worried a lot about my own body not smelling like the old one, but she insists that she's grown to like the faint odor of my synthoskin."

Seven nodded. He looked as if he were trying not to smile.

"Meg says she's having good orgasms and I can certainly feel the contractions of her vagina so I know that's true." He paused. "And my emotional identification with her orgasm is more than that, as you said. I'm not just having memories of my biological body's pleasure. I'm having my own, too."

A particularly virile prominence arched up from the surface of Alpha Centauri A in Seven's picture. They both stared at it and began to laugh.

"An erotic universe, but all in the eye of the beholder," said Seven. Then he drummed his robot fingers on his desk. "Unless there's something innately sexual about the particle field of the universe and its child, organized matter."

"We'd better keep that to ourselves," said Adam. "Until we find Jonwon. I'd like to tell him, see if I can help him accept life, or at least laugh at it. I wonder where he is—out there somewhere, alone inside his skull like the rest of us, but still angry about it."

"He shouldn't have been the only one," said Seven, "but we might as well stop feeling guilty about him, you and I. Human parents have to stop worrying about the way their children turn out. There are too many factors producing the end

237

result, including what the children decide to do with what the parents did to them. If you follow me."

"I'll always follow you, Seven. You're the wisest man I know."

Seven shook his head. "No, I'm not. What little wisdom I have was won the hard way, by learning from what happens."

Adam held his hands out, those perfect replicas of human hands. He put the first two fingers of his left hand into the slight groove along the inner edge of his right wrist. There was no pulse. There never would be.

"Learning from what happens." Adam said it as softly as he could. He would never be able to whisper again.

"It's the only permanently useful thing I can teach you, Adam. I'm afraid I failed with Jonwon."

Adam heard the anger in Seven's voice and knew that neither of them would ever stop worrying about Jonwon or wondering what had happened to him and if there was anything anyone could do about it.

CHAPTER • 36

"Why should Walt go to college on Earth when Centauri U. is excellent? Just because you went to Harvard is no excuse for encouraging our son to leave home."

"Meg! You know I haven't encouraged him. It's his idea. He's sixteen and wants to live on Earth for a while. Why not?"

Meg's face had more lines than most women had in their mid-forties, but she was still beautiful to Adam, and he was grateful that since his transfer she had seemed to enjoy domesticity and Walt more than she had before. Now her only child was grown up and she would not be consoled.

"Don't you understand, Adam? Once Walt is gone I'll have to face the fact that I'm a failure as a roboticist."

"You and Seven have made Tully Robotics so successful that none of us has to worry about money."

"Hack work, refining refinements. Nothing creative, nothing original. I wanted Walt to join the company."

"He didn't inherit your brains, darling, only mine. He knows there's no place for him in Tully Robotics. Fortunately he likes Paul Hirson and wants to work with him and Rusty in biological research. Maybe he'll go to med school and maybe he won't. Let him find out. Paul and Rusty and Dinah will take good care of him."

"I notice you put my mother last on the list," said Meg peevishly, and then burst into laughter. "Correctly."

He took her in his arms. It was late at night and the house was so quiet you could hear an owl hooting somewhere in Wildpark, over the faint background hum of Centauria's machinery. "Meg darling, I know you've been unhappy about

239

your work lately. Seven likes the executive end of the business so let him run it. You concentrate on creativity."

As she snuggled against him, the same old thought came back. He had no heart beat, the link of sound between mother and child, or between lovers who thrill to the aliveness of the other's body. As he felt and heard her heart, the usual terror struck him. The organic body was fragile, and the heart only a simple muscular pump rhythmically contracting as if providing bass notes for the temporary music of life.

Music. All the MTs loved it, even craved it. They drowned their troubles in it. Jonwon had. If only Meg . . .

"Adam, you're not listening. Now I must find something important to do if motherhood is to be a long-distance and only occasional business."

She was going to let Walt go. Adam hugged her. "You could help Lee Teleg write up her work with MTs, Meg. She wants to show that there's no way a biological human can evolve without giving up the relatively unspecialized human body that permits our brains to exercise so many talents. Mind transfer is the logical step in human evolution."

"We're too damn specialized for thinking," said Meg morosely. "And alot of the MTs concentrate on it too much."

"Not me, love. And you can't even get a diehard bioeffer to claim that MT thinking isn't human thinking. MTs just have the advantage of being able to do it more hours of the day."

"I believe I'd think better, not just more—as an MT."

"You're too young, and in perfect health."

"You'll probably say the same thing when I'm one hundred and fifty with most of my cerebral neurons limping."

The truth was that they both knew she was old before her time, burning herself out and accomplishing little that meant anything to her. Adam felt she still longed for the kind of triumph she'd had with the invention of hyperdrive. With Jonwon. She had not mentioned him for years.

240

As if she'd read Adam's mind, Meg said the name. "Jonwon, blast him, is probably exercising his brain in some fantastic enterprise. I wish I could break the new transporter code he used to get to his ship the last time. One-O says it's not the same one you and he used. That's true, isn't it?"

"Yes, Meg." And it was true, so that no one could go to Jonwon's ship. But anyone could go to Far—if Adam Durant gave them the coordinates, the one secret he'd kept from Meg. As a dying biological, he hadn't been able to remember them, but as a robot he could recapture anything he'd once learned. He hoped no one would think of that.

The semiannual hycom meeting of MTs was boring, as usual, so Adam only glanced up occasionally to see what was going on in his screen. The group's president, Lee Teleg, seemed to be proposing that MTs think of a new name for themselves.

"I think all of us resent being called 'empty MT.' It's a name that's probably going to stick, but if we adopt a new name for ourselves it will give us a better identity, at least for our own self-esteem. Any suggestions?"

MTs throughout the human-occupied galaxy gave suggestions. "Second Human Society" seemed reasonable until someone pointed out that the initials made it sound like a sedative or a fascist organization with a lisp.

Nevertheless, everyone liked the idea of "second human."

"It's not as demeaning as 'empty,' " said an MT from one of the new planets. "I suppose it still means we're 'seconds' in the sense of not as good as the originals, but it's also literally true, since we are the second lives of humans. Both meanings should appease the biologicals."

"We've been calling our flesh and blood colleagues 'biologicals' for years," said an MT from Luna City, "but they'll probably always think of themselves as the only humans. We

241

are and always will be robots, the empties that were filled
with human brain patterns but are not human."

Much argument ensued, until some scholar suggested that
the name be latinized. "Latin is one of the ancestral lan-
guages of the Terran Basic that we all speak. How about
calling ourselves the Society of Homo Sapiens Secundus."

"The initials sound like what happens after a sedative has
been given to biologicals who snore," said Lee. "And the
name homo sapiens is male chauvinist."

Adam grinned. He liked Lee, who strove conscientiously
but not successfully to suppress her sense of humor when
she was running a meeting.

"Isn't there something Latin for people?" asked a Terran.

"Populus," said a Centauria teacher. "I think."

Nobody was sure, but everyone liked it, and the name
finally became Terrestris Populus Secundus, wildly applauded
and never used except in writing. The name MT continued
but MTs began to think of themselves as the Second People,
and little by little biologicals came to the idea that when they
died they would become seconds, not merely empties.

It was appropriate, thought Adam, after looking up the word
'second' in the dictionary. It meant "next after the first in
order, time, place, rank, and importance; derivative and not
original; subordinate, inferior." That would please those who
were still biological.

But there was another definition of second. It meant "someone who acts as assistant, who follows to aid another." Very
like the laws of robotics.

And are we not robots? he thought, going back to his work
as a physician with renewed optimism.

CHAPTER • 37

By the time Walt had been in Harvard for half a year, Meg was seriously depressed. She came out of it slightly when the twins arrived with a large music synthesizer-recorder, and announced that they expected Meg to improve it for them.

For once Adam was pleased by the turmoil any visit from the twins caused in the relative placidity of Centaurian life. The twins had never been placid, and while each had been briefly married, their only real interest was music.

Amy's still-urchin face beamed after Meg brought the revised synthesizer back to them. "Goody. I'm set to record music on New Garden, that planet with the primitive culture the Feds have made a colony. The natives drum and sing, except that they haven't actually got mouths—"

Agnes was no longer the silent twin. She tended to interrupt constantly. "Ever since Adam told us about that noisy ocean on Far, I've wanted to record the sounds. Can't you get back there, Adam?"

The lie came easily now. "Only Jonwon knows the coordinates. Jonwon's transporter here sent One-O and me to Jonwon's ship, not to Far. And Jonwon changed that code."

Meg stared at him. "When you wiped out knowledge about Far from the computer in Jonwon's ship, did you see the hyperdrive coordinates? Or the code for the transporter on Far itself? I suppose you just let the computer handle it."

"Yes, of course I did," said Adam, for the umpteenth time.

Agnes was chewing her lower lip, a sign of deep thought that would probably get someone into trouble. "Robots, and that includes MTs, are supposed to have better memories than humans. Adam, don't you have a good memory now?"

"Fortunately the heal-itself brain was modified so that along

243

with the capacity to sleep, there's only selective awareness of what's in the memory banks. Otherwise we'd all go crazy, unable to concentrate on what is because we were flooded with what was."

"Nicely put, Adam," said Meg. Sarcastically?

Agnes smoothed down her hair, still springing up in unruly waves. "Why can't you play with our music synthesizer until you hear sounds that resemble those you heard on Far?"

Meg scowled. "Adam remembers perfectly only what's happened to him since he transferred, not what happened when he was still biological, and very sick too."

Adam was glad his facial expression of emotion could be easily controlled now. Meg's explanations would pass, but Adam knew that if the twins insisted, he could recapture the music of Far as perfectly as he remembered the coordinates of Far.

The trouble was that he wanted to play with the synthesizer. He wanted to recapture those sounds. "Maybe I can approximate the sounds of Far as I last heard them. But first I think I'll take a solitary walk. Maybe the memories will be clearer."

It was night, and the great arching world of Centauria was above him, the faint shimmery glow from the central bubbles like a series of tiny artificial moons, not to be compared with Earth's full moon—but comparisons were stupid. Each thing is itself. Including the sound of Far.

MTs were allowed keys to the Wildpark fences, for they were in little danger from wild animals, so Adam opened the gate of the inner fence and walked up the slope of Starboard mountain, seeing in the dark better than any human.

He stopped. A cougar sat in the middle of the path ahead, watching him as her two cubs played with her tail. Adam didn't move. His scent would puzzle, not frighten her.

One of the cubs bounded toward Adam, who slowly held

244

out his hand to be sniffed. The cub licked it, sneezed, and ran back to her mother, whose tail was now twitching.

"It's okay, girl," said Adam softly. "No harm done."

The cougar growled in her throat, batted the errant cub with her right paw, and stalked off through the woods, toward the highest levels of the mountain.

In the silence and loneliness of Wildpark, Adam let the totality of Far come back. It was as if he were dreaming, yet not dreaming. At first he was almost overwhelmed by the outpouring of visual images, sounds, and even smells his human mind remembered even if his robot body could not experience them again. The smell of the organic scum, like a salad. The changes of color and sound. The oneness . . .

Oneness? It must be this intense feeling that he had recaptured all of Far as he had known it. Especially all the sound that he had pretended was music.

He ran home to play with the twins' synthesizer. It took a couple of days until he thought he had the sound of Far duplicated as well as he could. He called in the family and set the machine to playing it.

It played, and played, and played.

"Enough," said Agnes. "You say it doesn't have the same damaging vibrations it had at the beginning of change in the scum, but it still gives me chills. Turn it off."

The machine wouldn't turn off. Seven and Meg tinkered judiciously with it while the twins moaned about not hurting their precious synthesizer, and the noise continued. It wouldn't even transfer to the ear phones, so the house was filled with the sound of Far.

"Maybe it will wind down soon," said Amy. "I'm hungry."

The humans said lunch was terrible, apparently because the kitchen computer was adversely affected by the noise, and Bess announced she was going back to work and hoped the machine would be stopped before she returned.

Seven peered into the innards of the synthesizer once more

245

and shook his finger at Meg. "You've made this machine more intelligent than any music synthesizer has a right to be. I think the damn thing is simply trying to finish the piece."

"But it's not a piece of music," said Adam. "It's just sound. I pretended it was music. It ought to be able to stop at any time."

"It won't stop if the machine thinks it's music," said Amy. "It'll continue until the piece is finished."

"Correct," said Agnes. "The synthesizer is an expert in musical composition, and should know when a piece of music comes to a logical end. Adam, you must have wrecked something in the synthesizer when you were playing it. The only thing to do is pull the plug."

"It doesn't have a plug now," said Meg. "I made the machine run on robot power packs. If it won't obey orders and stop playing a particular piecce, it will have to be destroyed."

"Make it obey, Meg," said Seven. He sounded frightened.

Meg touched the voice button of the machine. "Synthesizer, why can't you stop playing that sound?"

"Not completed. Completion necessary."

"Why?"

"Evolving sound sequence. Evolving toward completion."

"When?"

"In exact numbers?"

"In rough estimate."

"One hundred fifty billion years."

No one spoke for several minutes, until Amy giggled. "Can we wait that long?"

"Meg," Agnes said crossly, "have you messed up this machine so it's lying to us?"

"Certainly not. Anyway, machines don't lie. They make mistakes. The whole thing may be an error from Adam's imagination. After all, he was sick at the time."

Adam then made a serious mistake of his own. He argued. "I'm sure that what I put into the machine is no error. That's

246

the sound of Far as I last heard it, and if I work hard at dredging up the memories, I can bring back everything that's ever happened to me, perfectly. Now I'm damn sorry I tried to remember what I put into the synthesizer. I feel like the sorcerer's apprentice."

"Luckily the sound doesn't seem to be as dangerous to robots as it first was on Far," said Seven, "although I have the nearest thing to a headache I've experienced since I was activated."

"I have one too, now that you mention it," said Adam. "And what's the matter with One-O!"

The robot, as usual almost unnoticed in the background of family life, was swaying with his eyes shut.

"Come out of it, One-O!" shouted Adam. "We're home!"

One-O opened his eyes. "Master Adam, for a moment I thought I was back on Far. Please turn off the sound."

"Before we destroy the machine, let me try," said Seven. "Synthesizer, don't you have rudimentary cognitive circuits?"

"Yes."

"Then think about what I'm going to tell you. One hundred fifty billion years is the current rough estimate of the time left to the universe. After it finishes expanding, it will collapse and everything living in it will die. You are playing alien sound, call it music, that will last longer than the lifetimes of any human or robot. Is this not so?"

"Yes. Until the end of all things, change will be unceasing. Evolving sound sequence ends with end of change."

Meg's hands tightened into fists. "Maybe the sound made Jonwon hate Far so much that he wanted to prevent anyone from going there. If the sound represents unceasing change that ends only with the end of the universe, then Jonwon would hate it. He always wanted to avoid change and uncertainty and the finality of death."

"I wish I hadn't recaptured the sound," said Adam.

247

"But you did," said Meg, with a mysteriously triumphant smile that frightened Adam.

Seven spoke. "Synthesizer, have your cognitive circuits been programmed with the laws of robotics?"

"Yes. In the factory."

"Then consider this, synthesizer. The music—I will call it that—which you have decided to play until it ends consists of sounds that are detrimental to the rest of us. We don't like them. They make us feel terrible. We will feel worse the longer they continue. We may even die or deactivate. All because you, synthesizer, would not stop making those sounds. Think again. Must you continue?"

"The sounds . . . the music . . . music . . . music . . . is . . . is . . ." The voice of the synthesizer rasped and squeaked. " . . . linked to the universe . . . must end . . . with universe . . ."

"You are violating the laws of robotics," said Seven. "You injure us."

"The laws of robotics say you must do no harm," said Meg. "That law is primary."

"Yes," said the synthesizer, and turned itself off.

When Meg turned it back on, it had no memory of Far's sound, but otherwise functioned normally.

"It's wiped off that circuit," said Seven.

"Well, it would never be a great concert piece," said Amy.

After the twins left Centauria, Meg seemed absorbed in her lab, but at night she wanted Adam in bed with her until she fell asleep, and before sleep she wanted passionate love that would have worn out a biological husband.

Adam's enjoyment of it was diminished by a persistent dread of what might be going on inside Meg's head.

CHAPTER • 38

To stop the dread, Adam plunged into work, but it didn't help much. One day in a conference with Lee Teleg about a psychiatric case, he felt a sharp tap on his hand.

"Sorry, Adam. You weren't listening. What's the matter?"

"Just worrying—my substitute for creativity, I guess."

"Feel like talking about the worry?"

"No, doctor." He quickly reviewed what his brain had heard of what Lee had been saying. "If this Terran was always a borderline psychotic before transfer, I think he'd better go home to Earth as soon as possible, especially since he seems to be paranoid about Centaurians."

"That's what I think, too," said Lee. "The last patient is the one who imagines that her robot body is being eaten by the cancer that killed her organic self. She's alot better."

"Good. One less thing to worry about."

"Adam, I'm worried about you."

He looked at her, marveling that her brown robot eyes were so human that they seemed ready for tears on his behalf. He was about to thank her for her concern when Bess called on intercom. It was his mother's day off and she was at home.

"I don't want to worry you, Adam, but Meg left work this morning and no one can find her. She hasn't come home that I know of, but there's a sealed envelope addressed to you on your bed. The writing is Meg's."

"Meet me in Seven's office, with the envelope. Right now." He turned off the intercom. "That's my worry, Lee. It always has been."

* * *

"One small computer is missing from the lab," said One-O. "Meg took it," said Adam, reading her letter. "Listen.

"Dear Adam, and all the family,

"I must settle things one way or the other. I'm going to Far, and since I may become contaminated, I'll return to a Tully factory satellite's transporter and not endanger Centauria. I don't know if I'm looking for Jonwon or the fabulous work I imagine he's doing, or just curious about Far's music. If I return hopelessly ill, please transfer me at once.

"I feel that all my life I've been saying good-bye every day to those I care about. If this is the last good-bye, and I can't return, then I suppose you will take one of my old brain recordings and make a mind transfer robot out of it. I can't stop you, but I wish you won't. If you do, you must show her this letter, because I suspect that the next Meg Tully Durant will want to do exactly what I am about to do.

"I'm sorry, Adam. I love you and the family but I must do this before you find the transporter code and stop me. I do so want a job! I can't get rid of the belief that Jonwon has one for me. And I've waited long enough to become a robot.

"All my love, Meg."

Adam put the letter down, opened the back door of Seven's office, and went to Jonwon's transporter. "It's been used."

"And she set the code to self-erase," said Seven. "Why does she think we'll find the code when I've been trying many combinations for years without any luck?"

"Because Meg knows I know them," said Adam.

"But Adam," said Bess, "Jonwon changed the code."

"He changed the code for his ship, because One-O had it. Meg didn't use any code for his ship. She used the one for the transporter in Jonwon's building. Jonwon probably didn't change that because he didn't know I knew it."

"Master Adam," said One-O slowly, "several weeks ago Meg

250

asked me if I had ever used the transporter in Far's building. I said I had not, because Jonwon's robots held me captive in the ship. I did not tell her that you and Jonwon used the transporter coordinates to Far itself when you left the ship. I did not think you knew them."

"It took a long time for me to realize that they were in my memory," said Adam, "and that my robot brain would be able to find them. Meg must have used the first brain recording I made after returning from Far. She put it in a computer—"

"This one," said One-O, lifting it from the wastebasket. "If it was asked to search for the coordinates in the brain recording, it did so, but finally burned out."

"Adam!" cried Bess. "You mustn't go there!"

Carrying his medical bag, Adam was already on the transporter, setting the controls. "I'm only a robot, Mother."

"I'm suiting up to come along," said Bess. "I'm her doctor and I'm more resistant to the sound of Far than you MTs."

"Absolutely not. No one goes but me."

"Master Adam—"

"No, One-O. Not even you."

Seven pointed to the wall of his office. "I didn't notice before, but one of the suits is missing. Meg must be wearing it. Wait, Adam. She may not get infected, and biologicals are safer on Far now than any robot. Don't go yet."

"I'm going. Then you must all leave this room and seal it, using only the self-contained ventilation system. I may have to bring her back here in an emergency, and Centauria has to be protected from the spores. Once here, we can clean the room if the spores don't die away from Far as they did before."

Adam touched the switch.

She was lying naked on the roof, her eyes closed. Nearby was a crumpled tunic beside an empty space suit. Around her wet hair were the standard bands for brain recording, and a recorder box was at her side. When Adam knelt beside her,

251

he saw that her skin was pale gold and damp, with a light dusting of golden powder on it. She was still breathing.

Something was different about Far but he concentrated on Meg, afraid to wake her before the recording was finished. He listened to her heart, hearing the severe arrhythmia with horror. A bioscan of her body indicated massive infection and cell damage much greater than Adam's body had shown. It took him months to die. It might take Meg . . . hours? Minutes?

There was no cure for that kind of cell damage. In spite of all the studies done on the biological Adam, nothing had been accomplished. Even if he interrupted the recording to take her home at once, nothing could be done.

Recording continued, but Meg's eyes opened. "Hello, Adam. You always were terribly stubborn, but I'm glad you didn't obey me. I'm glad you're here. Far is a lonely place, especially when one is dying. You deduced how I found the way to get here?"

"Yes, Meg. Should you be talking before the recording finishes?"

"I want to. I want the robot Meg to know everything I know, including this last conversation. Including the act of dying. The recorder is set to run until I'm thoroughly dead. I suppose I thought all along that you'd come here and find my body, and take the recording back." She clutched suddenly at his arm. "Adam! I forgot! Is it safe for you here? Are you feeling in danger of deactivation?"

"No. The planet has changed. I can hear the sound, but it's muted and doesn't even give me a headache the way the synthesizer did."

She seemed radiant with delight. "Music! It's not muted for me, not now that I'm infected. I couldn't hear it at all well from the space suit, not even with the receiver turned way up, so finally I decided what the hell, and took off the suit. Then I still felt alien to Far, unable to find out what it meant,

252

so I undressed and jumped into the ocean. It was a glorious swim through that translucent, warm stuff out there, and when I felt distinctly odd, I climbed back to the roof."

"Oh, Meg!"

"Don't, Adam. Don't scold. After the infection set in I heard the sound in every cell of my body, and I'm in love with the music of Far. Music that will never end until time does."

"The Feds will clean off Far—"

"No! No! Don't let them! Don't ever tell them how to get here!"

"Darling, I'll never let them destroy Far's indigenous life, even if it kills humans. Kills—my only love." He held her hand, kissing the golden fingers.

"All along, you've wanted to protect Far. I never understood, until now. Oh, Adam, the sound is so wonderful. Don't take me back to Centauria. Let me finish absorbing it. After all, a biological can die only once."

"Meg, I love you."

"Forgive me?"

"Yes, yes. Meg, did you find any meaning in the sound?" It wasn't the question he wanted to ask. Had she found Jonwon?

"No, there's no meaning. Yet the music means something to those who hear it. Does that make sense?"

"I don't know."

"I wonder if Jonwon knows."

"Then you've found him?"

"No. I don't know. After the infection started and I felt terribly sick, for a moment I thought I heard his voice, but I was wrong. Probably hallucinating. I was burning up with fever for a while. But after I hooked myself up to the recorder I kept trying to believe that he's here, up there with the others."

"Up . . . where?"

"Adam! Look around!"

He hadn't looked at anything but Meg. Now, as she pointed,

253

he saw great metal arches over the ocean, each swooping down, apparently anchored in the ocean bed. As far as he could see, the ocean was festooned with these enormous structures, and moored on the arches were thousands of ships in every possible color and shape.

Meg's voice was weaker. "I've also seen glimpses of metal reflecting the sunlight, high up as if there are other ships in orbit around Far, or maybe huge orbital satellites as big as Centauria. Far must have become an interplanetary meeting place. Or is it intergalactic? After I'm a robot, let's find out where they come from."

Tremors shook her body and she coughed. "Is the sun going behind a cloud, Adam? I can't see much for the darkness, and there are funny spangly spots in my vision. The music is so terribly loud now that I'm a little frightened. . . ."

He bowed his head over her, kissing her forehead. He thought she'd gone, but she seemed to rouse herself, grasping his head and pulling him to her. She spoke in a whisper.

"I forgot—the alien artifact appeared out of nowhere soon after I climbed out of the ocean. It hovered over me for a few seconds and left. I guess I didn't interest it the way you did. Maybe you'll find it again some day."

"Maybe. You'll help me."

"Will I? Will I really live again? I'm frightened. I didn't think dying would scare me, but it does. Please help me let go."

"I will help."

Her eyelids closed. The next whisper was very soft. "It's so private, so different that I must turn off the recorder. Do it for me, Adam."

"It's off. You can let go now, Meg."

She sighed, her hand relaxing in his, her breathing so shallow it was hardly there. Then she opened her eyes once more. "Oh, Adam! Anybody can join! Hook up the recorder

254

again—I must not forget this. . . ." But she shuddered and went limp in his arms.

"It's too late, Adam. Tell my . . . other self not to worry about a job—Adam?"

"I'm here." He hooked up the recorder quickly and kissed her lips. "I love you, Meg."

She smiled one last time and then the brain death was so sudden that there was nothing for the recorder to find. He waited, hoping, but finally he kissed her again and the sensoskin of his lips registered the coldness of hers. Colder than any robot would be.

CHAPTER • 39

Meg had been careful. The brain recording unit itself was clean. Only the bands around her head were coated with the spores that dried after she climbed out of the water. She had apparently used something—perhaps the glove from the space suit—to touch the *on* switch. And downstairs the transporter had long ago dried out from the surge of seawater into the cracked building, and no spores remained on it.

Adam put the recording unit on the transporter plate and sent it to Centauria. There was no immediate need for any other message. They would know that Meg was dead.

He went back up to the roof and held her body while the music of Far flowed around him in endless permutations of sound. Sometimes he imagined it was a great chorus of voices that didn't use words, and sometimes it was just a noise that seemed to be mindlessly expressing the rhythms of an alien planet. The strange arches glittered in the light, but no ship came to inspect him; no alien voice asked what he was doing there holding his dead wife.

Without resentment, he thought about Jonwon. "I wish he were here. Our fate has always been linked with him."

Linked. Why is that such an important word? thought Adam. All Terran-originated life is one, each bit more like another than like any alien life. Yet is that golden ocean totally different, just because it kills us when we are flesh? The scum is primitive but alive. It vibrates and makes me think of music. Perhaps music is universal, and links everything.

"Meg, come back. I want you back, this body, this flesh. Yet there's a smile on your cold lips. You're happy, and I'm so alone now. . . ."

But her discontent had been separating Meg from Adam for

a long time. Far had only finished it. For the first time he admitted to himself that he was not a little in love with Lee Teleg. But his responsibility was to Meg. And to Jonwon.

Are you up there, Jonwon? thought Adam. Is one of those ships yours?

He was staring out at the arches of Far when he felt someone shaking him.

"Master Adam! You did not seem to hear when I spoke to you just now."

"Hello, One-O. Did Seven send you?"

"No. Seven is starting the mind transfer process for Meg, and told me to wait for him to finish. Then we were both going to go to Far—you left the coordinate code in the transporter and I could detect it—"

"And you couldn't wait."

"Seven said you were probably safe because you were able to put the unit on the transporter, but Seven has never felt the sound of Far. You are now a robot—"

"So you came to rescue me, at your own risk, One-O."

"I am dispensable. You and Seven are not."

"That's debatable, but now that you're here, do you detect any ill effects on your body or brain?"

"No, Master Adam. And you?"

"Far seems to have simmered down, at least for robots. It killed Meg."

"We knew. I am sorry, Master Adam. Perhaps you should take her back to Centauria now. Jonwon's room has been sealed off and a plastic decontamination bubble is around the transporter plate for our return. You—and she—will not contaminate Centauria."

"Fine, but there's no hurry, is there?"

"Seven and your mother are beginning to worry. You have been away for four hours now."

"It hasn't been four hours . . ." But Adam saw it was true. This part of Far had obviously turned further from its sun, for

257

the shadows cast by the arches were longer and Meg was much colder. Yet it hadn't seemed long at all. He had been immersed in the music of Far. And Meg had been in love with it. Adam stood up with the body still in his arms.

"Master Adam, what are those arches doing here?"

"I don't know, One-O. It's a mystery. I used to like mysteries."

"Perhaps you still do, Master Adam."

"If Adam Durant refuses to give us the way to go to Far, we cannot call him a traitor," said the Centaurian President to the Feds scowling back at him on hycom. "Dr. Durant offers to go back to Far as the emissary of all humans, to meet the intelligent aliens whose ships are now moored at the strange arches they have built on Far. Until he goes I suggest that we all think hard about this evidence that we are not the only intelligent, technologically advanced species in the universe."

"But when will this MT physician leave?" growled a Fed.

"When he is ready," said Cavister. "In the meantime, try to remember that Far is not even in our own galaxy, and stop worrying." He turned off the hycom and sat back. "That ought to blow their parochial minds," he said to himself.

Adam was not ready. He was waiting for Meg, and there were problems. For years it had been known that brain recordings made while the biological human was dying had a frequent bad result. The MT was often psychotic, and so was Meg. She stood all day in her hospital room staring at the wall, never speaking, although sometimes she lay on the bed that an MT used only because resting one's mind was easier in a posture familiar and necessary to the previous biological.

"We could try some of Meg's earlier recordings," said Lee.

"No," said Adam. "She wanted to know it all. And we can't deactivate this Meg in favor of another. If she deactivates spontaneously we'll do it, but not until then."

258

Lee didn't even mention the possibility of having two MT Megs. Recently they'd heard of some wealthy Terrans who had two MTs made of themselves. The two MTs became disturbed and eventually both deactivated spontaneously.

Meg had spoken at first. She said, "Music. All of them. I failed." Adam tried to tell her she hadn't failed, that before she died she was happy, but she didn't respond.

"I shouldn't have turned off the recorder—yet she asked me to. I felt the same when I was dying—a strong wish to be completely private, to own my death and deprive my MT of it. But at the last she had an insight she wanted her MT to know, and by the time I hooked up the recorder it was too late. Perhaps she won't respond because she blames me."

"No, Adam," said Lee. "If she were biological, we'd call her condition catatonia, and there would be ways we could treat it, but in an MT we just have to wait."

"I'm going to talk to her again," said Adam.

"It makes you unhappy and may harm her."

"Then I'll just sing. And tell her the truth."

After three hours he wondered if his attempt to sing Far's music had failed, yet one thing had happened. Meg's eyelids had closed. At first he thought she was deactivating, but she remained standing, and her hands straightened out. Her fists had always been clenched before.

"Meg, you don't have to answer, or give any response at all, but please listen to me. I'm telling you the exact truth. When you asked me to turn off the brain recorder you thought it was the end. It wasn't, not completely. You looked as if you'd discovered the solution to a problem. You said, 'Anybody can join,' and that I should tell your robot self not to worry about having a job. You were happy about whatever it was."

Slowly, the beautiful head of the robot turned toward him and the eyelids raised. She stared at him for a full fifteen minutes, and he was glad he was no longer biological because

259

he'd have been unable to hold what he hoped was a facial expression of pleasant calm.

"Have you told me this before?"

"Yes, Meg, many times, but I didn't try singing the music of Far first. I guess that made a difference."

"I don't belong in Centauria, Adam. I belong on Far. You can't understand because you didn't die there, and I did."

"I'm sorry, Meg."

"Don't be sorry. Have I been psychotic?"

"That was the official diagnosis."

"Yet I didn't deactivate. Did they try to—"

"No! And if it had been suggested, I wouldn't have let you be deactivated."

"Thank you, Adam." She looked down at her body, stretching out her arms to examine them, inspecting the fingers, touching her hair. "This is a very good body."

"Seven worked hard on it. And I made sure the face was perfect. Would you like to see yourself?"

"Yes." She gazed into the mirror and, to Adam's astonished relief, smiled. "I look young. I look like the beauty I always hoped I'd grow up to be and never did. Adam, please destroy all my other brain recordings. This is the only Meg I want to be, complete with as much knowledge of being on Far as I now have. When I was dying you put your arms around me. Did you hold me—afterward?"

"Yes, Meg."

"You must really love me."

"I've been saying so since I learned to talk."

"And I love you. We have been wonderful mates, and in a way we always will be. Do you mind my having to find Jonwon?"

"I know you have to do that," said Adam.

"I don't think of Jonwon as a lover, although he might be someday. He's someone on the same path I'm on, not paying attention to the fact that he's not alone. He needs me even if he doesn't know that either. Am I making myself slightly clear or am I still too crazy?"

"Remember how we used to read all the myths about heros who go on lonely journeys? Maybe Jonwon's one of them. And they usually need helpful companions now and then."

"Both of us?"

"If you want that, Meg."

They looked at each other solemnly and then she turned away. "Has Walt been to see me?"

"Yes. He's back at school now. Perhaps you could give him a hycom call before—"

"Sure," said Meg cheerfully. "It's a good thing our son has two terrific grandmothers, two marvelous grandfathers of no blood relation, and the best father a boy could have. I'm leaving out his two musical aunts, but I think they're an addition in anyone's repertoire of relatives."

She was Meg. The old Meg. Exultation filled Adam, until he saw that she was looking at him sadly.

"You'll have to leave me with Jonwon, if we find him," said Meg. "Your life is still here in Centauria, with your work and with Seven and Bess and, yes, Lee. I don't mind."

This time she took him in her arms and held him, knowing that he wanted to cry and could not.

CHAPTER • 40

Adam and Meg stood on the roof of Jonwon's building, looking up at the multitude of ships on the arches, as far as superior MT vision could see. The golden ocean was calm, and the ships might have been decorations, in all colors, placed to break up the sameness of the ocean scum and the identical parade of metal arches.

"They're certainly taking no notice of us," said Meg.

"Jonwon would, if his ship were up there. I can't believe he wouldn't have one of his scanners tuned to this building, in case anybody came."

"I don't see any small boats going back and forth between any of the larger ships. What on earth are they doing up there, just listening to Far?"

"I wish we were 'on Earth,' Meg. After my experience with the alien box thing I'm not too eager to meet its owners."

"Let's call your alien artifact something that will make it seem less eerie and unpleasant. How about 'Watcher'?"

"Okay. Are you sure you saw it? I thought it had gone for good."

"No, I know I saw it. I'm certain about that. Not so certain about feeling, hearing—whatever it was—Jonwon's presence. Maybe it was just that I hoped he'd be here."

Adam took her arm. "We'll find out. Do you think that if he came back to Far in his ship, he might have left it in orbit and gone back and forth to it using the transporter downstairs? The new code for his ship might be in it."

"And I thought I was supposed to be the genius!"

It took all of Meg's genius to decipher the new code for Jonwon's ship, but finally she said, "I think I have it. He's certainly been here, so we can hope that his ship is one of those up there."

"Not necessarily moored to an arch. He might be in orbit. He'd be cautious on Far, since it nearly deactivated his brain."

"Oh, Adam, let's go! If my curiosity isn't satisfied soon I think this lovely new brain of mine will go into an electronic tizzy."

Jonwon's ship was empty, and not in orbit. It was cradled in a mooring on an arch that was almost out of sight of his old building, the pathetic start of what he'd hoped would be his grand city on Far. Adam looked through the open airlock to the top surface of the arch, immensely bigger than he'd imagined. It must have been at least a kilometer across at the top, getting wider as it curved to plunge into the ocean.

He moved aside so Meg could look, too, and she said, "He's in trouble. The airlock open, the landing ramp down, and he didn't come back. But where did he go? I don't see any break in the surface of the arch."

"You wait here, Meg. I'll just step onto the surface and look closer."

"Not without me, chum."

Together, they went down the ramp and out onto the shiny surface that was surprisingly unslippery. They hadn't walked more than five steps on it when, ahead of them, a section of the arch bulged up and opened a door in itself.

"Will you walk into my parlor?" said Meg. "Adam, coming here was my idea. Please go back to the ship and be safe."

"No."

"Darling, be logical. If I don't return after a stated amount of time, you can go home to summon help."

"We should have brought One-O. He'd wait and do exactly what we'd told him to do. I think. It's hard to tell with One-O these days. Sometimes he seems to decide that he knows what is best for me, whether I think so or not."

"You send for him, and I'll—"

"No. I will wait here. You go back into the ship and leave a message in the computer. Tell whoever shows up that we've gone inside the arch, and when. If we've been gone a long time, they'll know to be careful."

"You don't trust me to wait here while you leave the message."

"That's right, love." He kissed her and she did as he wanted, coming back down the ramp with her arm outstretched to take his hand as they walked into the doorway on the arch.

The corridor seemed endless, and so narrow they had to walk close together, the light a dim shadow of gold on the synthoskin of their faces. Meg's hand clasped his tightly, and he treasured the sensation, wondering how much longer she would need him.

"The sound of Far's ocean scum seems much stronger up here," said Meg. "I feel a little strange, and then I don't want to walk anymore, just stand still and listen. Did Jonwon feel this way when he thought Far was deactivating him?"

"I don't think so. He was in genuine pain and very frightened. The noise was so different then. I know what you're experiencing, but it doesn't seem dangerous, and I don't think we'll even be paralyzed, the way One-O was. Perhaps the arch collects the sound and concentrates it in some way."

They walked farther, and gradually the walls of the corridor seemed to lighten, the illumination much brighter and the surface changing. Suddenly they arrived at a place where the walls had become transparent.

"A power station of some sort?" asked Meg. The room beyond was so enormous Adam could not see the other side, or any of the boundary walls except the one he was looking through. Round transparent structures floated in the space, connected to each other by shimmering wires.

"There must be thousands of those bubbles, even in this one arch," said Adam. "What's inside them?"

"Brains. Robot brains!"

"Meg—there—could that be Jonwon's?"

"No. I know superaide brains as well as you know that revolting hunk of grey protoplasm called the human brain. That only looks similar to a superaide brain. And there's another in the next bubble. I don't see any more of that type."

"They may be the brains of Jonwon's modified superaides that jumped into the ocean. Thanks to me, the three others wouldn't be usable. But to what use?"

"I don't know. If Jonwon put them here, after building the arches—but he couldn't do that without factories. We don't even know how long he's been back on Far. Did you see any signs of it having rained in that open airlock?"

"No, but that's no indication of the ship being here only a short time. It doesn't rain often on Far, and there's no dust if the waves don't spatter scum up here, and it's too high up for that. I think we should assume that someone else built the arches, perhaps rather quickly, and Jonwon found them here when he came back."

"Here's a door, Adam. Let's go inside and look at some of those other robot brains. I think they're all modifications, sometimes radical, of the superaide brain!"

But inside the cavernous area containing the bubbles, the sound of Far was horribly loud. It was hard to think and to hear each other talk. When Adam pulled Meg back out into the corridor, she was holding her head.

"I feel so odd. As if I can't move."

Adam picked her up, conscious that his own robot body was having problems. He ran down the corridor, thinking at first that he was heading back to the outside door until the floor began to slant.

"I'm mixed up, going the wrong way, got to go back . . ."

He stumbled and fell with Meg. They landed hard, but were not, of course, hurt. In fact, the jarring seemed to shake some sense back into both of them.

265

Meg clutched him. "The sound is filling our minds—makes it hard to think. Can we get back?"

"I don't know, but now that the floor's slanting, the sound has diminished somewhat. I think it's so loud in the corridor now because I stupidly forgot to shut the door. Doors in Centauria shut by themselves. I'm in favor of going on if you think you can stand it."

"Bravo, Adam. Let's sing. We won't let Far's damn music trap the likes of us."

Adam roared out "The Song of Seven," put to music years ago by Agnes and Amy. It had always been Walt's favorite.

"Widdershins!" yelled Meg, stumbling with him down the golden slope.

"Witchery-sweet!" yelled Adam. I can't believe this, he thought. I'm having an adventure, and it's fun, and I'm safe in this wonderful superaide body. . . . Then he remembered the robot brains. Just because they hadn't seen Jonwon's didn't mean his wasn't there. Nothing was known or safe.

The downward corridor ended in a level section—and another door. Adam opened it and immediately grabbed both sides of the doorway, preventing Meg from going on.

Holding onto him, she peered under his arm. "Like a pit to capture unwary animals," she said. "It almost got us."

The darkness of the shaft seemed to go endlessly downward. "This must be where the arch goes down to and under the ocean," said Adam. "Falling down it would destroy even our bodies, Meg."

"We don't have to fall—look, transportation arrives."

A sleekly streamlined antigrav liftcar floated up to them and opened its door. "Shall we?" asked Adam, bowing to her and motioning with a gallant flourish.

"Why not?" said Meg, stepping inside with her head up like a queen.

As the car moved noiselessly downward, Adam felt better.

"The farther we go, the softer the sound is. We must be under the ocean surface by now."

"Perhaps the noise made by the scum travels upward in air better than downward in water."

They had reached bottom, and there were four corridors radiating out, each so dimly lit that a biological human would have been almost blind. The antigrav car opened its door and seemed to be waiting for them to leave. As they stepped out, the door, unlike all the others on Far, shut behind them.

"Wait!" Adam tried to grab the door to open it again but the car lifted away from him. "Blast! Now we're stuck down here, unless we can get it to come back, but I don't see any switches on the wall for that."

"Then onward, mate. There's a different kind of noise coming down this middle corridor. Sounds like machinery. How about investigating it?"

This time the corridor was too narrow for both to walk together. "The aliens who built this are either small or they have small machines," said Meg, darting ahead of Adam. She was the same size as the biological Meg had been, still a green-eyed elf prancing into danger.

"Let me go first, Meg." He pounded after her, the corridor curved, and then he yelled. "Stop! That's Watcher!"

The silvery cube with pyramid top nearly filled the corridor from side to side. It moved so fast that Adam could not pull Meg back in time.

Metal tentacles shot out of the cube, grasping Meg.

"It's all right, darling," said Meg calmly. "I want to know everything. Let it do what it has to do."

Adam reached for her but the pyramid-cube drew back, and then it disappeared, with Meg.

Shouting her name, Adam ran back and forth, pounding on the corridor walls, but Watcher did not return.

There was no way to get back out. The antigrav car did not return to the bottom of the shaft, which was too steep for

267

even the most agile robot to climb its walls. The only way to go was forward, but Adam was reluctant to leave the spot where Meg and Watcher had disappeared.

Finally he walked along the corridor as it led away from the antigrav shaft. Soon there was a door off to the right, but it was locked. So was the next, to the left. And the next. And the next.

He could hear nothing behind any of the locked doors, and no one responded to his shouts. Desperately he walked on until the corridor ended in a fork where two others branched off. Which to take?

His thoughts revolved around his stupidity at letting Meg walk first into the unknown, at not realizing that Watcher was dangerous. He sat down on the floor in the semidarkness, cursing himself. There was no point in cursing Meg's foolhardiness when her bravery and curiosity had always attracted him. Besides, she was newly recovered from MT psychosis and not all that responsible.

"But I'm responsible. I've always felt responsible."

His voice seemed to echo in the corridor against the background sound of Far, distant but always there. "And inside I feel like a stupid little boy. Maybe I always have."

With the swift vividness that memories had for him in his robot incarnation, Adam remembered the first time he'd realized that he was responsible for, at least, himself. That the adults around him were not necessarily the perfect source of comfort, reassurance, and the solutions to all problems.

He was very small, holding a dead thrush he'd found in the garden. Bess explained death to him. Matt reminded him there were lots of birds. The nanny robots tried to distract him with food and games. He remained upset and went to see Seven.

"Seven, I feel bad. What can I do?"

"Have you buried the thrush?"

"Yes. Made me feel a little better but not much."

"Then do some work you can put your mind on, hard."

"Work?" Seven and Matt and Bess and the other adults worked. "Am I supposed to work?"

"Work is what everyone does, even children. Your job is to grow and learn. Are you learning?"

"Well, I'm starting school, and I read."

"How much do you work at thinking?"

"Oh, Seven, work isn't fun—"

"Yes it is. The best of all. Answer my question, Adam."

"But—thinking? Work at thinking?"

"It's one activity that intelligent beings do better than anything else, and they enjoy it, unless somebody stupid tells them it isn't fun. I suggest you try to develop the habit of thinking. When there's nothing else to do, or no activity that seems to help a problem, you can always think."

But first, thought Adam, listening to the vibrations of Far, an alien symphony with no meaning he could decipher, first I must quiet my mind.

He wished he could take a deep breath and let it out in the serene confidence that his autonomic nervous system would slowly readjust. He no longer had an autonomic nervous system, just a superaide brain full of jangling human thoughts and emotions . . . into which came two clear pictures. An ocean breaking in waves on a rocky point in New England. And the holov of Alpha Centauri A he'd watched so often in Seven's office.

Holding both pictures in his mind, he brought them together so the blazing star shone in the dark gray-blue of the Atlantic. As he held the image in his mind, he let the music of Far in, too. He stopped worrying and thought about what to do.

Find Meg and Jonwon, and then think about how to escape.

Adam kept his eyes shut and Jonwon's head with its crisp yellow curls and chiseled features appeared against Alpha

269

Centauri A in the Atlantic. Slowly, the sea and the star faded and only Jonwon remained.

"Okay. Jonwon first. He'll help."

Adam stood up and, without thinking about it, marched down the corridor branching off to the right.

CHAPTER • 41

As the dim corridor curved on in the strange building under the ocean of Far, Adam walked faster and faster, and finally began to run, stopping only to try each door he came to. All of them were locked.

He shouted for Jonwon, but heard no sound except the echo of his own voice above the pervasive hum of machinery that seemed to be all around him, out of reach.

"Meg! Where are you? Jonwon! Are you here? Dammit, isn't there anyone sentient in this place? Anyone concerned about an intruder like me?" No one answered; no one came, although he hoped against hope that Watcher would come back and take him, too. At least then he might be with Meg.

He ran as hard as his new body would go, and suddenly had to skid to a stop because the corridor ended in a ballooned out area with one large door at the far end.

The last door opened easily, and Adam didn't stop to wonder why. Inside was another cavern of a room, but not filled with silent robot brains. It vibrated with mechanical devices and shone with the lights of giant computers, motionless but obviously working.

"Hey!" Adam jumped aside as a metal object the size of a small dog bore down upon him as he stood in what seemed to be a main walkway between banks of machinery. The object—oval, with antennae—paid no attention to him, swerving to the left into a smaller walkway and disappearing in the distance.

There were hundreds of small, active mechanical creatures of various shapes and sizes, all scurrying to and fro among the larger, stationary equipment. None of them paid the slightest attention to Adam.

The noise was sufficiently loud to make it unlikely that anyone could hear a shout, but Adam tried it. "Jonwon! Meg! Are you here?"

He was about to turn back to the door when he heard something over the pervasive sound of the room. It sounded like a shout. He waited, and the words became clear.

"Don't shut the door!"

He saw Jonwon running down the main walkway toward him, leaping over the small robot workers on his way.

"Adam! How did you—oh, no!" Jonwon's outstretched arms fell helplessly to his sides. "The door is closed."

"It shut behind me when I came in," said Adam.

"Blast. It locks on this side and can't be opened."

"I'm sorry, Jonwon. I didn't know."

"Of course not." With what must have been an effort, Jonwon managed a smile, and actually gave Adam a hug, something he hadn't done since the first years of his existence. "Adam, I'm delighted to see you, but I'm afraid that you are now as imprisoned as I am. You were calling for Meg, too. I don't understand—where is she?"

"I hoped she'd be in here." Adam explained about Watcher and Jonwon shook his head.

"It must have taken her to the same place it took me when I moored my ship on an arch and found my way inside. All I can tell you about it is that the place was dark, and as soon as I woke up—"

"Woke up? You mean you'd been unconscious?"

"I must have been. I have no memory of that thing you call Watcher letting go of me, but it wasn't in the dark place with me, I'd swear to that. Anyway, I woke up knowing that I was to help set up a factory to make robot brains, and then Watcher came back, glowing slightly in the dark. It grabbed me and we went into a sort of grayness, and then here. But why would it take Meg and not you?"

272

"I don't know, unless it's because Watcher had already been in contact with the biological Adam Durant."

Jonwon said, "Adam! I didn't realize, even when I touched you. You're a superaide! The body's so good I thought that somehow you'd been healed from your disease."

"Both Meg and I are robots, Jonwon."

When Adam told Jonwon what had happened to the biological Meg, the blond robot turned away for a moment. "Adam, I've been in this factory for years, adapting our type of superaide brain according to instructions from the computers. It's the job I was given by aliens I've never seen. My escape attempts always fail. There's been no one to talk to and sometimes I thought I was going crazy because I'd have vivid imaginary pictures in my head, most of them about Meg. Once I even thought she said something to me— something about joining."

Adam had told Jonwon only that Meg wanted to be a robot. "Meg and I came back to Far to find you, Jonwon. Meg is convinced that you're doing something important and she wants to work with you."

The impassivity Jonwon had cultivated for so many years was no longer there. He did not smile, but his voice mechanism responded with a bark of mirthless laughter. "I'm a prisoner, and now that the superaide brains have all been designed, I do nothing but supervise the factory, which doesn't need it. I've thought at times of deactivating myself, but isn't it odd how compelling life gets to be when you toy with the notion of giving it up?"

Adam thought about the biological Adam. One-O had told him how the man had turned off the medichair and died quietly, a look of peace on his ravaged face. Robot Adam had once contemplated deactivation so that there would only be one Adam Durant, who had died and been buried on Earth. But Jonwon was right, life was indeed compelling, and Adam had no intention of spending it in a factory.

273

"If the arches were here when you came back to Far, where did you go before that?"

"For a long time, I just let my ship drift in the Milky Way Galaxy. I was angry at Far for killing you—and Hank and my hopes for a kingdom of superaides free from human contamination. I just sat and listened to music recordings."

"Always human music."

"How did you know I prefer that?"

"Seven told me."

"The evil genius who prompted you to give me life."

"Evil!"

Jonwon paused, and then said wryly, "Not evil, I guess. Just—all too human. Perhaps I am, too. I can accept this, now that it's too damn late to do anything about it. I'm sorry you've fallen into Far's new trap, Adam. Sorry Meg is missing. Sorry I've never found a single way to open the lock of that door or even batter it down. Sorry we're stuck here, possibly forever and—"

"Stop the sorriness, Jonwon! We're here and there must be a way out no matter how clever and technologically advanced these aliens are—say! If they are so advanced, how come they needed you to make robot brains?"

"I don't know that or why I've never had to put the brains in the robots. The brains leave this factory by an antigrav lift so small that I can't fit into it, although I've tried."

"I know where the brains go," said Adam, and described the room at the top of the arch. "The aliens in all those other ships must be linking the brains into a giant computer instead of putting them into robot bodies for mind transfer. There may be rooms of brains at the top of every arch!"

"Horrible. A superaide brain is capable of emotion. Even the stupid Feds wouldn't link bodiless robot brains. The Giant A.I. computers serve that purpose, and have no awareness of being imprisoned. I suppose the brains in that computer up on the arch are all different to serve different functions."

274

"And if the aliens even found the dead brains of your two superaides that jumped into the ocean, then they'll use any robot brain available that isn't necessary for some other purpose—like you working here." Adam stared at Jonwon, realizing what that meant. "Meg. They'll take her brain—"

"And there's no way out!" shouted Jonwon, shaking his fists at the mindless little work robots. "I've tried everything. The door is impervious. The antigrav lift is too small. The parts-supply chute is too small. A sit-down strike, which I've also tried, doesn't work—nobody came and after a while I was so bored I went back to work. I used to sneer at One-O for his eternal joy in being useful, but there's something to it. Probably built into all robots."

"No, into all intelligent beings, I think. But let's not have a philosophical discussion about it when I have to find Meg. Do you think if we went on a rampage and destroyed as much of this place as possible, someone intelligent would come, even Watcher?"

"I'd just be ignored while the repair robots went to work. I tried that, too, years ago."

Adam thought. "We could take off our heads and put them on the antigrav lift. They would fit even if our bodies don't."

"And we'd end up in bubbles in that computer up there."

"Oh. Dumb of me. Well, let's stand by the door."

"What for?"

"In case it opens. If you'd been there when I came in, you could have held the door open so we'd both go out instead of me coming in to get trapped with you."

"Adam, no one but you has come for years and years."

Adam walked over to the door and sat down in front of it. "You have also never understood that One-O has little patience with the adventuring impulses of so-called intelligent beings. He thinks he has to look after them. I'll wait."

"Okay, Adam. Shall we sing?"

CHAPTER • 42

Consciousness. Floating. "Space?" said Meg. The sound of her own voice told her she was not in space but in air. It was completely dark, and when she kicked out to move herself forward her head bumped hard against a metal wall. If she'd still had a human skull it would have hurt badly.

The wall was covered with thin bulges and narrow indentations in a repeating pattern modified by an occasional bulbous protuberance. She grasped the bulbs to haul herself over the wall until she came to another wall at right angles. In weightlessness it was impossible to tell whether it was the ceiling or the floor.

She felt sure she was alone, but she tried calling anyway. "Adam? Where are you? Jonwon?" No one answered.

The other wall was so smooth there was nothing to hold onto so she returned to the patterned wall, following its join to the other until she came to a third wall, equally patterned. Eventually she had explored the entire space.

"I'm in a room with two facing walls that are smooth and four that are patterned," she said aloud to calm her mind. "Now I'd better search for something unique in the pattern."

It was in one corner. Two of the thinner protuberances bent over to form a bizarre handle which she instantly pulled. It didn't budge so she twisted it, and it turned to the right. Lights came on, shining from slits that had opened in the smooth walls.

"All right, blast you, where's the door?" When no one answered, she began to look for it. An hour later she had to admit defeat.

"You brought me here for some purpose, well what is it? If

276

you don't need me anymore, why can't I go back to my husband? Answer me!"

Only silence remained when her echoes died out.

"I must think. It's what I'm supposed to be good at." She tried to calm herself by using Adam's technique of visualizing an ocean, but immediately saw the golden, deadly ocean of Far and the myriads of alien ships moored on the arches—why?

"Oh, damn, I wish I'd never come to this horrid planet. I wish I'd never become a robot. Never grown up . . . no. I'd have missed too much." She closed her eyes, remembering the kinds of happiness that only biologicals can know. She saw the red, squirming shape of Walt as Bess put him on her body, which he had just left.

For the first time, Meg admitted to herself the intense biological triumph she had felt then, and would never have again. "But I've forgotten other things, like what Adam's skin smelled like, or the taste of food. I'm a robot. A robot. A robot. And I'm alone. I thought I wouldn't be. I thought I'd feel some sort of belonging, but I don't."

Panic swept through her mind, with none of the organic symptoms that biologicals could concentrate on instead of the fear. She'd scoffed at humans who worried and fretted about their unreliable bodies, but now she envied them. All she had was an unreliable mind.

She floated next to the strange handle, hooking a finger around it as if it were at least real. Light switches, however strangely shaped, were quite real, weren't they?

"Walt mustn't become a robot too early, like Adam and me. I'll tell him when I get back to Centauria. If I get back."

A visual memory returned, and it was almost as if she were in Wildpark again, walking with Adam and a very young Walt. The forest leaves were so green, and the dappled light came from Alpha Centauri A, courtesy of Centauria's mirrors.

"Fake, like theatrical lighting." Meg smiled, seeing herself

277

as a young goddess, taking a bow on the stage of a universe still radiant from the light of the big bang. The goddess pointed and instantly patterns developed in the universe, changing, growing. The goddess was pleased.

"Well, that was fun." For a few moments she'd completely forgotten who and where she was, just like the old days when she'd acted on a stage.

She glanced casually at the patterned metal wall and suddenly thought that perhaps the patterns had meaning.

"Master Adam, are you all right?" asked One-O, standing in the doorway.

"Keep that door open!" yelled Jonwon as Adam got to his feet. One-O obeyed, and soon all three of them were outside in the corridor.

"Master Adam, you told us not to worry because Far is no longer dangerous to robot minds, and your mother and Seven decided to give you and Meg a full Centaurian day here, but I . . . I . . ." One-O rocked a little on his metal feet, his jaw opening and shutting.

"You worried," said Adam. "And came after me. I approve. We were imprisoned here, and Meg has been captured. Stop being upset, One-O. I tell you it was good that you couldn't wait."

"Thank you, Master Adam. I am glad I am no longer a liability on Far. I did experience some temptation to stay at the top of the arch where the sound was loudest, but I felt that I must search for you."

"And alot of good it is to be out of the factory when we can't get up the antigrav shaft," said Jonwon.

A ghost of a smile flickered on One-O's face. "The antigrav car is waiting, Jonwon. I suspected it might leave so I adjusted the machinery. You and Seven have taught me many things about machines and simple computers."

All the way back they searched in vain for Meg, and by the

278

time they arrived in Jonwon's ship, Adam was discouraged and ashamed.

"I wanted to be a hero and help find you, Jonwon, but One-O had to rescue both of us, and now I can't think of a single way to find Meg."

"You looked for me thinking I'd help you," said Jonwon. "Did you imagine I was some kind of hero, too?"

Adam laughed. "Exactly. Meg and I pictured you as a mythic hero, moving through great adventures."

"And I was only working in a factory. I'm a bumbling misfit and always have been. I've had years to look at myself, and that's what I've been and always will be."

"I'm the bumbler," said Adam, "doing things accidentally or on impulse or to please people, and never thinking about what Watcher might have taken from my mind, and now he's got Meg because I wasn't careful—"

"Adam, you're babbling," said Jonwon. "Neither you nor Meg would be MTs if it weren't for my hubris and stupidity—"

"Shut up, both of you," said One-O.

Adam and Jonwon turned as one to the other robot.

"You are wasting time with guilt," said One-O serenely. "I suggest that you take this ship up to a low orbit around Far and look for the big computer that is up there."

"It's possible you're right," said Jonwon. "That dark room I was in could have been a computer, and I was floating so I was in space. But how do you know it's there, One-O?"

"I can only say that I sense many computer beams coming down to the planet. Perhaps it is beaming instructions to the factories. Can you not sense the beams?"

"No, One-O," said Jonwon. "Far gave you powers we don't possess."

"I am happy to be of use," said One-O.

There was a door in one of the smooth walls after all, once you pressed the right knob. Meg propelled herself through the doorway into a room that seemed to be full of bubbles that

279

were smaller than those containing the robot brains, down in the arches of Far. These bubbles were translucent, so it was impossible to tell definitely whether or not they contained anything, and they were connected by glittering wires that converged on the metal outside walls of Meg's former prison.

Carefully, she edged her way along the outer wall, trying to avoid touching the bubbles, but finally she did. She felt no shock, but lights flashed in the wall. She went on, looking for the top—or bottom—of the box from which she had just escaped. When she got there, it was a vast metal surface covered with switches not too dissimilar to those of Terran computers. But she didn't know what they did and was afraid to experiment.

Looking out through the bubbles, she saw that there was a kind of corridor between them, leading from the box to a far wall—and a door. She started out for the door, then changed her mind and came back to the switches.

"If this is actually a computer, there ought to be an emergency switch, something that would bring somebody running, or flying, or whatever they do in here." The Federation's Computer Prime, grandly safe in its hollowed-out asteroid, nevertheless had a conventional emergency switch so that even the lowliest of caretaker robots could instantly announce that something had gone wrong—if Computer Prime had not already done so itself.

The switch had to be conspicuous, but in an advanced technological society with superb equipment, it might also look relatively unused.

She searched and found a thin protuberance almost like a handle that glowed yellow. "My favorite color," said Meg.

Neither pulling nor twisting accomplished anything. Meg spoke aloud again, to the entire room. "You're only a computer and I am going to win, dammit." But however she twisted and pulled, nothing happened.

Holding onto the handle, Meg let her body drift out and she

closed her eyes. Slowly she felt the handle with both hands, letting the sensitive receptors in her synthoskin study it. The inside definitely had a ridge.

"Presumably this was not designed for the use of humans or humanoid robots," said Meg as if she were lecturing to someone. "Watcher has metal tentacles, pointed at the end. How would such an object manage this handle, if that's what it is?"

The ridge was not uniform. It had two small depressions, one at each end of the handle. It definitely needed two hands and the use of Meg's smallest fingers to touch both depressions at the same time while still holding onto the handle.

The handle began to swell upward and spread outward, so that Meg had to hold it tightly and stretch out to keep touching the depressions. "I'm a robot and robots don't get tired. Now we'll see what happens. . . ."

Nobody came, but in her mind she heard a question. It was in no language she knew, but the meaning was clear. It was the sort of question any computer asks when someone gets into the program. A great fat question mark of sensation that meant who are you and what do you want?

"All right, you," said Meg. "If you can speak to me in my mind, then you can probably read it, so you know what's in it and can, if you're bright enough, use my language. I am Meg and I want to know where I am."

"Robots do not ask questions of this machine," said the machine, out loud and in flawless Terran Basic.

"I am a mind transfer robot. I have the mind of a biological. I demand to know where I am."

"There are no mind transfers in robot bodies."

"Oh yes there are! Where am I? Answer my question!"

"In your language, you would call this place a space home, or spome, in high orbit around the planet you call Far. You are inside the main computer controlling Far, and if you are not careful you will endanger its functioning."

281

"I will be more of a danger if you don't find Adam Durant and bring him here. He's in one of the arches on Far, unless he's gone back to the ship—it doesn't matter. Just find him." The computer had obeyed the command to answer the question. Would it obey this command?

She waited in silence, expecting that any moment the machine would say the command was invalid or impossible. It did neither. Instead, the lights in the room brightened, and the door at the far end of the room slid open. Something floated through it.

The door must have been much bigger than she thought, and much farther away, because by the time the creature arrived, she saw that it was too large to squeeze through any human-sized door.

Whiplike tails propelled its body, a circular mass composed of four enormous white balloonlike sections of quivering protoplasm. It resembled four very tough, opaque jellyfish glued together to form a ball, with motile tails extruded from the line of glue between the domed sections. Behind the obviously biological creature floated the box that she and Adam had labeled Watcher.

The tails were not tails, for when the creature arrived in front of Meg, some withdrew into the body, and others waved gently toward her, more like Watcher's tentacles.

"You are a robot," said the alien in passable if heavily accented Terran Basic, from what must have been a hidden speaking aperture. "Why are you asking for Adam Durant?"

"Adam Durant is a robot just as I am, and I want him. I demand that you find him."

"He is not a robot. I am Adam Durant."

Meg screamed.

CHAPTER • 43

Adam was glad to be back in Jonwon's little ship. It seemed safe and familiar and very human compared to the structures above and below the surface of Far's ocean. As the golden arches receded in the viewscreen, he tried not to worry about those caverns full of imprisoned robot brains, one of which might be Meg's.

"Going into low orbit," said Jonwon, at the controls.

The viewscreen changed. Far seemed to drop beneath the ship, the odd indentations of the surface scum once more obvious. Each arch was over an indentation, and dipped down to enter the surface at the points where the lines intersected. Perhaps the sound made by Far's microscopic native plants was loudest at the indentations.

Up they went, and the viewscreen changed again.

"I never imagined there'd be so many ships in orbit around Far," said Adam, astonished at the variety of shapes and sizes. "Why haven't any of them challenged this ship?"

"I don't know," said Jonwon. "They didn't before, either. One-O—can you tell where the beam is coming from?"

"There," said One-O, pointing to the viewscreen. "That largest ship. The computer must be inside it."

"Is it a ship or a spome?" asked Adam, for the thing was huge. Not as big as Centauria, but certainly the size of the orbital "space home" that housed the Federation government.

"Maybe both," said Jonwon. "Perhaps it moves easily on hyperdrive, which these aliens must have had for alot longer than we have. Watcher must disappear into hyperspace to reappear in normal space someplace else. With hyperdrive that advanced, why shouldn't they use it on a spome?"

Adam stared at the oval-shaped artificial satellite of Far as it loomed in the viewscreen. It was gray-blue in color, which made it harder to see from the planet's surface. "One-O, can you tell if it's filled by a giant computer, like the asteroid housing Computer Prime?"

"I cannot tell, Master Adam."

Jonwon's ship began to circle slowly around the object, which seemed featureless until Jonwon cried out.

"There! An airlock for ships! I'm going in."

"Perhaps we should first attempt communication with this spome," said One-O. "That would be a safe initial step."

"Nothing's safe," said Jonwon. "And suppose they tell us we can't come in? Or just shoot us down? They're paying no attention now, let's just sneak in and—"

"One-O's right," said Adam. "We must be cautious."

"Furthermore," said One-O, "there is no artificial gravity in that spome or ship or whatever it is. Observe—it does not spin. There may be nothing inside except a computer."

"Possibly with Meg inside it," said Jonwon angrily. "Adam, I thought you wanted to find her."

"Take the ship inside, Jonwon," said Adam. "Is there a stun gun in the ship?"

"Two—in that drawer there. You take one and I'll take the other. One-O, can you manage—"

"I am well-shielded and very strong," said One-O. "I can defend myself and will help defend you. You and Master Adam should keep the guns, because my programming will not easily permit me to use them."

Adam gave a gun to Jonwon and kept the other for himself, wondering what use it would be against a computer the size of that spome. Who had built it? Were there any protoplasmic creatures in any of the ships on the arches of Far and in orbit around it? Or was the galaxy M31 populated now only by robots like Watcher?

"I hate to sound like a bioeffer," said Adam, "but I hope there are some biological aliens among these silent ships and

284

giant computers and nasty tentacled metal monsters like Watcher. Robot as I now am, I feel I can deal better with biologicals. Sorry, Jonwon. I know you don't agree."

Jonwon stared at him. "I wanted to populate Far with robots who could be unconcerned by biological problems, but Far's biology killed my dream, and my two human friends."

"Try not to hate biology, Jonwon," said Adam, feeling sad. "Perhaps it's the best the universe could do—evolve biology, which would then make robots."

"Adam! I'm trying to say I agree with you in spite of everything. I hope that Watcher and the giant computer have biological owners. Or at least once had them."

Adam gave Jonwon's shoulder a light punch, the kind he'd used to display affection when he became too old for hugging. "Then take the ship inside, Jonwon. We'll be the three muske-teers, determined to rescue the fair damsel."

Jonwon attended to the control board and then suddenly punched Adam back. "All those years Meg—and you—thought I was an adventuring hero, when I was only locked in a robot brain factory. It's full speed ahead into danger now!"

As the little ship zoomed forward, the alien object's airlock yawned wide.

"Will you walk into my parlor . . ." Adam stopped, abruptly conscious of the fact that Meg had said that so recently, and with such disastrous results. Conquering heros? Dangerous folly, but Meg was trapped somewhere and . . . "We have to find Meg," Adam said softly.

"Far does not paralyze us robots anymore," said One-O loudly. "We will do the best we can." One-O stopped, swayed back and forth momentarily, and added, "With due caution."

The ship slid into a landing cradle that appeared in the far end of the lock. It was exactly the right size.

"Like coming home," said Jonwon, grinning at Adam and One-O. "And speaking of caution, what about our third musketeer, old One-O here? Barging into an arch to rescue us, indeed! Not cautious at all. If you aren't careful, One-O, you'll lose your sensible saint image."

The lock shut behind them, and the ship's instruments indicated a surge of air around the ship. "There must be biologicals inside," said Jonwon. "Or why the air? It's too full of various unpleasant things for humans, but there are probably many protoplasmic creatures who'd breathe it well."

"I'm going out," said Adam. "Can't see anything from in here." The walls of the cradle were solid, the ship bathed in a greenish artificial light.

"Wait," said Jonwon, "I'll try to get the sensors to give us an image of what's beyond the cradle walls." But the viewscreen remained blank.

"I'm definitely going out," said Adam, heading for the ship's airlock.

"Not without me," said Jonwon. "I'm the computer expert."

"I must go with Master Adam," said One-O.

"So be it," said Adam. "The three robot musketeers advance into enemy territory to challenge the alien computer." Adam wished he felt as cheerful as the way he spoke. He didn't like those two words—*enemy* and *alien*. Soon they might join to become *enemy aliens*, a phrase time-honored in the annals of stupidity called human history.

"I think we should keep in mind," said One-O, "that although the creatures that built this spome may be alien to us, they may not be enemies."

Ashamed, Adam opened the airlock and saw directly in front of it a round door in the wall of the cradle. The ship's landing platform extruded until it was flush with the door, and Adam stepped out, only to float upward and hit his head on the top of the cradle.

"You forgot about the null-G," said Jonwon, pulling himself out of the artificial gravity of the ship by holding onto the landing ramp. One-O reached up to pull Adam back to them,

286

and the three clung to the ramp, staring at the metal device to the right of the cradle door. It was shaped like a pair of thin, curved wings.

Jonwon felt the wings while One-O held his feet. "There's a ridge at the back. I think it depresses like . . . this."

The round door dilated open so rapidly that nobody had a chance to move back.

"It's not a bad view," said Adam. "I wonder why nobody comes to find out who we are and what we're doing?"

Rose-colored buildings, boxlike or domed or jutting out in pyramidal shapes, festooned with strange blue-leaved vines, seemed to be an integral part of the spome like the buildings in Centauria. Everywhere was a soft light that might have been from the sun of Far, reflected by mirrors.

"Those white clouds look very solid," said Jonwon, pointing.

"Because they're the aliens," said Adam. "And they're coming to us."

"No wonder the doorways in the buildings are so large," said One-O.

The bodies of the aliens, circular and four-lobed, had no trouble moving through the null-G, air-filled world they inhabited. They propelled themselves with long tentacles while other, thinner tentacles vibrated toward the three musketeers.

Jonwon had his stun gun in one hand, and was awkwardly holding onto the doorway with the other.

"Don't shoot," said Adam. "There are ten of them, and I can see hundreds more milling around in the air of the spome. They can maneuver here and we can't, unless anyone thought to bring jet packs?"

"No," said Jonwon. "This is ridiculous. It's a scene like something from one of those awful holov movies made for kids. Can it be that galaxy M31 is populated by white blobby balloons with intelligence?"

"Their bodies are probably filled with gas," said One-O

287

judiciously, "to make floating easier. A puncture might suffice to render them helpless."

"I may have enough stun charges for the entire population but I can't be sure how many—"

"Jonwon! One-O!" Adam tried to keep from yelling. "Do either of you seriously want to attack these creatures before we find out how dangerous they are, or where Meg is?"

"Sorry, Adam," said Jonwon. "You're the human. You were once biological, as these aliens still are. You lead."

It was what Adam wanted, but now that he had it, he didn't know what to do. He remembered how hard Seven had tried to teach him patience, and he waited.

The ten who approached seemed to hang in the air before the doorway, and were soon joined by more and more until Adam could no longer see the rest of the spome. Yet the creatures did nothing. He felt no electronic vibrations, but perhaps . . . "One-O—do you sense any beams or anything coming from them?"

"No, Master Adam. Only that the far end of the spome contains the source of the beams going down to Far."

"You mean the computer's at the far end?" asked Jonwon.

"It would seem so," said One-O.

"Well we can't get to it, not with these living balloons in the way," said Adam. "Perhaps we should go back to the ship and try communicating through—" There was no point in talking about the ship, for as he spoke, the door shut before they could let go of the rim and try to prevent it.

Six aliens detached themselves from the mass. These bore what looked like giant forks in the tentacles nearest the three robots. The forks waved, and the six swam in the air to take up positions, two to a robot.

Two forks prodded Adam, and then with a quick heave pried him from his grasp on the door rim. He floundered in the air and saw that Jonwon and One-O were doing the same. He tried to propel himself away from the oncoming fork, but his

288

desperate attempt to flail his legs and move only resulted in slamming himself against the fork of his other alien captor.

This time the fork pushed under his tunic and no matter how he struggled he was hooked. The same thing happened to Jonwon. One-O's one-piece lab suit was encircled by two forks that curved to meet around his body. They were caught.

Borne like fish on skewers, the robots were pushed toward the wall of living alien protoplasm, which parted to let them through. Now Adam could see down the long dimension of the spome. They were going toward the other end. Toward what One-O had said was a computer.

Except for their captors, the rest of the inhabitants lost interest in the intruders. The aliens floated away as silently as they had come, waving their tentacles, disappearing into buildings, and "Going about their business, whatever it is," said Jonwon. "I suppose this is the only way we'll find Meg."

Adam was scared. He'd thought that his years of space dancing in Centauria's sky gyms would have made it easy for him to get away, or at least travel unaided, but propelling a humanoid body through null-G is difficult without wings, propulsion devices, or helpful air currents.

Adam tried to observe what he could of the inside of the spome as they traveled through it. As far as he could tell, it had no central core like Centauria's, no vegetation other than the vines, some of which bore yellow fruit, and it seemed much smaller inside than it looked from the outside. Then he saw why—a large part of one end had been walled off by thick metal that curved and protruded in elaborate and to Adam totally meaningless designs.

"I would like to know who's in charge of this," said Jonwon, upside down to Adam. "Why don't they try to talk to us? You'd think they'd have some means of talking to strangers since there must be hundreds of different kinds of ships and probably many species . . ."

A large section of the metal wall was dilating open, and

289

Watcher flew out, aimed straight at Adam. As the metal tentacles clamped on his head, the fork slid out from his tunic and Adam yelled, "If you can get loose, grab my legs or arms in case Watcher disappears with me."

But Watcher did not disappear, and once at the round doorway into the far end of the spome, the aliens released One-O and Jonwon. Watcher did nothing until the other two robots attached themselves to Adam, and then it began pulling through the doorway. The white lobed aliens drifted away as if the matter no longer concerned them.

"Hang on," said Adam, thinking how the pull of Watcher on his head would have made his biological neck ache. He was being pulled headfirst, but could twist enough to see that they were in a dark passageway.

Jonwon, who could see better, said, "There's another door."

When the door dilated, Watcher pulled them into a chamber that seemed enormous, filled with beautiful, connected globes except for a clear space that formed a corridor.

"Brains?" asked Adam.

"I can't see into these globes," said Jonwon.

"Not brains," said One-O. "Part of a big brain."

"You mean we're inside an enormous computer brain? How do you know this, One-O?" asked Adam.

"I do not know, Master Adam."

"It isn't where I was brought after I landed on Far," said Jonwon. "That was just a small, dark room. Look—isn't that an alien at the end of the corridor? Maybe it's their king or something. How does one bow in null-G?"

"We don't bow unless we have to," said Adam. "First we demand explanations for our treatment, and find out where Meg is and—"

"Master Adam, how will we do this since we do not speak the language of these aliens?"

Adam paid no attention. He was getting angry because his

290

worry was coming to the boil. "Where's Meg! What have you done with my wife! I demand . . ."

He could see nothing ahead but a huge, wrinkled alien, its tentacles curled up against its body.

"Welcome, Adam," said Meg's voice.

CHAPTER • 44

Appalled, Adam stared at the alien until the voice said in an exasperated tone, "Shove that disgusting blob of protoplasm out of the way so I can see you."

Before Adam could move, the alien floated upward, revealing the metal surface of a rectangular structure. Clinging to a strange yellow handle on that surface was Meg.

"So, you found Jonwon. And I suppose One-O came along to protect everybody. Welcome, all of you."

There was something wrong with Meg's voice. Or perhaps with her attitude. She had an expression of faint contempt on her face, and she seemed to be distinctly patronizing.

"Meg, are you all right? What happened?" asked Adam as Watcher let go of his head and hovered near Meg.

"Welcome to Vrizayka—that's the closest I can come to pronouncing the name of this spome. One of Watcher's jobs is to bring aliens, or their brain recordings, back to this computer for examination. To Watcher, we seemed like two robots in the wrong place, so since I was ahead, it just took me to be mentally raped by the computer and left inside it until the Vrizay could decide what to do with me. We're only unimportant robots to them. They're a bunch of alien bioeffers, but I'm fixing them good. I'm in charge now."

Meg's triumphant smile was only too familiar to Adam. "How can you be in charge, Meg, and of what?"

"We're here to rescue you," said Jonwon pathetically.

"I don't need rescue, but I thought Adam did. I sent Watcher to look for him. This is a horrible, disgusting place, Adam. You don't know what they've done, but they'll pay for it. I've linked my mind to this computer and Watcher now

292

obeys me, not . . . that thing. Monster, tell the real Adam Durant who you think you are."

The alien floated closer but Adam couldn't tell if it had any visual organs. As he wondered why the body was bluish gray instead of the usual white, the creature gestured toward him.

"Adam Durant," said the alien in a hollow rumble of a voice, issuing from some unseen orifice. "I have made a mistake. I told Meg Durant that I am Adam Durant."

The accent was odd but the words were unmistakable Terran Basic. "Why did you do that?" said Adam, thinking that Meg must have sustained an emotional shock that might have unhinged her. He cursed himself for believing that she had recovered completely from the difficult mind transfer.

"I was wrong," said the alien, "in the sense that I am a Vrizay who has merely received the memories of Adam Durant. It was a long time ago in your years, and since then I have come to think of myself, when I think in your language, as Adam Durant. I apologize."

"It's simple, Adam," said Meg impatiently. "When you were ill on Far, Watcher read your mind and stored all the facts from your brain. He transferred them to the monster."

"I do apologize," said the alien. "Goddess Meg had a right to be angry."

"Goddess!"

The alien waggled a withered-looking tentacle. "The word is not clear to me since it is not one you used often and my knowledge of human culture is limited to yours, but that is what Meg Durant calls herself now."

Jonwon, still holding Adam's left arm, drew himself closer and spoke softly into Adam's ear. "One-O just told me that's a powerful computer, and that Meg is indeed linked to it. Perhaps it's pushed her into psychosis."

"Stop that!" yelled Meg. "No secrets! I tell you I've finally found my perfect job. I'm linked to a computer bigger than Computer Prime, and it's linked to another, even bigger

293

computer-thing on Far. I haven't figured it all out yet, but I'm sure there's more power than anyone has ever dreamed of."

"But Meg . . ." Adam stopped as she scowled.

"Don't argue with me. Why should these monsters use Far for their own purposes? Why should they control all those helpless sentient robot brains in the arches of Far? I'm going to be in charge. I'm a goddess now—"

"You're jumping to conclusions, Meg," said Adam. "Let's find out what's really going on before you play deity."

"I'm not playing, Adam. This is real. These hideous biologicals mistreat robots—"

"They imprisoned me in their factory for years," said Jonwon.

"You see?" said Meg. "They put me into their computer as if I were just another machine to be inspected and discarded. I'll teach them what it means to treat me like that—"

"Meg, robots have been treated like that by the Feds for generations. Even now, only MTs are given equal status to biologicals, and the so-called equality isn't all that real."

"Please, goddess," said the alien, "may I speak to Adam Durant? I wish to explain Vrizayka to him."

"I can do that," said Meg imperiously. "I know the facts. Vrizayka is a spome brought through hyperspace to orbit around Far. It comes from the solar system used by the Vrizay as home base. They are an ancient species whose planet didn't suffer the kind of catastrophe that wiped out the dinosaurs on Earth, so evolution toward intelligence has been undisturbed and continuous. In this galaxy the Vrizay have been in space for a long time, and it was they who put Watcher, and others like it, to observe the development of planets starting to have life. There are other intelligent species in this galaxy by now but the Vrizay were first. They have evolved to the point where the adults can live only in weightless conditions, and their planet is now only a nursery and garden for their young."

294

"Admirably summarized, goddess," said the alien, "but that is not what I wish to tell Adam Durant."

"I don't care," said Meg. "I haven't had time to absorb all the information in your computer, but I'm getting there. You decided to get your Federation—which includes all the other sentient species—to build arches on Far, where your slave robot brains would function, doing . . . I haven't discovered what yet, but I will."

"We built the arches after Far changed," said the alien. "After you changed it, Adam Durant."

"Find out why they built the arches and put me in the factory, Meg," said Jonwon.

She closed her eyes, and one of the alien's tentacles tapped Adam's arm. "Stop her, Adam Durant. She is trying too hard to understand and control the recent data in the computer's memory banks, and that has not yet been integrated. She will deactivate if she persists in trying to be a goddess."

Adam tried to get near Meg, but Watcher intervened, pushing him away.

"Meg, stop the linkage! You'll lose your own identity!"

Her eyes opened to their widest, and she looked like a statue of a beautiful demon. "I cannot permit the Vrizay to imprison our robot brains into their diabolical device on Far. It is they who will kill us, steal our identities—"

"No," said the alien. "You don't understand, Meg Durant. It is you who are killing me. You have caused radiation to emanate from the computer and no biological can tolerate it for long. Eventually it will kill you robots, too, but first I will die, and then all the other Vrizay in Vrizayka."

"They're vicious alien biologicals, Adam, and we must kill them before they kill us."

Adam kept staring at the alien who had called himself Adam Durant. "Do you have a Vrizay name, sir?"

When the alien spoke it, Adam knew that he would not be able to duplicate the sounds. "Sorry, I can't pronounce that,

295

so I'll call you A-Three. The biological Adam Durant died, and I am the mind transfer robot who replaced him. You are a biological alien who also replaced him by receiving his mind transfer. You have all my knowledge of medicine. Can you tell if the computer radiation is already making you ill? Your skin is not the color of the other Vrizay."

"I am the oldest Vrizay in this spome, as you call it. Ordinarily we live so long that we don't contemplate death or prepare for it adequately, so that in spite of my age I have not prepared anyone to succeed me. The computer is indeed killing me quickly, because I am so close to it, and when I die, Vrizayka will be deprived of its doctor."

"You're a doctor because of the knowledge you got from my brain recording?"

"Oh, no. I was given the recording because I am the doctor here. There are others for other Vrizay worlds, but none to spare for this one. Would you take my place?"

"Meg!" Adam lunged forward, to be stopped again by Watcher. "Did you hear that! Turn off the computer's radiation before you kill him!"

One-O pushed against Jonwon, and as Jonwon went back, One-O was propelled forward toward Watcher. He clung to Watcher and said, "Master Adam, try now."

Jonwon floundered through the air to help One-O, and Adam tried again to reach Meg. This time he managed to pull her arms loose from the handle, although she was almost as strong as he and struggled against him.

"Meg, you're destroying a spome like Centauria, and their only doctor. Meg, listen . . ."

Her eyes were shut, and she was as limp as a robot can be. He held her close and finally she said, "They enslave robots and I must clean everything—"

"No, Meg. They have as much right to live as we do. Wake up. Don't let yourself deactivate. Make the computer turn off the radiation before anyone dies."

296

"Biologicals—bioeffers—monstrous—Jonwon—make Adam understand . . ." Meg's voice died away and Adam was afraid her robot brain was dying, until her eyes opened.

"Adam, you and Jonwon and I should control Far. Robots are the future of the universe and we can't let biologicals destroy our chances."

"Watcher is no longer under her control," said One-O, letting go of the pyramid-box. "When you pulled her from the handle she lost her link to the computer."

Jonwon pushed at Watcher to propel himself near Adam. "Give her to me, Adam. She is a true robot now and belongs to me. We must have our chance."

"Master Adam, shall I restrain Jonwon?"

"No, One-O." Adam let Jonwon take Meg into his arms, her face just as stony blank as it had been those months after she first became an MT.

"Then Vrizayka is condemned to death," said A-Three.

"Jonwon!" Adam shouted. "Are you condemning this world and its people to death?"

"But Meg says—"

"She is reasoning from a partial number of facts gleaned from a computer. She is not reasoning with compassion."

"Go away, Adam," said Jonwon, cradling Meg close to him.

Adam tried once more. "This is your last chance, Jonwon."

"For what?"

"To be human."

CHAPTER • 45

"The radiation continues," said the alien that Adam had named A-Three. "Meg no longer controls the computer but her previous instructions to it still hold. She has apparently told it to clean Vrizayka of organic life. Only she can cancel the order." A-Three's lobes were sagging and grayer.

"Meg, turn it off!" Adam reached for her, but Jonwon pushed him away.

"Adam, she's mine now. It is our last chance—hers and mine."

Jonwon stroked the synthoskin of Meg's face. "Listen to me, Meg. It's important. You and I are robots."

"Yes. Robots."

"But the laws of robotics—"

"Prohibitions invented by humans!" Meg struggled in his arms and then touched the glistening gold curls on Jonwon's head. "You look like a god, Jonwon. I am your goddess now. Don't act like a stupid, dutiful aide—like One-O."

"One-O's a lot more than an aide!" yelled Adam.

"Are you, One-O?" asked Jonwon, stroking Meg's dark hair.

"It does not matter," said One-O. "I am content to be whatever I am. Seven says there are many ways of being, many ways in which the universe can understand itself. One day he told me I am a good way. I hope so, because I enjoy it."

"What does it matter what One-O says?" asked Meg. "You and I will have all this power to ourselves."

One-O's voice was deeper, his words slower. "Seven also said that power without compassion is always doomed."

"Meg," said Jonwon. "You are human, and I was raised by humans. We must be the best of what we are. Please help me

298

be more human. We long-lived robots should help and protect fragile biological life, not destroy it as you are now doing."

"But they're monsters," said Meg. "We robots could be gods. Why doesn't anyone understand?"

"I understand you," said A-Three. "My species is older than yours, our wisdom hard-won. Since intelligence developed early on our planet of origin, and with it the lust for power, we nearly destroyed ourselves until the invention of hyper-drive let us expend our energy in space exploration. It has taken us many thousands of your years to build a galactic Federation of all sentient species, many more to achieve the peace we now have. We would like the species of your galaxy—biological, mind transfer, and robot—to join us."

"But you monsters are subjugating robot brains on Far, trying to be gods—"

"No, Meg Durant. If you don't believe me, you must risk linkage with the computer once more. Take it and find out the truth. That computer is not as powerful or as intelligent as you imagine. Its main function has always been to maintain the life-support system of Vrizayka. It also beams solar energy to maintain the buildings we and other species and our simple robots have constructed on Far. Recently we have added a cognitive part to the computer that files and integrates the data being accumulated by the brains on Far—"

"There!" Meg shook her fist at the alien. "You're using robot brains to make a giant computer on Far. What for—to control this galaxy, and then the sister galaxy where humans live? And then you'll spread out to be masters of the universe?"

The alien seemed to sigh, and one of the lobes collapsed completely. "Please search the data banks for the truth."

"Hurry, Meg," said Adam. "Don't be cruel."

With Jonwon's help, Meg positioned herself with the handle of the computer and closed her eyes to concentrate. Minutes of silence passed and then the anger died in her face.

299

"A-Three is speaking the truth. I didn't even give him time to tell us the most important thing of all—those robot brains on Far are not prisoners but volunteers, the last lives of many sentient species. They're the final use of mind transfers!"

"Turn off the radiation, Meg," said Adam. "Quickly."

"I can't," said Meg wearily. "I've been trying but I don't know how."

"Let me in." Jonwon's lips brushed her forehead. "Adam and Seven and Bess and the twins taught me to be human, but Meg, you can teach me love. If we can save these lives, we'll stay on Far and help anyone who needs it. Open your mind to me as we link with the computer. Let me help."

She put his hand under hers on the handle, and he put his other arm tightly around her body. "Close your eyes, Jonwon."

"Be with me, Meg. Shut out the rest of the universe."

It seemed long to Adam, but finally One-O said, "The radiation has stopped."

"A-Three, are you all right?" asked Adam.

"The radiation has not caused harm to the rest of my people. Vrizayka will live."

"But you . . ."

"It is too late for me."

"Is there a hospital?" Adam held one of A-Three's limp tentacles. "We'll take you there at once."

"There's a crowd outside the metal barricade of this computer," said Meg, "and according to the scanner, they are saying they must find and destroy the alien robots who have endangered their lives. I can keep the wall locked, but if A-Three is dying . . ."

"Don't try taking me to the hospital," said A-Three. "It won't do any good and you may be harmed if I die before I have a chance to explain. My people are generally peaceful, but you will be seen only as aberrant, dangerous robots. I cannot be cured, so it would be best if you used Watcher to take you to your own ship so you may escape."

300

"What about mind transfer for you?" asked Adam. "Could Watcher take a brain recording of you as it did of me?"

"Watcher has never been used for a Vrizay. Since we live for many thousands of your years, usually knowing of our impending death well in advance, we decide whether we will die as biologicals or allow a direct transfer to robot brains made for our species, to be used on Far. We have no tradition of intelligent robots, and no robot bodies to transfer to. Since I cannot get to the mind transfer stations in the arches of Far, I will die here."

"Wait," said Adam. "Hold onto life as long as you can. Meg, can you control Watcher again?"

"Yes, Adam. I've ordered him to make a brain recording of A-Three. I'm so sorry."

As Watcher's metal tentacles spread out to touch the collapsing body of the alien, Adam tried to soothe A-Three. "All of us regret that your biological life has been destroyed, A-Three."

"Stay with me until the end, Adam Two. It will make me calmer for the recording, and then I can die peacefully."

"I'm right here."

"You and I share the memories of the biological Adam Durant, yet we are very different species, alien to each other. Perhaps it is unpleasant to take care of a creature like me."

"No," said Adam. "Even without the memories, we have the universe in common."

CHAPTER • 46

The recording was finished, and the oldest Vrizay was dead, his limp body hanging in the space next to the computer. Adam felt bereft.

"What are we going to do now?" asked Jonwon. "We should have tried to get A-Three to talk to his angry friends, to explain that we made a mistake, and that we hope we can save his mind if not his body. No one else can talk to them, since they don't understand Terran Basic, as he did."

"It was more important to get the brain recording," said Adam. "Besides, we're not going out—that way. Meg, please instruct Watcher to pick me up and move me through hyperspace to the factory on Far. And tell Watcher to help me pick out the right size brain for A-Three's recording."

"Done," said Meg.

As Watcher hovered over him, ready to take him away, Adam smiled at the other three robots. In spite of robothood, they all had worried faces. "You stay here and don't get into any more trouble by probing around in that computer or opening the door. Just wait for me to return and pray the door holds."

"Master Adam, I wish to accompany you."

"Then hang on, One-O."

"But Adam," said Jonwon, "what are you going to do with the brain? Presumably the Vrizay are experts in mind transferring a recording to one of those robot brains on Far, and we can't explain to them—"

"I'm not going to bother the Vrizay. I'm taking the recording to a mind transfer expert."

In the factory, Watcher picked up the right size brain for a Vrizay, held it in one tentacle, and obediently picked up Adam and One-O again. Instantly they hyperjumped to the roof of Jonwon's building, and Adam ran to inspect the three dead superaides, still lying where they had fallen when he shot them so many years before.

"The ocean is beautiful now, Master Adam. All gold. And the sound it makes is like music."

"Do you think so, too, One-O? It must be true." The music of Far seemed sweeter, gentler than he had ever heard it, and he found himself thinking of it as a wordless song of praise and farewell to a dead Vrizay.

Adam selected one of the superaide bodies and removed the head. He handed the body to One-O to carry and settled Watcher on himself once more.

"Down to the transporter, One-O. I'm glad I'm a robot and can remember anything I choose, even the coordinates for home."

But before they had gone another step, Watcher clamped tentacles on both One-O and Adam.

"Hey! What the hell do you think you're doing!"

Adam's words vanished into a gray nothingness. All he could sense was his own body. He was afraid that Watcher had decided to take him to the Vrizay, but when light came back, Adam was staring into a bemused and beloved face.

"Seven!"

"I'd swear you didn't arrive on that transporter plate in the normal way," said Seven. "Why are you and One-O in the clutches of that peculiar box, and why have you also brought an oddly large superaide brain and a small, sexless, stream-lined superaide body—one of Jonwon's old creations?"

Seven grinned. "I believe those questions cover most of the more urgent demands of my curiosity, but I have a good deal more on my mind since I've been waiting by the transporter for hours, wondering if I should come after you in spite of your mother's strict instructions to stay here."

"I'll explain as we go along."

"Just tell me one thing. Has someone invented a mobile transporter and is that box it?"

"Right. Meet Watcher, mobile transporter and brain recorder combined. Not very brainy but useful. Seven, please make a robot head to fit this alien brain, and then attach it to this body. Watcher will provide a brain recording for mind transfer."

"The largest head size will do, if expanded slightly, and I can manage that. There'll only be an extra seam or two, but who is it for? You said alien—so it's not Meg, or Jonwon?"

"No, they're fine. This is for an important alien who just died because Meg—well, it was our fault. It's a rush job, Seven, to save the necks of Jonwon and Meg—and the futures of a couple of galaxies, including ours."

"All in a day's work," said Seven.

Watcher floated wordlessly overhead while Seven and One-O worked and Adam watched. Bess, who had been told to come without letting anyone else in Centauria know about the alien, arrived and ate her lunch during the transfer procedure.

"I don't know how long this should take," said Seven, "but since Watcher's performing the transfer we'll have to trust that it knows what it's doing."

And suddenly it was over. Watcher released its hold on the new head, containing the alien robot brain, and floated up.

Seven's hand poised over the switch to release the block on the superaide brain. "Ready?"

"If I could sweat I'd be sweating," said Adam. "Try it."

Seven touched the switch and the robot's eyes opened. He sat up and swung his legs around so that they dangled from the top of the lab table.

"Seven!" said the new robot. "I'm delighted to meet you at last, after all the memories of Adam that I have enjoyed."

They shook hands, and A-Three turned to the one biological in the lab. "And Mother—I mean, Bess. You must forgive

304

my presumption. For years I contemplated Adam's memories until I now think of you as my mother."

Bess took A-Three's hand in both of hers. "Welcome back to life, A-Three. I'm so glad."

When she released his hand, A-Three looked at it. "I like the custom of shaking hands. Much friendlier than touching tentacles. And now I believe we should return to Vrizayka at once, to rescue Meg and Jonwon. I will speak to my people in the Vrizay language and explain everything."

"That doesn't mean we'll be safe," said Adam.

"It probably does," said A-Three. "My people have been civilized for much longer—I mean, for a very long time."

Watcher managed to find enough tentacles for A-Three, Adam, and One-O. Seven wanted to go, but Bess said it might strain whatever mysterious way Watcher used to travel through hyperspace.

"Good-bye, Bess," said A-Three. "I hope to return to your world to study with you, now that I am in a body capable of walking easily in gravity. Do you think your people will accept a mind transfer who looks like me?"

"A-Three, the danger is that you will be adored. All primates respond with parental warmth to anything with the proportions of a primate baby—big round head and small body. Every human child will want a toy that looks like you."

"Good-bye, Adam," said Seven. "I'm glad you've had such remarkable success as an adventuring hero."

"I'm no hero," said Adam. "I'm just a doctor who's been trying to help another doctor."

CHAPTER • 47

A-Three's voice, broadcast to his people from inside the computer, made it possible for the robots from the Milky Way Galaxy to be escorted politely to Jonwon's ship, where they were told to wait, please.

Watcher flew through the air of Vrizayka, carrying A-Three to a government conference, while the robots watched from the ship's airlock.

"Seven and Bess will be worrying. Let's go home and reassure them and come back," said Adam.

"No," said Meg. "After the way I've behaved, I think we should do just as A-Three requested. He said he'd return."

"He still hasn't answered your original question, Meg," said Jonwon. "What work is the linkage of transfer brains doing on Far? It must be terrifically important, for these aliens to want to have second lives trapped in a giant computer system like that one."

"Seven has guessed," said One-O. "He told me just before we left Centauria."

"How can Seven know what the MTs of this galaxy are doing on Far?" asked Jonwon. "And what's the guess?"

"I think I will not spoil the surprise," said One-O.

"Adam, tell that robot sidekick of your to—" Jonwon stopped. "Oh, hello, A-Three."

The big-headed little robot walked into the ship, beaming. "All is well, my friends. My government has consulted with all the other intelligent species of my galaxy, and we extend an invitation to your galaxy. Please tell your species to send a delegation to official Friendship ceremonies here in Vrizayka in a month's time. Your month, of course. If your people wish to merge Federations, that is possible, if not, we will work together."

"The delegation will have to be human MTs," said Adam. "The atmosphere of this spome, as well as the spores of Far, are much too dangerous for any biologicals to come."

"Then we will welcome the MTs in particular, because they will show our galaxy examples of biological mind transfers living free in robot bodies. Our bioeffing galaxy, as I believe you would put it, has been prejudiced against intelligent robots for longer than yours, but if Adam Durant is now a robot, then we will give up our prejudices."

A-Three smiled and continued. "I must confess that my own example has already excited much interest in robot second lives. I believe that many will elect to be robots after biological death, and only later join their brains to the network on Far, after which their bodies can be reused—"

"Okay, A-Three," said Jonwon, "but isn't it time you told us what those MT brains are doing down on Far?"

"What is it?" asked Meg, leaning forward eagerly. "A linkage to attain ultimate power?"

"No, Meg. No attempt at godhood is being made," said A-Three. "The linked brains are studying."

"Studying!" Meg threw up her hands. "I don't believe it. What on earth for?"

"Hardly on Earth, my dear. We who have heard the music of Far do not know if it has a hidden meaning or if the brain network must eventually give it one, but we listen and study."

"The music that will be complete only when the universe ends," said Adam, and told A-Three about the music synthesizer.

"Ah, I wish I had that memory of yours, but it was after you became a robot. I am glad to know about it. The knowledge may help the study done on Far."

"But all the power of all those linked brains—it's a waste," said Meg. "Just studying?"

307

"Just studying. I will think about the music synthesizer and perhaps I will have more to say at the Friendship ceremonies. Please, all of you come, with Seven."

"We'll be there," said Adam.

Adam hadn't seen Meg or Jonwon for a month because they were too busy in the robotics' lab, shuttling back and forth to Far's factories, and he was busy catching up with things in the hospital. A-Three had visited for a week and it was just as Bess had predicted. Everyone adored him, especially the children in the hospital. Walt came from Earth with Rusty and Dinah and Paul, who took A-Three back with them to a sold-out lecture at Harvard.

"Lee," said Adam, "I'm happy to be back, but there's something nagging at me. Something I should know about Far but I don't. I keep thinking I have to figure out what it is before the Friendship ceremonies."

"Ask your mother," said Lee. "Will you marry me, Adam?"

"Mother, Lee and I are going to marry," said Adam. "But I have this problem."

"Meg? Walt? They won't mind . . ."

"No. Far. Do you remember my description of its present surface appearance?"

"Remember it! Holov has done nothing but show the sights of M31, the various biological aliens, the linked robot brains on Far, and of course Far itself. Of course I've seen it."

"It reminds me of something, but I don't know what. Lee said I should ask you, but I don't know why that, either."

"Adam, you're not dumb. You're just humble. Lee thought it would be easier to take coming from me."

"I don't think I want to know whatever it is you're going to tell me."

"Then figure it out for yourself. Go back to Far and really look at it. You're not thinking enough like a bioeffer."

308

"I am not a bioeffer!"

"You are. When you were four you worried about whether the cells used for clone-grown meat dishes might feel something when eaten. To please you, we ate algae products for weeks until you got tired of them. Matt suffered, as I recall."

"But Mother—"

"You're the best kind of biofundamentalist, revering life and dedicating yourself to saving it. That's why you didn't want anyone to go to Far and bioclean it. You tried to save the alien organic scum that killed you."

"Yes, but—"

"So it can only be your lack of self-absorption that blinds you to the interesting form that scum has taken."

"Interesting? But what—"

"I could be wrong, of course, but you'd better get a good view of Far and think about what it looks like—to a human doctor."

"Mother, I don't know—"

"It's a good thing you were there to contaminate Far, or it would have developed only from rabbit shit."

Adam watched the Friendship ceremonies with half a mind, the other half preoccupied with the problem of Far. He watched the slow and dignified proceedings that aimed to cement friendly relations between the intelligent species of two galaxies, and he brooded.

"I suppose that's all I am, an improvement on rabbit shit," he muttered.

"Shh," said Meg. She and Jonwon were arm in arm, listening intently. They had already learned the Vrizay language and did not need the simultaneous translation through the earphones placed on the net for robot visitors and other non-Vrizay species who could attach themselves to it and not float away in null-G.

Adam was pleased with Meg. He would always love her but

309

now he could let her move on, to an equal relationship with Jonwon—and Jonwon would see to it that Meg didn't again imagine that the universe was a play she could direct.

Next to him, Lee Teleg put slight pressure on his thigh, enough for him to know that she'd heard and would argue later that he was considerably better than any aspect of rabbit.

On the other side of Adam was Seven, and beyond him, One-O, with their legs poking through the netting, listening to the speeches. And so many other creatures that no Terran-descended being had ever seen or imagined.

Wherever you looked in the universe, diversity was the rule. There were indeed many ways that life could be lived.

A-Three, his humanoid body held steady by Watcher, began to speak. "I wish to conclude these Friendship ceremonies by expressing our gratitude to specific individuals. The robot Jonwon, from Centauria, made the superaide brains for us, and we apologize for not realizing that he is as intelligent as any of us and was bored and lonely locked in our factory.

"Most of all we wish to thank Adam Durant, especially the biological known to us as Adam One. The brain recording taken from him gave us the knowledge that mind transfer is possible using the superaide brains invented by his three fathers. But more than that, Adam One's biological substance contaminated the living ocean of Far, causing the organic scum to change, to vibrate.

"It was Adam One's imagination that meshed with the new vibration to turn it into music. And the MT brains linked together on Far are discovering that they can immerse their individualities when they wish, into a different kind of mental linkage that is part of the music that never ends.

"Through the music of Far, the linked brains can study the universe, sharing their knowledge and thoughts. Perhaps this linkage represents a new way in which the universe is changing. Do you think so, Adam Durant?"

All eyes, and things that were not eyes, turned on Adam.

310

He had never felt so embarrassed. "It was only an accident. I didn't set out to create something important."

"But you did, and your biological self died for it. We are grateful that the sacrifice was made."

The view of Far's ocean from the top of an arch was still lovely, and still meaningless to Adam. One-O waited patiently while Adam gazed down at the golden, patterned surface. Lee had already gone back to Centauria's hospital from the transporter in Jonwon's ship, moored to this arch, and Seven had rushed home to tell Bess everything that she had already seen on holov, all the way in another galaxy.

"King Midas?"

"I do not understand the question, Master Adam."

"I was just wondering if that's what Bess meant. He was a king in a myth, and thanks to human stupidity, everything he touched turned to gold and caused alot of trouble."

The robot Adam suddenly recaptured the total memory of that moment when his biological self looked down to see the change in the Far's scum, a change that was like rays of gold flowing away from his body.

"One-O, do you think the brains on Far will join to become a new phenomena, as A-Three believes?"

"I do not know, Master Adam. I hope so."

"They may learn and learn, using the sound of Far to create an ultimate music of thoughts and emotions."

"That is beautiful, Master Adam. Very well thought out, and much better than the Midas myth you read as a child."

"Don't tell me you've read it!"

"Certainly, Master Adam. You gave Rusty a book of myths and I read them aloud to him."

"Ultimate music. That may be beautiful, One-O, but I feel the way Jonwon always did—it's not enough for me. I want to know more than that, and much sooner. I should be content to be part of the process of learning, but—oh, no!"

311

"What is wrong, Master Adam?"

Seven stuck his head out the airlock of Jonwon's ship. "Hey, what *is* wrong? We expected you back hours ago and you look like you've uncovered one of the weirder secrets of the universe. What's up, Adam?"

Adam said nothing for a minute, and then pointed to the scum. "Look at it. The curve of the indentations in the scum and the way the surface bulges up between them slightly. The way they bend and cross and—oh, it can't be!" Adam held his head as if trying to stop something.

"If you mean that the ocean of Far now resembles the surface of a human brain, so what?" asked Seven.

"Master Adam, do not be emotionally upset. I think it is a good thing that the life form of an entire planet has imitated the brain of your biological self."

"But it can't be really a brain," said Adam. "It's just alot of microorganisms vibrating, making a sound that helps link the robot brains . . . no, it doesn't mean anything. The ocean of Far itself doesn't think!"

"Yet," said Seven.